MW01268207

THREE TO LOVE

REBEL CARTER

VIOLET GAZE PRESS

All rights reserved.

No part of this book may be reproduced or used in any manner without written permission of the copyright owner except for the use of quotations in book reviews.

Copyright © 2019 Rebel Carter

Cover Design by Najla Qamber

Edited by Bria James & Jack Holloway

Published by Violet Gaze Press

20-22 Wenlock Rd

London

www.violetgazepress.com

✳ Created with Vellum

This book is for Romancelandia. Y'all never cease to amaze me.
I hope y'all enjoy the hell out of this steamy historical, okay?

CHAPTER 1

"*T*hat isn't how that works. That isn't how any of it works."

"And why exactly not?" Florence asked, eyes moving from her reflection to her sister who stood behind her. She'd been painstakingly applying rouge to her cheeks. She paused, the small pot of makeup in one hand, her powder puff in the other, and raised an eyebrow at Delilah. Her older sister was looking none too pleased with her at the moment, which could be truly vexing.

Clearing her throat, Florence thought quickly, trying to redirect her forward question into something...*softer?* A turn of phrase more palatable to Delilah's delicate sensibilities. Her sisters always had a way of getting in between her and her beautifully laid plans when they didn't agree.

This would not do.

"Ah, what I mean to say is, whatever do you mean dear sister?" She asked, keeping her voice at as gentle and agreeable a pitch as she could manage.

Delilah frowned at her and took a step closer. "Flo.

Absolutely not. I know what you're trying to do."
Evidently, she had missed the placating-meddlesome-
and-disapproving-older-sister's pitch by a mile.

Drat.

Florence lowered her hand and set down her makeup
with a heavy sigh. "Delilah, I have no idea what you
mean."

"You do, you little brat."

Florence turned away from the mirror and toward
Delilah with her arms crossed. "Now there's no need for
name-calling, Del." Her voice was flat, her face colored
with a slight blush and her lips pushed into a thin line.

Del's eyes moved over her face slowly before narrowing. "You're up to something. I don't care how mad you
get at me. I know it."

"Oh, you do, do you?"

Del gave a quick nod and pointed at the dress she was
wearing. "You're absolutely fit for a ball in that outfit.
Don't think I didn't notice just because Papa and Daddy
are too preoccupied to truly understand what's going on."

Florence smoothed a hand over the velvet skirt of her
gown. "Oh, this old thing?" She scoffed and patted at the
silk of her neckline, which was a touch beyond daring for
Gold Sky. The crimson silk and velvet dress left her arms
bare and her décolletage on display in an enticing way
that would have been pushing the envelope, even in New
York. In the setting of the city, her outfit would have been
seen as fresh, the marker of high fashion. But here? On
the frontier? It was positively scandalous.

Florence loved a good scandal.

She should. She'd been raised with a family that raised

no shortage of eyebrows and whispers outside of their bubble of happiness in Gold Sky. Here, in this westward town, she and her family had a place of acceptance and belonging. That was the way of all those who called the town home.

Life and society may not have agreed with the lot of them in the big cities, but in Gold Sky they were able to choose their own way. Free to love whom they pleased. Free to grow into whomever they might wish to be.

Florence knew she was fortunate to be blessed with such a home; that not every place was like Gold Sky. She knew there were rumors about her family in New York but that, due to her mother's family, the Baptistes, they were simply written off as *"eccentric."* New York's Four Hundred may not understand the life her mother had chosen, but first and foremost, her mother was a Baptiste, and that meant her choices were to be accepted, even if thought strange.

It might have bothered her if the joy and love of her family had been anything but sincere. But as it was, the affection and loyalty between her parents, all three of them, had served as an example of the very thing Florence hoped for as a young girl.

One person to love was fine and a rare thing indeed, *but two?* Two hearts that beat for yours? Now that was a miracle--a gift of untold value, and it was what Florence wished for herself now that she was a woman of marrying age. She was a woman in her prime and a good looking one at that. This would normally be an advantage in the ways of love, but Florence's needs were specific. She wanted those two hearts beating for her. To give

3

herself in the same way and have her love multiplied, not divided.

However, Gold Sky was not the place for such romantic overtures to be explored. Woefully lacking in eligible men for a lady seeking only one, but two? That was positively Herculean, even in such a place as Gold Sky. Florence patted the ribbons she'd intertwined in her updo and straightened her shoulders.

The women in her family were accustomed to taking on the insurmountable and making it their own. This would be no different. There was a dance tonight, and Florence was determined to make her best showing. Hence, her daring attire and efforts with makeup and hair.

"Where are you going tonight?" Delilah asked, tipping her head to the side. She could see from the set of her sister's shoulders, and the gleam in her eyes, that she was hatching a plan. But for what?

"To a social event."

"Which social event would that be?"

Florence turned back to the mirror and smiled at her reflection. She looked lovely and fresh--perfect for drawing the eye of two suitors. It was what she wanted. Two suitors, and one way or another, Florence was going to get what she wanted.

She raised her eyes and smiled into the mirror. "Why a dance of course."

It was common knowledge a dance was the perfect setting for romance. Tonight more so as it was a very special dance. Tonight's event was a singles dance. An opportunity for the unattached to mingle and enjoy an evening of frivolity. It would be the right atmosphere for casting her nets a little wider than she'd been previously afforded in her romantic efforts. Florence had been industrious, and was known for her enthusiasm in the pursuit of a goal, but for all her energy, there was little forward progress in her quest for two husbands.

"You cannot mean to entice two men into such an arrangement."

"Such an arrangement?" Florence's hands went to her hips and she pursed her lips. "It's a dance, not some sordid crime ring, Delilah."

"A dance? You really think I'm so naive as to believe that's all you have in mind for tonight?"

"Yes, yes, I do."

Delilah crossed her arms in answer, her sharp eyes missing nothing, so flinty was her sister's gaze that Florence nearly buckled.

Nearly, but *not quite.*

Instead, she beamed at Delilah, gray eyes practically sparkling. "Unless the town-sponsored singles soiree intends to be the site for a nefarious syndicate, which it does not, then yes, it is just a dance. And I haven't a clue what two men you are referring to." Her voice was cool, even, it was the picture of collected respectability, but Delilah remained unconvinced. Florence abhorred her sister's attention to detail.

"I know very well that you've been on a spree of getting acquainted with the eligible men in town," Delilah said, shaking a finger at her sister and making Florence frown.

"I wasn't aware that I was expected to keep a nun's hours. I am, after all, a woman in her prime."

"You are, Flo, and I know what your preferences are in the way of matrimony. We all know that you wish for what our parents have, but you are going about it entirely wrong, and this dance will not fix it."

Florence stepped back as if slapped and blinked rapidly against the prickling sensation of her eyes. She would not cry. She knew her sister was only looking out for her. Delilah always did, always would, in her role as the protector, the sternest and most serious of them all. But Flo did not want practicality and rational planning or forethought.

Not tonight.

Tonight was about her heart and giving in to all the soft possibilities that came with believing in love. Florence rejected her sister's logic, and instead, chose romance and drama. She chose the chance that she would meet her matches--two men with room in their heart for her.

"That is your opinion, and you are welcome to it." She shook her head and smiled, pulling the drawstring of her evening bag tight over her knuckles as she continued to speak, feet moving her over the creaking floorboards of her room until she was at the door. "I intend to enjoy myself this evening, and I hope to see you there, Delilah. You might even have a bit of fun at such an event."

Florence turned and left the room. Her parting words to her sister were meant to sting. They both knew it, and she bit her lip at having said them. Delilah was well aware of her penchant for severity, and it wasn't kind to poke a sore spot she knew her sister to have.

The same could be said for Florence's romantic nature. Her sister knew that truth, too. She sighed heavily, walking toward the door. Her dress no longer felt so grand, nor her steps as light. She had meant to leave earlier in the evening when her sister and fathers had been present, but she had been distracted at the thought of what wonder a carefully applied coat of rouge might do for her complexion. She wished she had left and avoided the discussion of tonight, and Florence's marital preferences, all together.

She continued walking, mind swirling darkly around her conversation with Delilah, when a pointed *"ahem"* caught her attention. She turned to look through the archway to the parlor on her left and froze, seeing her mother sitting beside the fireplace in one of the three ever-present hearthside rocking chairs.

Her mother's dark head was bent over a book, reading glasses perched on her nose as she "read," though Florence noticed that her mother did not turn the page.

"Mama, I didn't know you were home." Florence went to the door.

"I've been home for some time," Julie said, raising her head, brown eyes fixed on her in reproach. Ah, so her mother had heard her argument with her sister. *Drat it all.* She'd never be able to enjoy tonight's dance after this conversation.

"That's...good," Florence ventured, and her mother hummed, closing the book in her lap and taking her reading glasses off with a sigh.

"She only loves you--wants the best for you."

"She doesn't understand, Mama."

"Might not, but do you, Flo?"

Florence's eyebrows knit together in confusion. "What do you mean?" She walked into the room, unsure of what her mother was getting at, but she was sure it would take longer than a quick chat. She sat in her father's rocking chair and leaned toward her mother.

"I don't understand the question," she ventured when they had both been silent for a moment.

"I mean, do you know what it is that you wish for in a marriage?"

"I want what you have," Florence blurted out, the thought escaping her lips faster than she could follow it, and she blinked in surprise. "I mean... I want the love and happiness you and Daddy and Papa have, but it's..."

"It's what?" Her mother put a gentle hand on her shoulder, and Florence gave her a weak smile.

"It's difficult to find a match, or in this case, matches."

"Suitors are hard to come by," Julie conceded and patted her shoulder gently. "But there is no use rushing it. You do look lovely, though. The finest dress this town has ever seen by far."

Florence smiled, this time it was genuine and warm. She caught her mother's hand and kissed her knuckles. "Except for you on your wedding day."

Julie laughed. "Oh, I don't know about that, sweetheart."

"That's not what Papa says."

"Your papa's soft-hearted, Flo. We all know it."

Florence giggled and leaned back in the rocking chair.

It was Forrest's and suited the big man just fine. She ran a finger along the worn wood and smiled. It was familiar and comforting, the place of so many happy memories. The hearthside with all three of her parents had always been the center of joy for their family and oh, what she wouldn't give for such a place in her own home.

"It's true, but he loves you and Daddy. Loves us, too, and I just," Florence swallowed hard and looked up from the chair to her mother. "That's what I aim to have for myself. I know Delilah doesn't understand it, but I hope that you can, Mama."

"I do understand, sweet girl, but it is a difficult thing to find. The men you match yourself to must, first and foremost, love one another. It cannot be lopsided," Julie motioned with her hands in the way of a scale tipping. "For a marriage such as ours, you cannot be what binds them together. They must choose and love each other as well. That's where you've been erring, Flo."

Florence tipped her head to the side and froze. How could she have not seen that one crucial step? "Oh heavens no, what have I been doing?"

"You've been finding two men that you think are compatible and attempting to push them together. Do not think I haven't noticed your matchmaking tendencies as of late."

Florence frowned. She had taken an interest in the male friendships of Gold Sky, but with far less pure intentions than the men involved realized. They thought she meant to increase the amount of fraternal companionship and camaraderie of the community, or so she had proclaimed. Florence's intentions were nothing of the kind and were, at their heart, purely romantic, even if she had failed miserably.

In the weeks she had been seeking a suitable pair of men, she had managed to create four lasting friendships and what she thought was the start of a new business venture amongst them. The business would be a success, whereas her love life was quite the opposite.

"At least the men of Gold Sky have been finding common ground more easily these days. There's been a decided downtick in the number of arguments and gunfights," she finally said. Her mother burst into a hearty round of laughter, and the sound made Florence feel lighter after her argument with Delilah. It was hard not to smile when her mother laughed as she did now, and before long, Florence was laughing along with her.

"Your act of civil service aside, of which Seylah and your fathers will be appreciative, I have this advice for you, Flo." Her mother's voice was serious, her brown eyes contemplative as she looked at her daughter who was now wiping the mirth from her own face. She sat up and looked at her mother with a quick nod.

"I'm ready, Mama. What is it?"

"Do not force the connection. Find the place where love exists and ask for room."

Florence blinked at that. "Ask for room?" She tried, not sure how the words were meant to be taken, but knowing that they sounded as confused as she felt.

Julie nodded, sensing Florence's confusion. "Yes, ask for room. Be patient in doing so, but find the love first. Take that with you tonight. Do you understand?"

"Yes, I do," Florence lied, hoping the words would

make more sense on her walk to town. She stood from her seat and smiled at her mother who was beaming at her from where she sat. "I'll ask for room."

"And look for love," Julie helpfully added.

Florence nodded. "Yes. Look for love and find it before anything else."

"That's my sweet girl. Now don't take your argument with Delilah to heart. I suspect she'll be along tonight. Enjoy yourself and apologize when you can to your sister. I expect you home at an appropriate hour."

Florence pursed her lips. She hated appropriate hours and curfews, but she said nothing, instead opting for a quick bob of her head and a barely there: "Of course, mama." She turned to go but stopped. "I love you," she said over her shoulder, looking back at Julie where the older woman sat with her book in hand.

"I love you too, Flo. Now go and find your loves. Tell Rosemary I said hello."

FLORENCE ROCKED BACK on her heels, hands tucked behind her back, as she surveyed the dance floor. The dance was being held in the grand hall of the town theater. The space was normally reserved for high profile events, such as speeches from the mayor or other elected officials, when the town saw fit to have a gala, wedding receptions, and to celebrate any productions that came to Gold Sky.

Florence remembered the construction of the building, she had been a girl of six, and there had been plenty in the town that had laughed at the efforts to bring such an ornate and delicate building to the town.

"This is a working town. Not a frilly city."

"A waste of timber is what it is."

Mrs. Rosemary had been undeterred in its construction. The snide comments of some townsfolk sliding away like water off a duck's back. The woman was never one to be concerned with the opinions of others. She did as she pleased--always had and always would.

Florence was enthralled by her. She raised a hand and waved at Mrs. Rosemary when she spied her across the hall. Mrs. Rosemary's blue eyes lit up, and she bustled across the room with arms outstretched.

"Flo, oh you look ravishing! I am so pleased we chose to go with this color. It suits you perfectly." Mrs. Rosemary enveloped her in a tight hug. The smell of jasmine and cinnamon that was uniquely Mrs. Rosemary surrounded them, and Florence sank into the other woman's embrace.

"You are a wonderful designer. It's not difficult to look ravishing when you are the one dressing me." She gave a little twirl which delighted Mrs. Rosemary no end, who laughed and gave a little clap.

"It's even easier to look skilled as a designer when the model is so lovely. You and all your sisters take after your mother. I could dress you all in plain linen and every man in this town would lose their hearts."

Florence blew out a raspberry. "I am unconcerned with every man. I search only for two."

"Oh, is that so?"

"Yes, but I can't seem to find a pair that are up to the

task." Florence looked out at the dance floor and paused. All around the walls of the hall were hung with ribbons and glittering streamers which were pulled into the front of the room to delicately frame the crystal chandelier that hung from the middle of the room. Paper and silk lanterns added drama and warmth to the room. Tables laden with finger foods and crystal bowls of red punch were on theme, as were the paper heart cut-outs that covered every surface. Florence was surprised the servers were not attired as mini-cupids, and she smiled as one appeared in front of her offering her a refreshment. She nodded her thanks, accepting the small glass and took a sip before letting out an appreciative hum at the sweet taste.

"That's love's arrow," Mrs. Rosemary told her, nodding at the glass. "A little like a gin blossom, but with a splash of amaro."

Florence raised an eyebrow, sipping the ruby-colored drink and nearly coughed at its strength.

"How much of a splash?" She asked, taking another sip.

Mrs. Rosemary waved a hand and plucked a cup from the server's tray for herself. "Oh, measurements are such a dreadfully droll thing. You can never have too much amaro. Royalty drinks it, you know. It must be good for one's constitution."

Florence giggled and nodded. "Sound logic, as any that I have ever had the pleasure of hearing." She sipped her drink and Mrs. Rosemary stepped closer to her, a hand going to Florence's arm.

"Now, Flo, you were commenting on romance and men and," she raised her eyebrows and inclined her head.

"I am not one to let that conversation slip away. What were you saying?"

"I was commenting on the lack of pairs that I can..." She bit her lip, remembering her mother's words, "ask for a place in," she said finally.

"A place, you say? I could think of a pair of suitors who might be...amenable to such an arrangement."

Florence nearly spit her drink out. She whirled towards Mrs. Rosemary, nearly spilling her cocktail. "Do you mean that? Truly?"

Mrs. Rosemary smiled and gave a tiny dip of her chin in a nod. "I do."

"Where? Who? Are they in attendance tonight?"

"They are, but you might find it a bit difficult to get them to admit what they are searching for."

"But *why?*" The incredulity in Florence's question was palpable, and a few bystanders looked towards them in confusion.

Mrs. Rosemary gave a little laugh and looked at Florence. "Not everyone was raised to be as outspoken in their preferences, nor did they have the kind of home life you did or have the gift of growing up in a town such as Gold Sky."

"Ah, you do have a point there." Florence forced herself to be calmer. It was true that she was blessed to have been given this place as a home. She turned, scanning the dance floor, hoping to be able to spot the men Mrs. Rosemary meant. Surely she should be able to find them on her own.

"I see you straining your eyes, Flo. Look to the left corner by the silk lamps. The pair of young men there are very much in love, but have it in their mind to find wives when I'm quite sure they would do well to take one between them."

Florence's mouth went dry. She saw them. "They're beautiful." A pair of men in fine suits, cut just right and no doubt the work of Mrs. Rosemary's hand. Florence could spot the other woman's touches anywhere and saw it now in the matching charcoal suits they wore. One was red-haired, his hair pulled back in a fashionable knot, and fair-skinned. She wondered if he wore his hair loose and what it might feel like under her fingers. The other, a brunette with hair as dark as night. She suspected him to be of Mexican descent from the warm brown tone of his skin. He turned toward her, and Florence nearly dropped her drink. High cheekbones, full lips, and dark brown eyes met hers from across the room.

"Oh," Florence breathed when he smiled at her. The man beside him turned at a slight nudge and he too smiled in her direction, green eyes lighting up when they met her shocked gaze. She had thought she would be able to withstand the attention of two men, but here she was nearly melting like a candle from warmth in these two men's smiles.

"Come with me." Mrs. Rosemary took her elbow and began forward startling Florence out of her smile induced stupor.

"What are you doing?"

"Introducing you. Every proper lady needs an intro-duction when there are eligible men to be considered."

"But--" Florence made to dig her feet in and found out that Mrs. Rosemary was surprisingly strong.

"But nothing. You wished for two suitors and I have found them."

The march toward the men was quick, passing in the blink of an eye. Florence was tongue-tied as she found herself suddenly standing in front of them. Mrs. Rosemary inclined her head to the men.

"Hello, gentlemen. I'm so happy to see you here."

They both dropped at the waist in exaggerated bows that Florence might have found silly on anyone but them. She watched as they took turns kissing the offered hand Mrs. Rosemary held out.

"We thank ye fer creating such an opportunity for us, Mrs. Rosemary. We are forever indebted to ye for all yer hard work." The red-haired man spoke, and Florence nearly swooned at the Scottish brogue she heard in his voice.

"Brendan, you are too kind. Now, it is time for me to return the favor you bestowed upon me by introducing you to one of my dearest friends. Florence Wickes-Barnes. She's the sheriff's daughter and a fine young lady. She works for me in the dress shop as a seamstress and is one of the most talented I have ever had the pleasure of teaching. Sharp as a whip. And," Mrs. Rosemary paused in her praise, "very welcoming to different expressions of love." She winked at the men and her meaning could not be misunderstood. This was no normal introduction.

It was one of romance.

Florence bit her lip meeting the men's eyes to see they were looking at her with slightly rounded eyes. Neither man moved, standing stiff as boards, and Florence swallowed down the feeling of an impending shriek in Mrs.

Rosemary's direction. The other woman did what she wanted. That included having a blunt manner of speaking. One did not get the luxury of accepting Rosemary Stark piecemeal. It was either the whole woman or nothing. As such, Florence forced a smile to her lips and cleared her throat, stepping forward. She would smooth this over as well as she was able.

"Pleased to meet you both." Florence held out her hand to them, anticipating a handshake, but neither man moved, still staring at Mrs. Rosemary as if expecting the other woman to suddenly perform an acrobatic routine. Her hand shook slightly from holding it out, and Florence fought against the wince she wanted to give. Her plan for recovering the introduction falling flat as neither man came forward to take her hand. She would have to think of another way to form some kind of relationship with them.

Florence cleared her throat, delicately, and moved to step back but was stopped when a hand reached out to clasp hers. It was a gentle grip but firm. The feel of calloused fingers on her knuckles had her heart beating wildly. She wanted to thread her fingers with his but instead, she stood still and smiled at him, waiting for him to speak, like the lady they all supposed her to be.

"Pleased to meet ye Florence Wickes-Barnes. My name is Brendan Black." His voice was lovely. Dark and warm, rich like honeyed whiskey. She gazed at him curiously. There was something about the man that was closed off even as he touched her. Florence could have sworn he was in a different room, not a foot in front of her with an air of indifference that clung to him like the wool of his suit.

"Good evening, Brendan."

"This is my partner, ah," Brendan stopped and cleared his throat. "My *business partner*. Anselmo Ortega."

She looked to where Brendan gestured and Anselmo smiled at her, taking her other hand in his. Her fingers twitched in his grip and breathing was suddenly a feat. How was she to maintain the facade of a lady with both Brendan and Anselmo holding onto her hands.

Smiles were one thing, but touch, that was an entirely different matter.

"Pleased to meet you, but there is no need for you to call me Anselmo."

"Oh?" Florence asked, voice dropping an octave when he came forward and placed a kiss on the back of her hand. "Then what am I to call you?" she asked.

"Beautiful women get special privileges with me. Call me Ansel," he told her, smiling up at her where he was bent over her hand.

Florence managed a nod of her head. "Ansel."

Mrs. Rosemary tittered beside them and leaned close, kissing Florence's cheek and gave it a pinch as she drew away. "I'll leave the three of you to it then. Please enjoy the singles dance." She turned and swept away with a swish of her skirts before any of them could speak. When they were alone, Ansel squeezed her hand.

"Florence is a lovely name." He was still holding onto her, and Florence cleared her throat, drawing her hand away before anyone noticed. Though she wanted two suitors, two husbands, she did not wish to draw anyone's attention before she was good and ready.

"Thank you," she said, in her most demure tone, and

aimed a smile at both men. "When did you arrive in our fair town?"

"Month before last, but we have mainly been at work. Brendan here is absolutely horrendous for keeping us working. This is our first true reprieve from the business."

"And what business might that be?"

"Mining," Brendan said then, his voice had gone a touch gruff. "We're here to mine. We have a site outside of town and with the railroad? It's a lucrative move for us." He touched Ansel's arm then stepped back from her. "If you'll excuse us, Miss Florence."

"But only for a moment," Ansel interjected, quickly shooting her a wink. "We would never leave a fair lady such as you for too long, Florence."

She nodded, watching the men step away. Their heads were bent together as they spoke. Whatever the subject was, it was serious. She edged closer on the pretense of admiring the cluster of silk lamps beside her, but was unable to catch their conversation other than the hushed tones of their voices. Somewhere behind them on the stage, the band began to play a waltz and she nearly cursed. Now was not the time for music. She was trying to eavesdrop and how was she meant to do so with that infernal music playing?

Florence turned to the side casting a furtive look in the men's direction. Brendan was touching Ansel, his hand splayed across the small of the other man's back. The touch was slight but it was intimate as was the way Ansel turned leaning into the other man as they spoke. These were the touches of lovers. Mrs. Rosemary was right.

"How am I to ask for a place with them over there?" Florence whispered, sipping from her drink. The burn of the liquor was masked by the sweet flavor but it warmed her all the same as she contemplated her options. Ansel was amenable to her, she could see that. Brendan would take a bit of effort but she could manage it if only they were to--she stopped her spiral of thoughts when they turned and started back toward her. The men were coming and she needed to collect herself if this was going to go right.

She smiled at them when they came to a stop in front of her. "Is everything all right?" She asked.

"Yes, of course, nothing but a bit of business," Ansel replied, taking a glass from a passing server. He held out the drink to Brendan and smiled at the man. "Isn't that right?"

The other man nodded sipping from the drink but said nothing.

"Ah, well, I hope you've been having a lovely time in Gold Sky. I grew up here and there's no other place like it."

Ansel nodded sipping his drink. "We've come to see that. Mrs. Rosemary has made it abundantly clear that all styles of living are welcome here."

"She does take it upon herself to be the unofficial welcoming committee," Florence conceded.

"You have two fathers," Brendan said suddenly, startling Florence. It wasn't a question. It was an observation and she paused, giving the man a shrewd look.

"Yes, that's right. I have two fathers. The sheriffs in town."

"Is that what Mrs. Rosemary meant by you being accepting of all types of love?" Brendan asked, earning an elbow to the gut from Ansel.

"Brendan, this is not what we talked about," he hissed but Brendan shrugged and rubbed his side.

"We are not fighting over one woman," he shot back and Florence raised an eyebrow.

"And why would you be fighting over anything?" She asked in confusion.

"Because we aim to marry."

"As do I," she informed them.

Brendan crossed his arms and took a step closer. His emerald eyes were intent on her and she found she enjoyed the attention. "And there is only one of you, but the two of us. How could we not fight over you?"

Florence laughed, raising her glass to her lips and taking a sip. "That's quite easy, gentlemen. I aim to marry the pair of you."

She'd never been one to mince words. It was best the men learned that now.

CHAPTER 2

"*P*ardon?" Brendan asked, looking taken aback by Florence's statement. She smiled at him, growing bolder when she saw that Ansel was also smiling at the red-haired man at his side.

"I aim to marry," she repeated, eyes moving between the men.

"The pair of us?" Ansel flicked a finger between himself and Brendan as he gave her a charming smile. It was just a slight upturn of his lips, a smirk more than a full smile but it was enough to make Florence flush.

"Ah, yes, that's the order of things," she managed when she had recovered enough to speak again.

"And how do ye intend to do that?" Brendan questioned, hands going to his hips as he considered her. He was a large man with broad shoulders, his red hair reminded her of flames, of what the sun looked like just before it set. The red hues of it moving from ginger to auburn in the lighting of the hall. His hair was beautiful and Florence had to concentrate on the man's question rather than thinking of what his hair might look like free from the knot he wore it in.

"Pardon?" She asked, echoing Brendan's earlier question.

"How do y'mean to marry the pair of us when there is only one of you, flower?" Brendan's tone reminded her of what boots on gravel sounded like and she nearly dropped the glass she had been holding to her lips at that one word: *flower.*

"That's not my name," she offered weakly, her heart fluttering wildly in her chest. Was he meaning to use an endearment or had he simply misheard Mrs. Rosemary? Florence desperately wished for the former. It would, she was certain, help a great deal in moving forward with her proposition for the men, but there was no fixing it.

"Aye, tis not, Florence, but you are one all the same, are ye not?" Brendan asked. Florence shivered at that. The man knew her name but he chose to call her flower. Her grasp on maintaining her image as a lady weakened and she took a quick step away with a forced titter of laughter, though it came out far too high pitched to be considered natural.

"I'm not sure I know what you mean," she said when nothing else came to mind. Brendan's eyebrows knit together and he stepped closer offering her his hand.

"I'm sure yer words will come to ye quicker than y'think. Dance with me." There was no question here. It was a statement. A decree and Florence was stepping forward and slipping her hand into his before she could stop herself.

"Yes," she breathed, letting him draw her closer. He handed her drink off to Ansel.

"Mind that," he told the other man who snorted and waved a hand at them.

"As you wish, *darling*," Ansel drawled, voice clinging to the endearment in a way that had Florence's breath coming short. She looked at Ansel over Brendan's shoulder as the couple spun off and felt a heat spread through her body at the look in the man's dark eyes.

Desire. Want. *Need.*

It was all there for her to see, for any that looked upon him, and Florence was made giddy by it. A laugh escaped her lips as Brendan guided her through the throng of dancers already moving in time to the lively music being played.

"Now, flower, tell me this plan of yours. There is a plan, isn't there?" Brendan asked, leading her through the dance. He was leaning close, his breath a warm puff along her neck as he spoke and Florence bit back the moan that nearly slipped from her at the sensation.

"I hadn't thought that far in advance," she admitted, looking up at Brendan.

"That so?"

"Planning isn't my strong point. I'm more a woman of action so to speak."

Brendan chuckled, spinning her. The gesture caused her skirts to fan out around her and Florence felt positively ethereal. Light and desired, like the women in her romances. She eyed Brendan as the man brought her back to him. How was it that he had turned the tables on her so easily? He smiled down at her, a lock of ginger hair falling over his brow as he did so.

"You look very dashing," she told him, her hand tightening on his shoulder to stop from brushing it aside.

"Dashing?"

"Handsome," she clarified.

"I've been called many a thing in my life but dashing was never one of 'em."

Florence gave a snort of disbelief. The sound was unladylike, but it was true to her feelings. "That's a lie."

"I tell no lies," Brendan replied. They parted then. Hands outstretched towards the other as they moved through the dance steps that placed them side-by-side.

"I find that hard to believe, sir." Florence smirked at Brendan over their hands. There was no denying the tension building between them, the feeling growing from the touch of hands, the trail of fingers on bodies in close orbit. She had never felt this...aroused from the simple act of dancing with a man. She was not naive to the pleasures of intimacy, and yet, somehow Brendan was filling her with an ever-growing need, with only a simple dance.

So lost in her thoughts was Florence that she gasped at the sudden sensation of Brendan's hand sliding down to the small of her back, his palm flat against her body, his arm behind her as he stepped around her. The feel of his broad chest brushing her shoulders proved a formidable distraction but Florence recovered and managed to follow the steps.

"Distracted, flower?" His voice rumbled like thunder down her spine. The feel of it grounding her in the moment. There would be no getting lost in her daydreams now, no matter how pleasant her imagination could be.

She turned her head to look up at him. "I assure you, my attention is all yours."

Brendan chuckled again, turning her to face him as the dance ended. "Too soon," he murmured, raising her hand to his to kiss the back of it. "Thank you for the dance," he told her and for a wild moment, Florence thought he meant to leave her.

If he did, she would follow him, the move would bring attention to her, maybe even cause a few to whisper but Florence didn't care. Those who whispered hadn't danced with Brendan Black, nor had they gotten lost in the heat of Ansel Ortega's eyes.

She had. She would willingly attract attention for a minute more with the men.

But then Ansel was there with her drink in hand and an inviting smile on his handsome face. "Your drink." He handed it to her with a flourish, the gesture bringing a smile to Florence's face.

"Thank you," she murmured. Ansel beamed at her as she sipped.

"You both looked...perfect," he said, nodding at the dance floor behind them. "I would say perfectly suited."

"Did we?" She asked.

"More than suited," Brendan added. He put a hand on Ansel's shoulder and stepped closer, both of the men in front of her forming a wall of masculine beauty that Florence wanted nothing more than to lean into. She forced herself to stay as she was and took another quick drink of her cocktail.

"You're a beautiful dancer," she told Brendan.

"It's easy when my partner is so willing," he replied and Ansel chuckled, turning to look back at the man behind him.

"You've changed your opinion then?" Ansel asked.

Brendan lifted a shoulder in a shrug. "That depends on the lass. She says she has a plan to marry us both."

Ansel's eyebrows drew up. "Oh?" He looked at her, stepping closer until Florence was very nearly pressed between him and Brendan. The music and chatter around her faded into the background, until it amounted to only the vaguest of impressions. "What's your plan then?"

Florence swallowed hard, fingers tightening on the stem of her glass. "Well, I suppose the first step is to beguile."

Ansel grinned. "You're doing a fine job of it. What follows the beguiling?"

"An outing, where," Florence's eyes cut to the side, taking in the swirling colors of the dancers as they moved across the dance floor, "where I am able to proposition the pair of you."

"And then?" Brendan reached out and tweaked one of the golden ribbons woven through her hair.

Her eyes drifted closed at the sensation. "Well, I suppose negotiations would ensue before anything else would occur." She opened her eyes to look up at both men. "The end result would be marriage of course," she finished with a pleased smile.

"I have to say, I quite like this plan." Ansel looked to Brendan. "Don't you?"

"Aye, I do."

Florence raised an eyebrow at him. "You were not so agreeable before our dance."

"Aye, that was before ye cleared up the part where we'll not fight over ye. I have no intention of losing Ansel on account of any woman, no matter how bonny she be."

She crossed her arms and tilted her head to the side considering the men. They cut a fine image, the pair of them with their contrasting complexions and striking features. Brendan's green eyes served to set off Ansel's brown and ochre, the way they stood close with Ansel just a couple of inches shorter than Brendan. Florence would be able to kiss Ansel just by tilting her face to his, but Brendan's would require her to raise herself up on her toes. She wished to be between them rather than where she stood, but it would have to do for now because, for now, she had both men's attention. She basked in it like a cat napping in the sun and smiled boldly when a passing woman cast a curious look their way.

"You were here looking for two women then?"

Ansel gave a quick nod of his head. "A foolhardy thing to do, but Brendan has always been headstrong." His eyes cut to the other man and Brendan scoffed.

"I was doin' what I thought appropriate."

"But you know about my family, yes?" Florence asked.

Brendan nodded. "Aye."

"Then why would you think two women necessary for the pair of you to live long and happy lives full of matrimonial bliss?"

Brendan whistled. "Matrimonial bliss? Now that is something far bigger than finding a wife."

Florence hummed. "On account of you wishing for a husband as well?"

Brendan laughed and Ansel shook his head a smile on his face. "She has us figured out, now then. What do you think of that, darling?" Ansel asked, his eyes on Brendan, voice soft in a tone reserved for lovers.

Florence had never been more thrilled.

FLORENCE BLEW out a heavy sigh and leaned close to the silver-backed mirror. She had excused herself to "freshen up," but what she needed was a moment alone to collect her thoughts. She had come to the singles dance with the mission of finding a pair of eligible suitors. Florence had never expected the night's events to exceed her expectations and all within the first hour of her arrival.

"All is well," she whispered, and fanned herself with her evening bag. She was overheated and she had scarcely danced in the past hour. How was it that she was this out of breath and flush-faced from mere conversation? She straightened at the thought. It was not a mere conversation. Not when it was with Brendan and Ansel. The men were enigmatic, seductive, and intense in a way that had Florence feeling drunk though she had only enjoyed one of Mrs. Rosemary's cocktails.

And yet for all the attraction she felt for the men, there was a sweetness to them that was unexpected. An open manner that had urged Florence to open herself to them and to know that they returned the gesture in kind. The trio had spent the early night dancing that soon turned into deep conversation. Ansel had procured a small table for them in relative peace from the excitement of the dance. There they were able to talk openly and freely, and Florence learned they had indeed come to the dance with a similar goal to her own.

They wished to marry and start a family. Though Brendan had thought it must be done separately.

"There are not many places as accepting as Gold Sky," Brendan told her, leaning back in his chair with a serious look on his face. "We thought it was too good to be true when we heard of yer fathers."

"I told him it was to be believed but you'll see that he's headstrong," Ansel told her with a pained look. "There was never any need for two wives when one would suit us."

Florence looked down at her hands and then swallowed hard. "So you are in love then?"

"Aye, we are."

"Yes, very much so."

Florence was glad to hear it. They should be in love. Everyone should. But there was still one question she needed to ask of them. She raised her eyes to theirs.

"And you still," she cleared her throat and continued on, "still desire to have a wife. To truly have her?"

She hadn't thought of this when following her mother's advice. To look for love where it already existed was one thing, but asking for space in it was another exercise of vulnerability she hadn't anticipated. What was she to do if the men only felt love for the other? What would she do if there was no place for a woman, not truly, in their hearts and lives?

Florence wished to be cherished and desired in her marriage. It would not do for her to be a wife in name only.

"If ye mean do we crave to take a woman in our bed between us to share the answer is yes."

Ansel sighed and rubbed his temples. "Must you be so crass?"

"She was asking ye know it as well as I do."

Ansel's lips pursed and he leaned forward in his seat towards Florence. "What I think Brendan is trying to say is that we do, indeed, desire a woman in the romantic sense. We have been known to share a lover when they have been amenable. Our deepest desire is for our marriage to follow suit."

Florence nodded and smiled when he placed his hand near hers. Not touching, not really. Their fingers were barely brushing. Her pinky to his thumb, but that was more than enough for Florence. Even if they were to begin a triad relationship in earnest, they would have to follow the rules of a proper courtship in public.

Gold Sky was accepting, but what it was not was lacking in propriety in matters of the heart.

"Now, flower," Brendan began, pulling her attention back to him, "what do ye think of having the two of us?"

"All my life I watched my parents, all three of them, live and love in perfect balance. Their love only seemed to grow the more they shared it and I want that for myself. I do not think I could be married in any other way. I have had no prospects to pursue until meeting the both of you." She smiled at them, making sure to look each man in the eyes. She wanted them to see how sincerely she meant her words. That this was not a passing fancy.

It was her life. *Her heart.*

And she longed to share it with them.

"I desire nothing more than to explore this with you. With the both of you."

Brendan smiled at her. "Then it seems our next step is an outing. That was step two in her plan, was it not?" He looked to Ansel.

"It was, and if I'm not mistaken, there would be a proposition extended to us on said outing, but I am to assume that is if all goes well?" He looked at her expectantly.

"Yes, that's about the measure of things," Florence croaked, her throat suddenly dry. Ansel and Brendan nodded in agreement, the gesture so synchronized that Florence imagined they had done it hundreds of times before. She wondered what other things they shared and felt a bubble of excitement at being allowed to discover it all for herself.

"Florence?" A voice called out to her, pulling all three's attention to the speaker. Florence sat up and pulled her hand back into her lap when she saw who it was.

"Delilah!" she exclaimed, hopping up from her seat and rushing forward to embrace her. "You came."

"I did. Mama thought it would be good for me to get out of the house." Delilah's eyes moved from her to the men still seated at the table. "You made friends," she observed.

"I did. The most wonderful friends!"

Ansel stood from the table and extended a hand to

Delilah. "I am Anselmo Ortega, and this is Brendan Black," he said, taking Delilah's hand and motioning back at Brendan who was standing from his seat and welcoming Delilah with a quick nod.

"Pleased to meet you," Delilah answered as she accepted Brendan's hand as well. Florence nearly giggled when she saw that the men had caught her sister in a position very much like the one she had found herself in earlier. A hand taken by either man, Delilah seemed just as struck by them as Florence had been.

"I-ah, may I have a word with my sister?"

"Of course, of course. I will get you refreshments while you visit." Ansel moved forward, taking Brendan's elbow and the men left, but not before they both sent a shared grin Florence's way. She was in the midst of returning it when Delilah yanked her close and down into a seat.

"Who are those men?"

"Friends."

"Those are not friends, those are men. Now who are they?"

Florence smiled with feigned innocence. "Now, dear sister, why can I not be friends with men?"

"One man? That would be fine. But two?" Delilah held up two fingers accentuating her words. "Two is a plan, Flo. And two devastatingly handsome men is a promise."

"A promise of what?"

"Of you getting into mischief."

Florence stuck out her tongue. "A courtship is not mischief, Del. I do wish you would be a bit more accepting of my choices."

Her sister's eyes widened. "You're in a courtship? Already?"

"Well, not yet. I suppose that will come after I proposition them."

Delilah looked ready to faint. "Before you *what?*"

"Don't worry, it's all on the up and up. I swear it. I've discussed it with Brendan and Ansel."

Delilah bit her lip and sighed. "Florence, do you know what you're doing?"

"I do. I spoke to Mama about this and I know that you don't mean for us to fight, but if you cannot understand my choices, cannot accept what I want for my life then I fear we will never be at peace again."

"I don't wish to fight. I love you, Flo."

Florence's heart softened at that. She had always been close to Delilah. Their contention over Florence's choice of love match had proven to be an unexpected obstacle in their relationship.

"Why do you not want this for me?" she asked, and Delilah winced.

"It's not that I don't want it for you. I do not want you getting hurt. Our parents have something hard to find, and it would be hard to watch you chase after it only to be let down. I only want you to be happy, Flo."

She put her hand on Delilah's arm. "I know. I love you, Del."

"If those men are what you want, then I support it." She held up a hand when Florence's face lit up and she waited for Florence to settle before she continued to speak. "God help them if they hurt you. I will hunt them

34

down and make them pay. I do not care if Seylah is the surest shot out of us. I will shoot true. I promise you."

Florence laughed and blinked back the tears her sister's words brought on. "Oh, Del, that's so sweet."

"I love you, Flo."

"I love you too, Del."

They embraced, arms tight around the other as they laughed. It felt good to reconcile, and Florence let out a happy sigh feeling lighter now that she and her sister were at peace again. Delilah pulled back and gave her a smirk.

"How did you manage to find the two most handsome men at this dance?"

"They are dashing, aren't they?"

"Utterly breathtaking. I thought I might faint when they both held my hands."

Florence giggled. "They did the same to me. It is an unfair weapon to use on unsuspecting women."

"Remember to keep your wits about you with the pair of them pursuing you," Del advised, and Florence waved a hand.

"We still have an outing to enjoy. We could find that we do not suit, and the whole thing will be done before it begins."

Delilah rolled her eyes and sighed. "You know as well as I do that will not happen. They are enamored with you."

"How do you know that? You've only just arrived."

"I am in possession of eyes that see, Flo. It was obvious the second I set foot in the door that they had eyes only for you." Her sister's tone was imperious and under normal circumstances, Florence would have railed against it, but as it was, she did not hate it. Rather she was eager to hear more.

"Do go on, sister," she practically purred, leaning towards her sister, elbows on the table and tucking a hand under her chin. She smiled at the look of consternation that passed over Delilah's face.

"You're particularly trying at times, Flo."

"As are you, Del."

Delilah's lips turned up in a smile and she laughed. "Point taken. Now, Flo." She jerked her chin towards where Brendan and Ansel were walking towards them. They seemed to be taking their time, or rather, they were being forced to as every unattached woman---of which there were many in attendance, had taken the initiative to introduce themselves to the men.

Florence blew out an agitated sigh watching a woman fawn over Brendan, but the Scotsman looked unaffected. His green eyes moved over the woman before he looked over her head towards their table. She sat up when their eyes met and Delilah chuckled.

"I was nearly fit to wax poetic on how those men are enchanted by you but there's the proof." Delilah tapped a finger on the table, watching her sister and Brendan gaze at the other like smitten fools. "Even as he speaks to another woman, his attention is solely on you. It's quite romantic."

"It is, isn't it?" Florence sighed happily.

"I take it they are in love?"

She nodded, looking away from Brendan to her sister. "They are and I would have it no other way."

Delilah's shoulders relaxed slightly at that. "I'm relieved. My one greatest fear was the men you chose for yourself would not love the other as husbands. A marriage like our parents have would not work if their love was only for you."

Florence nodded and squeezed her sister's hand. She could hear the concern in her sister's voice, and suddenly her mother's earlier talk with her fell into place.

"Do not worry, Del. Mama saw to it that I understood exactly what was needed for a triad marriage and I am confident that I have a chance at a fulfilling and happy courtship with Ansel and Brendan."

"And then...marriage?" Her sister asked.

Florence looked away and back toward the men. They were only a few feet away now. She paused, weighing her sister's questions carefully. Could she see a marriage with them? It should be a weighty question, one that she had no business answering after knowing the men such a short amount of time, but Florence found the answer came easier than she could have ever anticipated.

"Yes," she answered, voice steady and sure. She looked at Delilah and smiled giving her a quick nod. "Yes," she said again.

"Then I am happy for you."

The men had joined them at the table by now. Each one flanking where Delilah sat. Her sister winked at Florence as she stood and excused herself from the trio.

"Enjoy your night, Flo." She turned to the men and wiggled her fingers in a goodbye. "Good evening, gentlemen. A pleasure to meet you both."

Ansel gave her a slight bow. "The pleasure was all ours, Delilah."

Brendan nodded, a hand over his heart in farewell. "Likewise."

Delilah left them then and Florence looked to the men as they moved to take their seats, one on either side of her. Florence sighed happily and settled back into her seat. The three of them sitting as they were felt *right*.

She knew they were embarking on something new, something with the potential to change their lives forever, for better or worse. Tonight was a night of possibility and potential, there was an undeniable attraction blooming amongst them, and Florence was eager to see it grow and mature. Hopefully, it would have the chance over many more nights shared, just like this, albeit in far quieter settings.

For now, however, she would enjoy tonight.

CHAPTER 3

*F*lorence sat in her room. The night's events playing in her mind. It had been eventful, to say the least. Enough to make a woman think she'd gone mad, or at least that none of it had been real. Her night with Ansel and Brendan was far too close to the perfect romantic fantasy she had daydreamed of. A magical night of dancing, a gorgeous dress, perfect decor and the entire night in attendance at an event where she met not one, but two eligible men.

Two men that were interested in pursuing her together. She licked her lips and stood from where she had been brushing her hair. They had an outing to plan. The particulars of it were vague at best, but she trusted the men to remedy that soon enough. Brendan and Ansel were men of action, or at least they presented themselves as such. Florence preferred to take them at face value until she was given a reason to believe otherwise. She quite liked the idea of two capable and interested men.

She shrugged out of her dressing gown, blew out her

lamp, and went to her bed. The light from the moon illuminated the bed and Florence rolled onto her side looking out into the pale light. It was a full moon and as pretty as it was, she was restless. Sleep would not come to her easily this night. Perhaps her restless energy was to blame on the feeling that overcame her when Florence thought of Ansel and Brendan. A warm feeling unfurled in her belly.

Exhilarating and relaxing ... and *pleasurable.* There was no explaining the sensation the men inspired in her other than lust. It was the only explanation, and could be the reason for her sudden bout of energy.

She frowned and shifted. Florence wondered what Ansel and Brendan would do if they were aware of the sensations the mere thought of them brought on. Her warm skin, the fact that she knew her sleep would now go fitfully, why even in her bed clothes she felt too constrained and short of breath.

Heavens knew what would happen when she was properly outfitted to play the part of a chaste lady. She swallowed hard, turning and punching at the pillow before shifting again. Florence did not much like having to placate other's expectations of her, and her propriety and reputation were two things that weighed on her the most.

She did not understand why two such cumbersome and unhelpful ideas should hold a woman back from living freely. Propriety would not help change a broken wagon wheel or shoe a horse, neither would her reputation save her from a blizzard, but here she was on the frontier and expected to heed etiquette.

Florence knew she was luckier than most to have the family that she did, a mother that encouraged her, sisters that challenged her, and fathers who let much go "unnoticed" when she took to one of her moods. They allowed Florence the freedom to grow, but it did not mean that she did not still feel held back in some way.

"Stop being so dramatic," she whispered to herself. She squeezed her eyes shut and worked to steady her breathing. How her thoughts had turned from lust to brooding over her predicament was quite worrisome. Florence needed to better train her thoughts if she were to be up at this hour of night losing sleep.

And without even a salacious thought to show for it.

Brooding over how she had a loving family, or suddenly two highly desirable romantic prospects when she started the evening with none, would not help her to be well rested the next day. Dark circles and shadowed features were the surest way to reveal that she had spent a restless night—and her family would notice. Nothing escaped her sisters' observations, even if her parents missed the signs. Though she much suspected her parents would refrain from asking after her less than refreshed appearance purely out of politeness.

Her sisters were in possession of no such reservations.

Florence breathed deeply, the heave of her chest and the following exhale relaxed her body slightly. She took another breath and her muscles loosened a bit more. Slowly, the tension left her body, each rise and drop of her chest allowing her to sink further into the mattress until she was able to drift away to a dreamless sleep.

THE NEXT MORNING, Florence realized that her efforts had been in vain because she did, in fact, appear unwell. Her complexion was splotchy, eyes puffy and there were the tell-tale circles beneath her eyes that had her groaning in frustration. Her sisters would never let her get through her coffee before the interrogation started.

They would think she had been brooding.

She knew it.

Florence went through her morning routine, dressing slowly and taking care with her toiletries, but there was no amount of rogue or carefully pressed powder to undo the hours of thinking, *not brooding*, Florence had entertained the previous night. She nodded at her reflection and made for the door.

"Yes, thinking. A wise woman thinks, and that is what I was doing," she told herself as she descended the stairs. "Thinking, thinking, thinking." Florence's foot had scarcely hit the last step when Rose's voice called out to her.

"Why ever are you muttering to yourself?"

Florence whirled towards her sister's voice and nearly fell from the step. She clung to the banister managing to right herself at the last possible moment. Rose's laughter was particularly vexing as the other woman descended the stairs above her.

"Why the scowl?" Rose inquired when she came close enough to look her sister in the eyes. "And are you well? You nearly tumbled to the floor just then."

Florence grit her teeth and pushed herself away from

the banister. She descended the last step with as much dignity as she could manage.

"I am plenty well," she said with a toss of her hair.

Rose scoffed. "Mmm, is that so? Well then why don't you tell me why I heard there were two men enamored with you at that little dance you went to?

Her mouth dropped open in shock. "How did you hear of that already?"

"I have my ways." Rose smirked and continued on, walking into the dining room. She looked over her shoulder at Florence. "And all who attended were all too willing to talk."

"Oh they were, were they? Those meddlers." Florence muttered, making a mental note to stay clear of as many busybodies in Gold Sky as she was able. It would be a challenging task. As she was one herself, but who could blame her? Gold Sky was not without its entertainment, if one knew where to look.

If Florence were honest, she just didn't much like that her sister had heard from town versus herself. In addition to meddling and busybodying, Florence adored a good reveal.

Damn those people and their loose lips.

"Don't pull that sour face," Rose said, turning an appraising eye to the kitchen counter where fresh biscuits sat cooling on the stove. Seylah must have been up before them judging by the coffee that was also brewed. Having a law woman as a sister could be rough on one's nerves but there were also perks.

"You are just upset that you didn't get to tell me yourself, admit it," Rose said and poured herself a cup of coffee with a smug look on her face.

Florence opted to shove a biscuit into her mouth. Under normal circumstances she should have been in heaven. The biscuit was of their Aunt Violet's recipe. Flaky, light, and decadent. But as it was, the biscuit was serving no more than diversionary purposes. She arched an eyebrow at her sister and continued to eat her biscuit.

If she were chewing then Rose wouldn't be able to see how right she was.

"Chewing isn't going to save you from having to comment at some point."

Florence raised a shoulder in a shrug and grabbed a plate and another biscuit. She took her sweet time buttering it. When Rose looked fit to be tied she finally turned to her and smiled sweetly.

"Perhaps there is some truth to your assertion." Florence sipped delicately from her coffee and took her plate to the small kitchen table that sat to one side. It was a far cozier spot than the formal dining room. A place where they had squeezed tight in her early years, enjoying the warmth from the stove while they enjoyed a meal together with plenty of laughter and smiles. They still took to having coffee and tea at the well-loved kitchen table, and her mother enjoyed breakfast cooked by her fathers there once a week.

It was a fortunate thing her fathers enjoyed cooking and that they had a wonderful cook, Agnes Pine, otherwise not one of them would eat. Her mother never had been any good in the kitchen, but thankfully Agnes took to teaching them all a bit of this and that, ensuring

Florence and her sisters knew enough to get by in the kitchen.

Rose considered her sister over her cup of coffee and sat at the table. "In what way?"

"In the way that you are entirely correct, but is it too much for a woman to disclose her own whereabouts in the land of romantic overtures?"

"And what overtures have there been exactly?" Delilah asked, coming in the kitchen door. Florence sighed, raising her cup in greeting to her sister.

"You know the measure of them as you were in attendance," she reminded her sister. Del chuckled and made her way to where the coffee and biscuits sat.

"Ah, yes, your suitors," she said, buttering a biscuit. Rose sat up with an excited clap of her hands.

"So it is true then?"

"Why are you acting surprised? You said the townsfolk had already enlightened you to my current romantic status," Florence asked in confusion, but Rose waved her off.

"You are prone to dramatics. I thought it best to piece together what I had heard at the mercantile this morning."

"And what were you doing at the mercantile this morning?" Delilah asked. "You're not one to wake early unless it is a dire circumstance and it is hardly seven this morning."

Rose blushed looking flustered at the question. "That is personal."

"No more personal than my night at the dance." Florence crossed her arms and pinned Rose with a stare. "Now tell us what you were doing there before breakfast."

Rose blew out a sigh and shook her head. "Absolutely not. We are not discussing my morning errands--"

"Mystery emergency, I think you mean," Delilah pointed out, taking a seat next to Florence.

"When it's all boring and mundane, I assure you--"

"I think you're right. It must have been rather secretive too with the way she's blushing."

Rose set her coffee down with an exasperated sigh. "You two are so trying. How is it that we are siblings?"

"Just lucky, I suppose," Florence said with a wink.

"Blessed we all are," Delilah deadpanned.

Rose glowered at them. "More like cursed, I say. You nosey little hens."

"That's quite an accusation. You were all too happy to discuss my suitors," Florence pointed out.

Rose rolled her eyes at her sister and pointed a finger at her. "That's because you would be absolutely put out if I did not go to such effort."

"She's right, you know." Delilah sipped delicately from her cup giving her sister a knowing look. Florence hated that look. It was the look all older siblings, especially sisters, had mastered to perfection. The kind that let their youngers know they had them entirely figured out. Delilah had always been the closest to Florence, and vice versa. The affection of their relationship made all the more obvious in moments such as these when the sisters were locked in a battle of stares and wills.

"I detest that smug look," she told her sister.

Delilah raised an eyebrow. Florence's lips pursed. The staring match persisted before Rose groaned at her older siblings.

"The pair of you are ridiculous. Now, do get on with it. I am dying for details!"

Florence was the first to break eye contact. The little sound of triumph Del made at that was nearly enough to set her across the table at her sister but Rose snapped her fingers.

"Attention here, dear sister." She pointed at Del. "And you stop poking at her, you know she cannot resist it."

"I can resist...it," Florence spluttered.

"Prove it. Tell me about your suitors."

"Fine, I shall. And let me say that the night was absolutely perfect. Mrs. Rosemary worked a miracle in the hall. It's a grand place, all right but with her eye for detail? Absolutely stunning! Oh, and the music was heavenly. I never danced so much in all my life."

"With two men?" Rose asked hopefully.

Florence nodded eagerly. "Yes, two wonderful men. Each beautiful in their own way."

"What are their names?"

"Anselmo Ortega and Brendan Black."

Rose hummed. "Well, with names like that you do indeed have my interest. Are they as dreamy as they sound?"

"Even more so," Florence sighed and leaned back in her chair thinking of the night she had spent in the men's company. "Ansel, he has me calling him that, you know. Is gorgeous and utterly devastating."

"He is quite charming," Delilah conceded, and Rose frowned.

"I hate that I haven't met them. Now tell me about

Brendan Black. He sounds like a villain from some old vaudeville act!"

Florence tapped her cup in consideration. "No, he's no villain but he is the more closed off of the two. A bit gruff but I know there's something softer to him. I saw a glimpse of it last night, but for all that, the man is sensual."

Rose paused and then cleared her throat. "Sensual?" she asked, voice scarcely above a whisper. Florence nodded eagerly.

Delilah joined in when Rose gave Florence a questioning look. "Very. Enigmatic, I would say," she added.

"Oh, my," Rose breathed.

"Oh my indeed. And I have plans for an outing with the pair of them this week. Why I cannot wait to see them in the light of day. Last night was the first time I had seen either of them."

"I was curious about that," Delilah said. "It was odd to me that they came out of hiding for the dance."

"Oh, I think we both know that Mrs. Rosemary had more than something to do with their sudden appearance," Rose said with a laugh. "If it were up to her, we would all be happily married and anchored to this town." There was a note of disdain, of bitterness, and both Delilah and Florence looked at their younger sister in question.

Florence's eyebrows knit together. "Why do you say that as if it were a bad thing, Rose?"

Rose was silent for a moment before she sighed. "I just mean to say that there is a life beyond Gold Sky and that-that I would like to see it. I want more than this town has to offer."

"You wish to leave then? In earnest?" Florence asked, not believing what she was hearing. Yes, Rose had always thrived in New York City when they visited their grandparents, she had been right at home on the fashionable and bustling streets, easily kept up with the changing social scene and that year's trends, and when they journeyed to Europe?

Why the woman was nearly inconsolable when their summer in Spain was over just the year before. How it was that neither Delilah, nor Florence had ever considered that Rose might wish to permanently leave Gold Sky, was beyond either of them. They looked to each other then and saw that they were not alone in their understanding. Rose did not simply enjoy traveling, she was well and truly restless.

"We had no idea," Florence rushed to say just as Delilah was saying the same.

"I'm so sorry, Rose, you should have told us," Delilah said, reaching for her hand and giving it a squeeze.

"And upset everyone?" Rose shook her head. "No, I couldn't do that, at least not until I was sure."

"You've become sure then?" Florence asked quietly.

Rose gave a quick nod of her head. "Yes, working in Mrs. Rosemary's shop has really helped me see that Gold Sky, even when I am operating in the most cosmopolitan and free environment available, will still be stifling. I have to leave town, and soon."

"Why soon?" Florence asked.

Rose picked at her dress and sighed heavily. "There's an opening for an apprentice with a theater company. Grandmother has connections. If I leave before spring then I'll have plenty of time to settle in and learn how they do things before production begins."

Both sisters sat blinking in surprise at Rose. Delilah's mouth had even fallen open. Florence reached over absentmindedly to push it closed before she turned her attention back to Rose.

"Then you mean to leave within the next few weeks?"

Rose gave them a quick nod and raised her eyes from where she still twisted her fingers in the fabric of her skirts. "Yes. I plan to stay through Christmas and the New Year, but after that...well, yes, that's the measure of things."

"When will you tell everyone?" Delilah asked, recovering her wits and ability to speak.

"I thought at dinner in a few nights. Perhaps when Papa and Daddy are in high spirits and it won't be so sad."

Florence chewed on her bottom lip. She knew Rose was scared, she could hear it in her voice, the slight tremor there. Going somewhere new was terrifying, leaving one's family, even if to go to their grandmother and grandfather could not be an easy decision.

Not for anyone, even if they did have Rose's wandering spirit. Florence would do her best to make sure Rose had as easy a time as could be expected.

She smiled kindly at her sister and gave her hands a quick pat. "I'll help."

"You will?" Rose looked surprised at the offer.

"Of course I will," Florence said, she elbowed Delilah. "And so will Del, isn't that right?"

Del looked like she wanted to protest but one sharp eyed glare from Florence had the other woman bobbing her head in agreement. "Yes, ah, yes, I'll help. We'll help."

"I expect Seylah will be agreeable to it as well. She is an advocate for going your own way. Her voice will have weight with our fathers and mama."

"That's good," Rose murmured and gave them both a tight smile. "I hadn't thought of that. I kept thinking…" she waved her hands at herself and then shook her head, "I kept thinking of how I would manage it alone but now it sounds almost achievable."

"You're never alone," Florence told her. "You will, no matter where you go, be our sister."

"She's right," Delilah said. "And that means we are there to help you at every turn."

Rose swallowed hard and blinked back tears. "You're both being so sweet. And now, when I'm about to leave, of all times. How dare you!"

Florence laughed merrily. "That was all part of our dastardly plan. Then you'll miss us so much you'll never miss a holiday."

"I suppose that is true." Rose sniffled and then laughed shakily. "I'll be here for the holidays and then I'll try to come back during the break times. I heard summer in New York is awfully quiet, you know…"

"Well, when you put it like that, it'll hardly be like you were gone at all."

Delilah winked. "We won't even know you were gone. It won't be so scary, you'll see."

"I know it won't but it will be an adventure. I just wish it wasn't so far away. But enough about me," Rose flapped her hands at them, "I want to hear more about this Anselmo and Brendan. How did they meet you? Are they attached to one another?"

The turn of conversation was quick and without preamble but Florence knew why. She could see the unshed tears in Rose's eyes shining bright in the early morning light. Her sister was near tears, if they did not change the subject she would lose her battle at keeping a brave face.

"Yes, they are lovers and I am doing as mother advised me in this hopeful triad courtship," Florence answered, following her sister's change of topic without so much as batting an eye. She would not make this harder, she would not. If that meant they mooned over Anselmo's dark eyes, or Brendan's beautiful dancing, then so be it.

"A triad courtship. I like the sound of that. What is it that mother advised you to do?" Rose asked, picking up her coffee cup and taking a quick sip. Her emotions were, for the time being, under control and this time, when Florence continued on, it was a slightly more genuine tone.

"She told me to find love where it existed already, and to then ask for space."

"That's quite simple," Rose observed. "I like it."

"I find it perfectly suited to taking two husbands. I do not know why I did not see it sooner."

"Perhaps because you wanted to craft the perfect triad, which led you to trying to fit two strangers together like mismatched puzzle pieces," Del said and Florence sighed.

"I do not need to be reminded of my folly, dear sister."

Del hummed but said nothing while Rose giggled away. The morning continued on as it had so many times before, with the women laughing together, heads bent close as they spoke, and simply enjoying the others' company. As girls these mornings had seemed infinite, seemingly endless and in bountiful supply. But now as women, there was one stark truth they all were slowly coming to understand: nothing stayed the same, and for that reason each moment must be cherished.

Rose's announcement was proof of it and Florence endeavored to enjoy each and every minute together, for in its fleetingness, it was made all the more sweet.

CHAPTER 4

*F*lorence had just left the Sheriff's office. It had been her number one destination after she'd finished breakfast with her sisters. Seylah hadn't been at breakfast to hear Rose's big news, nor hers for that matter, and as the eldest Seylah was expected to stay informed of the sibling goings-on.

It was her duty.

Florence grinned, remembering the aghast look on Seylah's face at the news of Rose's plans to leave, though it only took a moment before the other woman was sighing and leaning back in her chair, the pose reminiscent of their Daddy's posture.

"Can't fault her for wanting to spread her wings, now can I? Of course I'll help."

And then there had been the matter of discussing Florence's designs for romance and subsequent marital bliss with not one but two husbands by her side.

"I should have known you had your mind made up on the matter. It would suit you I think."

Except when Seylah had said that, Florence quite expected her older sister thought Florence's dance card to be woefully empty. She had meant to tell her the details of Ansel and Brendan, but August's sudden arrival from patrol had tabled the matter entirely. Sharing salacious details, sparse as they were, was not to be done in front of a man she considered her brother. Besides, Florence was under no illusions that August would be able to keep it from her fathers.

The last thing she needed was for her plans to be over before she'd had time to hatch them. Or was it eggs? How did the saying go again about counting and carefully laid plans? She paused considering it, but none of the turns of phrase sounded quite right.

"Chicks perhaps?" she mused. She would need a cleverer way to describe her intentions when it came to both men. Florence's intentions were of a particular romantic slant and she would have to work doubly hard to keep from showing her hand too early. There was no question that she desired both men. They were attractive. Their features were beautiful on their own but *together?*

Together the men were heart stoppingly striking. Florence could easily imagine herself at their side, or between them...She flushed at the thought and cleared her throat. She must get herself to rights, her plans depended on it!

"Chickens, I need to raise chickens," she advised herself as she hurried along. "Do not crack the eggs, Florence."

"Eggs? Are you meaning to take on poultry?"

Florence whirled at the voice and came face to face with a smiling Ansel. "I, well, perhaps?"

"What would they call you then?" He rubbed his chin. "A mistress of poultry, I think? What about a chicken farmer?"

She laughed and took a step closer to him. All around there was bustle and activity, the energy of Gold Sky was endless these days but all of it seemed to fade away to naught when Ansel smiled as he did at her.

"Can you even farm a chicken?" she asked.

"My lady, you can farm anything if you simply believe."

"But the terminology seems a tad off. I think I much prefer mistress of poultry."

He stepped closer until they were only a handspan away from the other. "And why is that?"

She shrugged. "I think it has more drama and import to it. A farmer? Now anyone can be a farmer. No drama to it. But a mistress of poultry," Florence swirled her finger in the air with a wink, "takes a very special type."

"Are you that type?" Ansel asked, the merriment leaving his eyes. His voice took on a huskier tone until it reminded her of the previous night. She suddenly was not on the boardwalk but was at his side dizzy from their last turn on the dance floor with the taste of Love's Arrow on her lips. How had they gotten here? From jokes to a tension that smoldered and made her want to close the distance between them until there was scarcely room for the other to breath without their bodies touching, hearts beating close together, lips moving slowly closer until...*until...*

"Florence?" Ansel looked concerned and he leaned down to study her. "Are you all right? Was it something I said?"

She shook her head, hand flying to her chest in a bid to steady her heart. "No, no, I merely was swept away by the possibilities of," she paused here, voice stumbling over what she would say next, "I ah, of poultry farming."

"I thought you said farming had no drama to it."

"So I did, but there is something to be said for the quaint life, now isn't there?" she asked moving to the side and giving off her best impersonation of a woman fascinated by hustle and bustle, when in truth she saw none of it, heard not scarcely a shout nor wagon wheel turn on its way past. The only sound Florence was aware of was Ansel's voice. She tucked her hands behind her back and smiled, looking out unseeingly to the busy avenue when he finally spoke.

"I agree with you, Florence," he said, and she nodded.

"You do?" Her mind came back to her then, the cocoon of want she had felt for Ansel cracking when she thought of Rose's announcement. Her sister wanted more, no, she wanted different, Florence reminded her. Life in Gold Sky was not for her younger sister but it did not mean it was less.

"Yes, the appeal for something simpler though," he gestured at the activity in front of them. "I would not call this place simple," he added. Every person moved at a determined pace, the wagons that moved past were laden down with goods, stagecoaches arrived with newcomers and the train whistle from the nearby depot sounded, signaling the arrival of yet more goods and people to Gold Sky. The small frontier town was growing, going through a proper boom, Florence frowned when she realized that her home would not remain the same forever.

Nothing did.

"No, I believe you're right, this isn't a simple small place anymore at all, is it?" she asked, voice soft now. She felt unshed tears prick her eyelids and she silently cursed. Her emotions felt wild and fragile, even for her, but she supposed that is what happened when one's sister announced her plans to leave for a life far away. A life that did not include morning coffee and biscuits. She sniffled and shook her head, hands coming to clutch her skirts. She rocked back on her heels with a little laugh, "I'm sorry, I'm probably giving you a fright, aren't I?

"No, no," Ansel murmured. He held out a handkerchief and with a gentle hand on her elbow guided her out and away from the foot traffic of the boardwalk. "Here, take this, Florence."

"Thank you." She took the handkerchief and dabbed at her eyes. "I found out a very shocking thing today and our talk of a simple life, and of how much Gold Sky is changing, and quickly so, brought the news to mind," she explained.

"Would you like to tell me what the news was?" Ansel's voice was soft and when Florence looked at him she only saw concern shining in the man's dark eyes. He truly meant his worry, and the delicate way he did not pry into the matter endeared him to her all the more.

"My sister, Rose, is leaving us in a few weeks' time for New York City," she said, fingers twisting in the handkerchief as she spoke. "She is the youngest among us and I worry. But it was the thought that somehow life in Gold Sky was far too simple for her that hurt me. I know it isn't true," she quickly went on with a shaky laugh, "my sister loves our home. This is not about her rejecting us, or this place, but more the fact that Rose desires to grow into someone else. I understand."

"But that doesn't mean your emotions aren't...raw, yes?" he asked, giving her a sympathetic smile.

She nodded, wiping away another hot tear. "Yes, that is the measure of it. I know logically why Rose must go, but my heart has still not caught up. It was all a surprise, you see? I used to quite think I loved surprises, thrived when presented with them, but this has me reconsidering."

Ansel hummed. "Surprises, while they can initially shock, can be good. Take for instance the surprise of meeting you."

Florence blinked at his words. "Meeting me?"

"Yes, meeting you," Ansel nodded and turned to face her then. They were standing in front of the newspaper office, an awning stretched the length of it and Ansel smiled leaning back against the wall. "Meeting you, Florence Wickes-Barnes was quite the surprise for Brendan and myself."

"How do you mean?"

"We never anticipated the gift of meeting a woman that would agree to have the both of us." He looked at her then, his dark brown eyes moving slowly over her face as if memorizing the planes of her cheeks and curves of her lips, as if they would somehow save him. The look was

59

like a delicate graze of a finger and Florence shivered under the attention.

"The idea of having two men is not one for delicate sensibilities, Florence, even in the best of circumstances, but not one but two foreigners with an interest in mining?" He chuckled, giving a light shake of his head. "A women that would have us needed to be far more than adventurous and open to new...experiences," his voice caught on the word and Florence blushed knowing full well what Ansel was intimating, "she would also willingly live on the frontier, she would be ready to endure the attention of such an arrangement, and most of all she would have to appeal to both of us."

He crossed his arms and looked up at the awning, a faint smile pulling at his full lips. "The differences between Brendan and myself are severe, there is little we agree on apart from mining."

"You agree on each other," Florence pointed out and he looked away from the awning to her.

He nodded slowly. "Quite right, we do agree on that. Love is foolish and blind. You do not get a say in where your heart leads you."

"And yours led you to Brendan."

"As soon as I saw him in Scotland, I knew." Ansel snapped his fingers. "It was instant. We both knew in that single moment. I, well, we have never felt that for another."

Florence's heart squeezed painfully. She was glad to hear Ansel's words, even to the point of nearly swooning at the thought that he would recognize a man he could love on sight, but she also felt another equally potent emotion.

Disappointment.

She wished to elicit such emotion and words from Ansel, from Brendan, from both of them. Florence had known from the second Mrs. Rosemary singled out the men, even from the distance of an entire dance hall, and three refreshment tables to boot, that these men would be important to her. That they were ones she could love, wished to, in fact. It had all felt very big to her, a tide of attraction and desire that nearly bowled her over at first sight, but how would her feelings seem to men that had fallen in love instantly? Would they think her silly? Inexperienced? Her mother had advised her to find love where it existed and ask for a place, but would her place always be tinged with a bit of sadness?

She smiled brightly at him. The gesture at odds with the storm swirling in her chest. Florence would not dwell on her melancholy. Ansel had shared a truth with her and she was grateful for it.

"That's wonderful," she breathed. "I am so happy to hear you found him as you did."

Ansel nodded. "I agree. Thank you for letting me speak so frankly to you, Florence. If you have time I would share another truth with you."

"Do tell."

Ansel pushed away from the wall of the newspaper office and moved towards her until he was standing in front of her. "My second truth is the first was a lie." At her furrowed brow, he leaned down until his mouth was near her ear. "I can no longer say that I have never felt it for another. I have felt that same sense of knowing, like a lightning strike to my heart. I felt it when I saw you Florence. We both did."

A startled gasp escaped Florence's mouth and she leaped back, hands out to steady herself lest she trip over her skirts. "Do you mean that? Truly?"

"I tell no lies." He was smiling at her, one that was light and mischievous, it matched the merriment she saw in his eyes. "I swear it is true." He raised his hand in an oath but Florence held out her hand and extended her pinky.

"Swear on it. A pinky swear is the only type of pact I recognize," she informed him. No doubt the effect of her having three sisters, but Florence swore it was the only legally binding manner of conducting promises and truths short of appearing before a judge.

And what lady had time to summon a judge?

Ansel chuckled but he moved forward and hooked his pinky with hers. "I swear it. I felt the same as I did when I saw Brendan, as he did when seeing me for the first time. and once more when we saw you first."

Florence hummed, adequately appeased, but when she moved to take her pinky away, Ansel tightened his hold. "But I have a question for you," he said.

"What is it?"

"Did you feel as I described, towards the pair of us?"

His question was direct. Florence adored directness.

"I did. Unequivocally," she replied, voice steadier than she thought possible. "I swear it."

Ansel flashed her a warm smile and dropped her hand. He extended his elbow to her. "May I escort you to your next destination?"

"You may, sir."

The pair were off then, blindly walking as Florence had no more errands to run. Ansel said nothing when they circled past the newspaper office twice more. Each content in the other's company, the time together well spent and a gift, oblivious as they were to the fracas of Gold Sky's streets.

CHAPTER 5

*F*lorence breathed out a sigh and leaned forward placing her palms on her dresser. She was home now. The time spent with Ansel had passed in a pleasant haze. It had been a good use of time for her, though she wondered if the same could be said for Ansel. The man was no doubt busy, especially given the opening of the mine he and Brendan had poured their hearts and sweat into was nearly upon them

They must have wandered the streets of Gold Sky several times over before he had taken her to lunch.

"A man must eat, must he not? And if I do so with a beautiful woman, then Brendan will simply have to be suffer jealously while we enjoy a meal." He'd winked then and pulled her chair out for her signaling an enjoyable meal and companionable time for Florence. She was loath to end it but the rumbling of thunder overhead had Ansel hurrying to escort her home. While a thunderstorm was less than desirable, it may have been for the best as it made bidding Ansel goodbye far easier than Florence might have found otherwise if there hadn't been an impending deluge looming overhead.

Florence's eyes moved to the window. She watched the rain fall outside for a moment before her eyes closed and she let out a sigh. Now that she was inside, the rhythmic sound of rainfall soothed her, though not nearly as well as Ansel's company had. She smiled and opened her eyes, it was impossible not to smile when thinking of the man. She might have gone right on thinking about him forever if a knock hadn't sounded at her door.

"Yes?" Florence called out, turning away from her dresser and towards the door that was opening to reveal a smiling Rose.

"Do you have a moment?" She asked, coming into the room. She looked shy, so unlike her usual self that Florence felt a twinge or concern.

"Are you all right?" She asked coming forward.

Rose tucked a lock of hair behind her ear, green eyes sliding to the side before they darted back to Florence. "I'm scared, Flo."

"Rose, what—" Florence's voice was cut off when her sister rocketed across the room to throw her arms around Florence. She squeezed her tightly, tightly enough that Florence coughed and struggled to breath from the force of Rose's body colliding with hers.

"I'm scared!" Rose wailed, turning her face into Florence's neck. Rose sniffled and muffled a sob.

"What on earth is going on?" Florence gasped. She leaned back from her sister and gave her a confused look.

"I know that I-" she hiccuped, a sob escaping her as she continued to talk, shoulders shaking, "I know that I said I wanted to leave Gold Sky. I know I sounded like I knew what I wanted but I don't know what that is anymore."

"Rose, oh, it will be all right," Florence soothed her. She put her hands on her sister's shoulders and gently squeezed her reassuringly.

"Will it?" Rose asked, sniffling still. She wiped at her eyes and let out a shaky laugh. "Will it, Flo? I'm not like you, or Seylah," she wrinkled her nose, "and I'm certainly not like Delilah."

"Meaning?"

"She's entirely too severe, I don't think I can recall when she last relaxed, and we both know that--"

Florence stifled a laugh. "That's not what I meant unless you think that of all of us?"

Rose crossed her arms and gave her sister a wry smile. "I meant that you all know what you want out of life, and I-I have yet to truly understand what I want other than that it's not...not..."

"Not here?" Florence supplied gently.

"Yes, that it's not here!" Rose snapped her fingers and then laughed shakily. "What I want is not here." She held up a finger and continued. "I did entirely mean what I said about Delilah. If the woman continues on as she is, then she will entirely lose her way. I am quite concerned for her."

Florence pinched the bridge of her nose. "We are not focused on Delilah or her penchant for overworking herself. Let us stay focused on the matter at hand, which is your sudden crisis."

"Yes, that."

Florence pulled a face. "Yes. *That.* Now do go on, Rose."

"I am to leave for New York in a few weeks time but I haven't the first clue what will happen to me once I arrive--"

"No one knows what the future holds, Rose."

"Or what my work will actually be. I won't know anyone and--"

"You will know Grandmama and Grandfather."

"They are my family, and I cannot rely on them for introductions to everyone, or for my social engagements. I must be responsible for making my own way," Rose insisted.

"It's quite all right to be scared. If you were not scared, I would wonder after you."

Rose turned to her sister from where she had taken to pacing the length of her room. "What do you mean?"

"Any time anyone does anything new there's room for fear. It is normal to the process of growing," Florence told her with a little flourish of her hands.

"Growing?" Rose spun back around, pacing once more, with a fraught look on her face. "Is this what growth feels like?"

"Yes, yes it is." Florence tucked her hands behind her back and watched as Florence stayed in motion. If the woman moved any faster she would be a blur. Florence squinted at her sister who was little more than a swish and flash of skirts.

"Growth is uncomfortable. It always is," she offered.

"I have no taste for it," Rose muttered crossing her arms and moving to stare out the window. Florence let out a sigh of relief. She would have become dizzy if she'd been forced to watch for one more moment. "Why can't the hard part of moving be behind me? I would love for it to be well into the summer."

"Why is that?"

"If it were, then I would be settled into the city. I would be well within the production, and by then have a life in New York but now..." she shook her head and sighed, "now I have nothing."

Florence laughed and came to stand beside Rose. "Now, who is being dramatic?"

"Birds of a feather..." Rose replied with a smirk.

"Indeed, but I am the elder of us, you know."

"By a scant year. That is truly nothing in terms of wisdom."

"Oh, it is, is it?" Florence asked, a hint of mirth in voice. She nudged her sister gently and smiled at her. "It will be okay, even if it doesn't feel as though that is true at the moment."

"How can you sound so certain of it?"

Florence smiled and looked out the window. The storm was still raging outside, rain drops ran down the glass of the window in rivulets. Her eyes followed the rain as the sisters stood close together in silence. It was peaceful in this moment, her own worries, the earlier emotion of the day, the sisters' fears, they all ceased to exist in the quiet.

It was simply the pair of them. *Sisters.*

"Give me your hand," Florence said. She held out her hand, fingers extending, palm up, open and waiting for Rose to take. Rose slipped her hand into hers and

Florence squeezed tightly. They held hands in silence, both watching the rain outside when Rose spoke.

"It will be all right," she whispered.

"Yes."

"Thank you."

Florence looked at her sister and smiled when she saw Rose was still watching the rain. There was no hint of the worry or fear she had worn on her face upon entering Florence's room. She was smiling, as she should be with an adventure awaiting her.

"Always."

FLORENCE PURSED HER LIPS. Despite her advice to Rose, she found that growth was an uncomfortable and inconvenient occurrence. The current instance of said growth was staring her right in the face in the form of one Mrs. Winthrop, newly arrived to Gold Sky via Boston by way of what Florence had come to think of as the accursed railway line. She had only started to think of the railway as accursed after making Mrs. Winthrop's acquaintance, or more precisely it was well within Mrs. Winthrop's most recent fitting that Florence wished away the Gold Sky depot with her entire being.

If the depot did not exist, the railway would have never come to town, and if that had never happened then Florence would not be standing in front of an irate Mrs. Winthrop.

"I very clearly asked for a tapered skirt, not this." The woman extended an immaculate nail towards the hobble skirt she wore. Florence had a tape measure and a mouthful of pins, the latter stopped her from cursing at Mrs. Winthrop, but it didn't not stop the frown that pulled her lips down.

"Are you frowning at me?" Mrs. Winthrop's voice was shrill. It carried well. It was, Florence estimated, a very good voice as the lady was one of the foremost auctioneers in town. She knew Mrs. Winthrop came from old money, that the small birdlike woman with features so delicate and fine that Florence wondered how she managed to fill an auction house with her voice so fully and completely that any who heard her would swear it was not Mrs. Winthrop's vocals but that of the esteemed almighty.

When Florence was silent Mrs. Winthrop clapped her hands. "Answer me, Miss Florence. Are you frowning at me?"

If the woman ever sought to give up her career as an auctioneer Florence was quite sure she could make a real run of joining the sheriff's department. There wouldn't be an outlaw alive that would be able to withstand the woman.

Florence gave a quick shake of her head. "N'mamph," she managed to get out around the pins and said a silent prayer. The woman narrowed her eyes at Florence and then turned away, launching back into a long list of critiques she wanted Florence to see to before she considered the clothing fit and final. Florence knew the demands were ...a bit much, but they would serve to make her a better seamstress and designer.

If she could meet Mrs. Winthrop's demands, then

Florence could do anything. She would have to do it with a smile on her face to keep the woman happy and that was precisely what Florence aimed for, mouthful of pins and all. Blessedly, the rest of the fitting went well enough and Mrs. Winthrop left with the semblance of a smile on her face, which was more than Florence had expected to see.

All in all, it was a success. She worked to set the shop back to rights after the appointment. Florence hummed as she worked, mind straying to thoughts of Ansel and Brendan. It had been three days since her talk and lunch with Ansel, and she had not heard from either man since. Under any other circumstances, she might have become worried or fearful her suitors had lost interest, but with these two special men she knew she had nothing to fear. Her spirit told her so, but even with peace in her heart Florence was still becoming restless. If Florence were an inanimate object, she would fancy herself a hairpin trigger. Every sound caused her to leap out of her skin, the jangling of the bell above the door with each new shopper alone causing her to jump from fright.

Florence was on edge, there was no other explanation for her behavior. She squeezed her eyes shut and rubbed her shoulders, rolling them in a bid to relax. The morning and early afternoon had been a bit frantic, but now there was nothing but quiet with few shoppers to occupy Florence's attention.

She rubbed her temples and sighed. She may as well start on the alterations Mrs. Winthrop had demanded. "No time like the present, I suppose," she murmured, moving towards the back of the shop where Mrs. Winthrop's dress, a blue silk evening gown, hung from the fitting form. If she worked steadily she would make decent progress today putting her far ahead of next week's deadline. Florence had just begun to set her pins when the bell at the front of the shop signaled a new shopper's arrival.

"Just a minute!" Florence called out to them. She was pushing the pins into the form, her mind making note of what was to be done when she heard the low sound of male voices. She froze and turned to look over her shoulder. She had thought the newcomers would be ladies intent on new garments, perhaps even the older women from church coming to check on their ordered hats but what she had not thought to see was the now familiar forms of Ansel and Brendan. They turned in tandem towards her, warm smiles on their faces when they caught sight of her and Florence swore she had never been presented with a more beguiling sight.

The pins fell from her mouth in a clatter, all thoughts of alterations and measurements flew from Florence's head in the face of not one but *two handsome* men, er, not men but suitors. There wasn't a woman alive that would manage to keep her wits about her with Ansel and Brendan's undivided attention directed at them, but Florence had been raised to rise to any and all occasions.

She thrived under pressure. Brendan and Ansel were just such a situation. And she intended to rise to them.

"Good afternoon, gentlemen." She put the measuring tape on the dress form and made her way forward in slow, deliberate steps, ones that were measured and not at all rushed. Ladies did not rush, and Florence was determined to do her best to maintain her image as a lady.

"Florence," Ansel greeted her with a bright smile. He looked so at ease among the fabrics and clothing that Florence couldn't help but laugh. "What?" he asked.

"You," she said coming forward until she was only a few feet away from either man. "Most men are not so inclined to come into our little dress shop here, let alone look so at ease," she told him.

Brendan turned from the assortment of ready-made blouses he had been inspecting. "Aye, and not many men in town are like the pair of us."

"Meaning?"

"Meaning that Brendan and I have an eye for quality workmanship." Ansel smiled at her and nodded at the display dresses. "Did you make these?"

"Not all of them, but some," Florence said. She watched as Brendan nodded looking back at the clothing to his left.

"Yer talented," he said. It was a statement, not a question and Florence felt her cheeks burn. She was pleased but also was not accustomed to a man complimenting her work. Her skill was known among the women in town, but the men largely missed how well her seams were formed, or the attention to detail in the suits they wore, nor could they be found to comment on the flattering fit their wives and sisters enjoyed after an appointment with Florence.

Too often Florence's work was seen as busywork, something for her to do until she found a husband...or husbands. In truth, she loved helping Mrs. Rosemary with her designs, she enjoyed helping dress the ladies of Gold

Sky for the simple reason that it made them happy, even at the expense of her skills going unnoticed.

"Thank you," she whispered.

Brendan nodded. "Yer welcome."

"We hope it's not overstepping to come here," Ansel said, giving her a concerned look.

"Why would it not be okay?" Florence asked. She couldn't imagine a day that she didn't want Brendan or Ansel here, and complimenting her to boot. She was pleased they were here, so she told them so. "I'm happy you came, and with words of flattery no less."

"It's not flattery if it's true, lass. Ever thought of going in to business on yer own?"

Florence blinked in surprise. She was talented and enjoyed her work but she had never thought of leaving Mrs. Rosemary's side. She couldn't imagine what her days would be like without the blonde woman's infectious energy.

"No," she admitted.

"Why not?"

Her brow furrowed as she thought it over. Business on her own? That seemed...*wrong?* No, not wrong, she just had not thought about it, she decided.

"I'm not entirely sure why, but I never have thought of striking out on my own." She glanced around the shop and shook her head. "Mrs. Rosemary wouldn't know what to do without me and she taught me everything as well."

"Ah, so you feel indebted." Ansel reasoned. Florence shook her head. No, that also didn't seem right. She didn't owe Mrs. Rosemary. They were more family, mentor and teacher, co-conspirators on more than one escapade—that was not a dynamic of imbalanced scales.

She shook her head once more. "I wish to be here with Mrs. Rosemary, that's why I've never considered my own dress shop. It wouldn't feel right without her. I love her."

Brendan hummed in appreciation. "Now that makes more sense." He waved a hand as he continued forward towards her, "Ye protect a valuable feeling such as that. A precious relationship you have with the lady then."

Florence nodded. "I do. I love her like another mother. I wish to be nowhere but here."

"Then you should stay right where you are." Ansel gave her a reassuring smile. "She's lucky to have such a talented designer and dress maker working with her."

"Indeed," Brendan agreed. He was beside her now and Florence swallowed hard at his closeness. She could smell him. Juniper and clean with just a hint of sweet, was that honey? She sniffed and he chuckled. "Like what you smell, flower?"

She flushed and cleared her throat with as delicate a sound as she could manage while blushing. "You smell nice."

"What do I smell like?" Brendan asked. Green eyes stared into hers and her mouth went dry.

"Juniper and honey," she answered without hesitation.

"Ah, so ye smell the effects of my cleaning then." He nodded knowingly and raised his cuff to smell it. "That's quite nice, I think."

She laughed. "It is," she agreed before she asked, "Now what brings you two gentlemen to my shop?"

"Aimed to ask ye on our outing."

"We had hoped you would tell us a time and date when you were free."

She clapped her hands excitedly. "I hoped you would be by for us to plan it. I wasn't quite sure where to find you to ask myself."

"And ye would have taken it upon yerself to ask us?"

"It's the twentieth century, my good sir and I am a modern woman who knows what she's about."

Brendan laughed then. Threw his head back, a hand to his chest, shoulders and big body shaking with a full-bodied laugh that had Florence giggling along and Ansel laughing as well. His laugh was more restrained, smooth and light, like fog over water. The two sounds delightfully twisted round the other until she could not imagine them separate. She wondered how long it would be until her own laugh sounded wrong without the accompanying brash and flowing sounds of happiness.

"Aye, so ye are, flower, so ye are." Brendan's green eyes were dancing with merriment, the effect worked to soften his entire demeanor. He was a muscular man with a body and hands hardened from mining but when he was looking at her like this Florence swore he looked years younger. She glanced at Ansel to see that he wore a similar look of contentment. He too, looked carefree and far younger. She liked the look of it on them.

"Since it is winter. The dead of winter, in fact, we much thought you would enjoy an outing to the play-house. There is a production in town. A Midsummer Night's Dream."

Florence's heart soared. She adored the play, had eaten up every word when it was assigned as an extracurricular in school. She had longed to attend the newest production but had somehow not found the time. This was absolute perfection for an outing.

"And we are in possession of opera box seating for the event which would make a night for the three of us more enjoyable, no?" Ansel smiled at her then and Florence swore she would have agreed to anything. Opera box seats for a night out then were easily agreed upon and without thought.

"What night shall we go?" she asked, bouncing on her toes and scarcely able to contain her excitement.

"We have the tickets for tomorrow night. Are ye free?"

Florence nodded vigorously, all thoughts of ladylike behavior tabled for the time being. She could attempt to act the part in public but for now, when it was just them? She was happier to simply react, rather than think too much on her behavior.

"I am! I am free and could not be happier at the invitation."

"The pleasure is all ours." Ansel bent low and took her hand, surprising her. The gentle brush of his lips against her knuckles pulled a slight gasp from her lips. He looked up at her, brown eyes warm and soulful. She could fall into them and never want for another thing. *Ever.* Of that she was sure.

"Charmer," she accused, but there was no way around the delighted look in Florence's eye.

"I think ye enjoy it," Brendan told her from over Ansel's shoulder and she shrugged, helpless to deny his words. She did enjoy it. She was thoroughly enjoying every minute of her time with the men and she could not wait to revel in tomorrow night's activity.

Ansel straightened, but not before pressing another kiss to the back of her hand before he passed her hand over his shoulder and into Brendan's hold. The feel of both men's touch, so close their fingers overlapped, gently sliding over the back of her hand and over her fingertips until Brendan had firm hold of her and Florence forgot how to breathe.

She watched as Brendan lifted her hand to his mouth and kissed it, directly over the spot Ansel had only moments before. A shiver moved over her, up her legs and down her spine at the slight brush of his lips. To any that passed the shop windows on the boardwalk outside, Florence was simply receiving amorous but chaste attentions from eligible men.

It was not a kiss to her lips, nor were they standing inappropriately close, with Ansel a respectful distance away, Brendan crowded close to Ansel, a hand resting on the other man's shoulder, Florence's hand held to his lips with the other.

In truth, anyone who thought this a chaste interaction knew precisely nothing in the way of men and women. Brendan released her hand and Florence took in a shaky breath. A shaky laugh escaped her lips as she patted her hair uncertainly with the hand both men had just kissed.

"Until tomorrow night, flower," Brendan told her, inclining his head to her. Florence nodded, not trusting her voice, she quickly found it, however, when Ansel said, "We shall call on you tomorrow night at seven o'clock--"

"No!" she blurted out, her hands coming up to gesture

wildly as she rushed to close the few steps between them. When her path looked to deposit her right into Ansel's arms she thought better of it and took a hasty step back.

Brendan crossed his arms. "And why not?"

"I mean to say that won't be necessary, gentlemen. You don't have to walk me from my home to the theater."

"That is what is expected of a suitor," Ansel pointed out.

"A *proper suitor*," Brendan added, and Florence winced, not missing at the emphasis he put on word proper. Her shoulders came up, nearly touching her ears as her body tensed. She squeezed her hands tight when she saw the way the men stepped close together, closer together and away from her. She could tell where their minds were going and she didn't like it, not one bit. If they thought she asked to meet at the theater because she was ashamed of them, then they had much to learn of her.

Though…

Though she knew she could not fault them, not in a world such as they lived in, not everywhere was Gold Sky. The fight deflated out of her slightly at that. She would have to put this conversation off until she had the words to explain.

"I will make my way to the theater and meet you there for the show, ah, if that is amenable?"

She looked to Ansel hoping to see that her plan was still a very good one for their outing even if it didn't have them calling on her in the classic sense of the word. If her family was within the same room as the men Florence didn't know if she would survive it. She would have to endure it at some point, but she thought it more prudent to embark on such a test of endurance once she was able to keep her wits about her when in the company of her suitors.

She could scarcely think when they both touched her. What would she do when her family's teasing was thrown into the ordeal? And even worse, when her fathers caught sight of Ansel and Brendan. They would size them up immediately. She knew it. There would be questions, her mother would have ones of her own to be sure, and Lord only knew what her sisters would do if given the opportunity. Delilah meeting the men was all well and good because Del was calm, level headed and prone to listen far more than she spoke.

But the rest of her family? No, all together the Wickes-Barnes' clan were another matter entirely. She gave the men a sincere smile willing them to see that she had a completely reasonable justification for suggesting they meet at the theater.

Ansel pursed his full lips and she knew he didn't like it. Judging by Brendan's still arched brow he was of the same opinion, but still she remained hopeful. Brendan cleared his throat and Ansel looked his way. The men shared a meaningful look that Florence recognized from the shared glances her fathers shared. When they did it she found it maddening but now she tolerated it if only to buy herself a few more seconds to think of how she might explain to them that--

"We agree," Ansel said, shocking her.

Florence relaxed slightly and nodded quickly not willing to try her luck. "Oh that's wonderful! I cannot wait for our time at the theater."

The men exchanged another look but this time they smiled at her and she knew they would understand once she found the words.

"Until then."

"Flower."

The men left then and the door scarcely closed before Florence sagged against the table behind her with a shaky sigh. She squeezed her eyes shut and forced herself to breath. She would explain to the men why she had asked to meet them at the theater.

After a night together spent in good company with wonderful entertainment and quiet conversation in dimly lit closed quarters such as an opera box, her reaction would make sense, and once they met her family, she knew they would understand her heart---her heart that was quickly coming to reside between the pair of them.

CHAPTER 6

*F*lorence hurried down the lane towards town. She had gotten so wrapped up in getting the rouge on her cheeks just so that she hadn't noticed the clocks' tell-tale ticking towards her intended assignation. She nearly stumbled at that thought.

This was not an assignation.

It. Was. Not.

This was a very proper and ordered outing, all scheduled and agreed upon in the light of day and in her place of employment no less. A night with her suitors, spent in an opera box, to take in 'A Midsummer Night's Dream' was an entirely respectable occasion for her to be concerned with her skill at rouge application. Even still, with the moon overhead and the lane and avenue leading to the play house eerily empty Florence's conviction that she was not on her way to a scandalous assignation wavered. Gravel crunched beneath her foot, the sound of it echoing in her ears on the empty avenue.

The night was so reminiscent of the one where she

had gone to meet Robert all those years ago. She had been just as excited, just as concerned with rouge and its benefits to a woman's looks, or in her case a smitten girl.

Then, she had been just as sure that her engagement was not an assignation, when in truth, it could have only been defined as classically scandalous. Robert had been secretive, thrived on it and Florence now knew it had been a large measure of the attraction the couple had shared. It hadn't been star-crossed love or anything worth cherishing.

It had been curiosity, lust, and a thrill.

For the both of them.

In spite of that, Florence had been the one to pay with her reputation, not Robert. He'd fared just fine in the town before he left with his family to go back east the following year. She supposed she had as well, but it was tough on a girl caught in the arms of a boy she didn't consider high on the marrying list. Even in a town as open and accepting as Gold Sky there were limits. Social expectations and decorum to follow. This wasn't a place where the rules of society and convention did not exist, even if the citizens of Gold Sky refused to allow anyone to be excluded by them.

One such convention was not to be caught in a compromising position with a person you did not intend to marry. Florence and Robert had not behaved as expected, but given that Robert was a boy "of that energetic age," and Florence was the daughter of two gun-wielding law men, even the town gossips had quieted in quick order.

That hadn't meant Robert's father, a newcomer to the

area, hadn't called Florence a "reckless girl." She'd heard him that night when they'd emerged from their stolen moment in Robert's parlor room. It had stung more than Florence dared to admit, but she was only a girl of sixteen and her heart was tender.

"It's not as if any of them have not thought with…" her mother had cleared her throat and given her a tight smile, "less than logical parts."

"And what parts would that be?" Will drawled from where he sat beside the hearth. "The part of her that does the thinking, or the part that does the feeling?"

"I don't see why they have to separate," Forrest muttered, looking as if he wanted to be any place other than where he currently was. He gave her a kind smile. "It happens, sweetheart."

Will snorted but was silenced by a stern look from his husband. "I seem to remember us gettin' up to all sorts of things when we were her age," he said.

"We were fools."

"We were *happy*."

"Am I reckless?" Florence whispered. The pain in her voice was plain for them to hear, her wide eyes and slightly shaking shoulders enough to cut through any talk of what was proper and what was not. Her question had stunned all three of her parents and the room was silent for a moment before Julie had sprung into action crossing the space in only a few steps.

"We love you. It's only sex," her mother sighed coming forward to give her a hug. "Nothing to fuss about, isn't that right?" Julie had turned giving her husbands who were still locked in a battle of glares a stern look. She cleared her throat when neither man answered. "I said isn't that right?"

Her fathers had broken their silent battle then to look at their wife and daughter and instantly softened. Will sighed, rising to his feet and coming forward to hug Florence tightly. "Ah, hell, anyone runs their mouth in town and I'll string 'em up. You didn't do anything wrong, Flo."

That hadn't meant that some in town viewed her dalliance through the same lens as her parents. She knew to them she appeared *easy.* What that entailed, she wasn't sure, but Florence knew she didn't like it. It didn't seem right for a person to be labeled so easily, but the best defense was a good offense, or so her fathers had taught her. Florence had learned to lean into the role she knew some assigned to her even if they hadn't the backbone to speak it out loud.

If they saw her as a girl with little respect for social mores, then she would truly put on a show. Florence took to all things dramatic, anything with flair and romance to it, she loved and adorned herself with it like fine silks and fur. She wore it as only a Queen would deign to wear a crown and before long she believed it herself.

If there was a scheme or commotion, the people of Gold Sky knew that Florence was never too far behind. They expected the drama from her. It was one of the reasons no one saw her true heart and seriousness about her work at Mrs. Rosemary's. To the town it was just a bit of frippery and pretty that Florence was known for, but to her it was a crafted skill honed from years of diligent practice. Somehow that made her bid to follow proper etiquette and enter into the role of a lady all the more important, even if it felt like play acting for the public's eye. It was hard to explain, but she wanted to prove that she was not the careless woman some thought she had grown into. She wanted to show that what she was building with the two men interested in her was real and true as anything anyone else might experience.

Her love should not be seen as less, simply because it was with more than one person.

The thought of such a thing made her mouth taste of ash. She knew her mother would tell her that it "didn't matter what anyone thought of her", and that "she knew her own heart and that should be proof enough."

Even so, Florence was still driven by the urge to present herself as steady and true in this romantic pursuit. She hadn't much thought on it when she'd been going through her options in the way of Gold Sky men but that had been before Ansel and Brendan had been real to her, before she had known them and certainly before she had felt as if lightning had struck her heart in the midst of the singles soiree.

Before Ansel and Brendan, Florence's designs had all been an idea, a possibility of what *could be*. She had flitted from man to man, trying to pair them this way and that on paper or in an outing, which had resulted in more than one new male friendship. That had all been well and good. There could never be enough fraternal community and camaraderie on the frontier, now could there? But now that the men were real Florence had little taste for coulds and maybes.

She was wholly dedicated to ensuring the success of

what *would be.* The role of a lady seemed the most secure avenue to her desired outcome. It would just be like she had done all those years ago when she had embraced her place as the *'reckless girl.'* Few outside of her family saw her as she truly was. It wasn't all bad, she supposed. It kept those who were genuine close to her, like Mrs. Rosemary. She saw Florence truly as she was, and for that she was grateful.

Florence hoped to add Ansel and Brendan to those precious few before long. It was tiring being like this. Despite her loving family, isolation was a heavy thing to carry alone, and lately it had weighed her down like a millstone about her neck. She would give nothing more than to cut the rope from her body and be free.

She pulled her fur wrap closer over her bare shoulders. The low-cut blue gown she wore was lovely, offering the right amount of décolletage while staying respectable. It clung to her curves just so before falling in a small waterfall train behind her. She'd sewn and designed it herself and knew it was just the thing for a night at the theater, but it did little to protect her against the winter chill. She was thankful for the fur wrap her grandmother had gifted her the Christmas before.

The feel of the soft fur beneath her fingertips worked to soothe her frazzled thoughts. Thinking of Robert was not the way to stay in high spirits for her time with Brendan and Ansel. The clock tower at the center of town chimed signaling the time and she cursed, nearly sprinting around the corner. She was definitely late. Ladies were not late, neither did they run, but that could not be helped when the play was set to begin in only a few minutes' time and she was late.

Florence was huffing by the time she entered the theater. She sucked in a deep breath and patted at her hair, worried it had come free of the pins she had painstakingly used to keep her updo in place. She had wanted to look perfect for tonight and a headful of wild curls did not play into her plan for perfection.

She had a moment's pause to look herself over in the grand silver backed mirror of the theater's entryway before Mrs. Rosemary bustled by and caught her arm.

"You look ravishing," she said. Mrs. Rosemary reached out to touch an errant lock of hair with a slight smile. "Absolutely lovely, dear."

"Thank you." Florence looked around worriedly. She had hoped to see the men, her men, upon entering the playhouse but another cursory look around the grand entrance showed them nowhere to be found.

"Looking for someone?" Mrs. Rosemary asked, noticing the frown on Florence's face.

"Yes, well two someones."

"So this is an after-hours arrangement then, hmm?" Mrs. Rosemary sounded excited but Florence grimaced at the little lilt in the other woman's voice. She looked at her and bit her lip.

"No, not exactly. It was all arranged properly you know."

"But where's the fun in that, dear girl?"

"I just mean to say that...it's, well--" she stopped abruptly and cleared her throat. She was already late for the production and there wasn't enough time to explain her heart to Mrs. Rosemary. "Nothing, nothing. I just haven't the faintest idea where they are but I suppose they must have gone on without me due to my tardiness."

"I think not. There they are." Mrs. Rosemary nodded behind her with a smile. "And they found my mister as well it seems." Florence nodded, the gesture coming out calm enough despite the sudden thumping of her heart. Ansel and Brendan were coming down the stairs, glass cut tumblers filled with amber liquid in their hands, with them was the only man capable of matching Mrs. Rosemary's energy and wit: Mr. Anthony Stark. He was a good man, smart and not intimidated by the challenges of life on the frontier. Florence couldn't remember a time that Mr. Anthony was without a smile on his face, just as he was now. He threw his head back and laughed along with Florence's men as they ambled towards Mrs. Rosemary and herself.

"Don't they all look handsome?" Mrs. Rosemary sighed, watching the trio.

"They do," Florence admitted. The blush on her cheeks deepened when Mrs. Rosemary nudged her in the side with her elbow and winked at her.

"You are one very lucky lady."

Florence nodded but said nothing until the men were in front of them. Ansel bowed low and Brendan mirrored the gesture a moment later.

"My, my, you have these men whipped into fine shape, Flo," Mr. Stark laughed and came forward to kiss her cheek. "A pleasure to see you. You're a vision tonight, darling."

"Thank you, Mr. Anthony." Florence smiled and hugged the older man. "You look dashing as well."

He let out a sigh and smiled. "Dashing. Do you hear that dear?" He looked to Mrs. Rosemary. "I am being quite swept away by this vision of youth and beauty."

Mrs. Rosemary cleared her throat. "And what of me, dear?" she asked with feigned consternation.

He laughed and came forward to take his wife's hand. He raised it to his lips and kissed the back of her hand with an elaborate bow that laid the man nearly so low as to see the tops of his wife's shoes. He looked up at her. "You are, and always will be, the belle of the ball."

"And what if we are not at a ball?"

"Then you are the Queen of any space we happen to occupy. If it be a bar, the bar, if it's a ballroom, that too. You claim all spaces in between but none so lovely or grand as my heart." He raised a hand to his chest and squeezed it with a grimace.

Mrs. Rosemary giggled. "You may rise, sir."

"Ah, thank you, thank you." He kissed her hand again and straightened, coming to stand beside her. "Any longer and you might have found me properly prostrate. I thought my back would give out just then."

"Oh, Anthony." Mrs. Rosemary swatted his arm but the man raised his hands.

"I tell no lies, my dear. Right on my face and in front of the younger folk as well. How terribly embarrassing that would have been, but enough of that. How would you speak on the gentlemen, Flo? They've been quite anxious for your arrival. I thought they would faint due to the stress before you graced them with your presence."

She turned to Ansel and Brendan offering them an apologetic smile. "I do apologize for that. I lost track of time and well, I am very sorry. I hope that we can still attend the production as planned. I would feel awful if it was ruined on my account."

"Nothing to worry about Florence. Our seats allow for flexibility. The entire box is ours for the evening."

"Oh, you have an opera box now do you?" Mrs. Rosemary clapped her hands, clearly delighted by the news. "We do as well. I had thought to invite you all to share it but let's head on up together instead." She motioned towards the stairs with a bright smile. "Shall we?"

"Let's." Florence moved to follow Mrs. Rosemary but then Brendan and Ansel were there beside her and offering an arm each. She paused, unsure of what to do but a quick jerk of Mrs. Rosemary's head to either men had her springing into action. She slipped her arms through theirs and smiled at them. Ansel leaned close and kissed her cheek, his lips lingered for a moment longer than was polite and Florence shivered when he slowly drew back. The gesture was slight, his lips staying close to her skin, breath puffing warm and tender across her sensitive skin. The barest brush of his lips had her seeing stars and she gripped the arms of both men tighter at the gesture.

She had suddenly become as uncoordinated as a newborn foal. If there was a woman alive that could remain steady and sure in the face of such seduction, Florence didn't know her, in fact she did not, no could not, pretend to even remotely resemble her.

Perhaps it was good that she had come in late. She

didn't know if she would be able to keep from falling to her suddenly shaky knees if the playhouse had been bustling with other theatergoers. She continued to climb up the staircase supported on shaky legs and her suitors sturdy touch. When they were in front of their respective entrance, Mrs. Rosemary turned to them and gave a little wave.

"Go on in and enjoy the show! Perhaps we can all enjoy an aperitif together after the play?"

Florence nodded with a smile. "That sounds lovely. Thank you for the offer."

Mrs. Rosemary bounced on her toes excitedly and gave one more wiggle of her fingers to the three of them before she spun towards the door and vanished inside with her husband in tow.

"We are just down the way." Brendan nodded to the door at the end of the hall. "Last one there."

"How lovely!" Florence was excited. It had been a good deal of time since she had enjoyed a production and even more so since she had done it in the privacy of an opera box. She glanced at the men beside her, they were still close to her, their touch burning her through her clothing. She swallowed hard and forced her thoughts to stay in the present. She was here to enjoy a performance, not indulge in her less than wholesome thoughts.

Ansel led the way into the opera box, and when the pair of them weren't touching her, crowding her as they had just been doing, it was far easier to breath. A lady's main weapon to keeping her wits about her surely had to be oxygen.

Without oxygen all else failed.

CHAPTER 7

*F*lorence stood in a small area of the opera box. It was well appointed with velvet curtains hanging from the front of it, the crimson fabric framing the balcony. Its edges were adorned with golden tassels which gleamed dully in the theater's lights. Florence's fingers itched to touch the tassels. She wondered what they would feel like under her touch; would they feel as decadently beautiful as they looked?

Sumptuous, silken and smooth under hand, or perhaps the golden thread would be made of sterner stuff. Her gaze slid from the golden fringe of the velvet curtain to Ansel and Brendan where they stood ahead of her at the front of the box. The men's heads were bent close together as they looked out into the theater. They were looking towards the stage, the twinkling of the overhead lights casting them in perfect relief. Florence smiled watching them as they stood close together, Ansel's hand rested on Brendan's arm, the redhead was laughing at Ansel's words. She liked seeing them together as they were, happy and carefree. She liked the way both men were...softer when in the other's presence.

She came forward tentatively. Though she wanted to be with the men she was loath to interrupt the joy they shared. It was much easier to stay where she was and observe, but that was not asking for space. She could not remain apart from them if she wished to be *with* them. And for that reason Florence came forward, her steps steady and sure as she approached the couple.

"This is quite the view," she said when she was closer to them. Her voice signaled her approach and they looked back at her still smiling. The sight of them made her heart clench tightly in her chest. They were beautiful.

"Aye, it is," Brendan said. He cleared his throat and then offered her a smile that was a little less free, a little more stiff than the one she had shared with Ansel. "But not so lovely as you."

"Thank you." Florence inclined her head at his compliment. She ignored how stiff his words sounded, this was all new to them after all.

"Have a seat," Ansel said, coming to her side and guiding her to one of the plush seats nearby. "Here you can sit between the pair of us. Wouldn't want Brendan getting lonely if I keep you all to myself tonight, now do we?" Florence's face flushed at his words. They were skirting on flirtation and her body lit up at the hint of Ansel's interest. He paused and looked at her with a curious look. "That is if you find it agreeable?"

Florence smiled, taking the hand he offered. It was nice to be thought of as this, to have both men on either side of her. The heat of their bodies was a comforting presence, and she basked in it like a cat laying in the sun. There was no other place she would care to be than right where she was.

"I find it very agreeable, *sir*." She took care to stress the title of sir, made an effort to pull it long as her voice dropped just an octave so that her tone was husky and inviting. Florence had enjoyed her fair share of attention from men. She knew quite well the effect she had and now, in the comfort of the opera box, she wielded said power with impunity.

In the hidden nook of an opera box, one did not have to choose to be a lady if one did not wish to do so.

Although...

She furrowed her brow at the mere thought of what a lady was and was not. It did not seem that being a lady allowed a woman to pursue a bit of excitement. She supposed those who considered such a role important would not think it appropriate for a single woman such as herself to be alone with not one, but two men. She raised her eyes to meet Ansel's as he guided her between the two men.

His dark eyes were on her. Warm and attentive. His hand light on hers as she sank down into the plush velvet of her seat.

"Sir?" He tilted his head to the side, a smile tugging at his lips. Ansel looked away from her and out to the stage, his gaze moving over the crowd taking their seats below. "Are we back to such formalities?"

Florence grinned and bit her lip. She folded her hands in her lap considering his question. "No," she said after a moment, "I think not. Certainly not if we are to enjoy such close quarters."

"It is rather intimate, no?"

"Very."

He looked back at her, gaze flitting over her before landing on Brendan. The ginger haired man was silent, arms crossed as he sat beside them observing. "What do you think?"

"Me?" Brendan asked, His voice was gruff, but there was a gentleness to it that pulled at Florence, demanded she come closer. The din of the theater goers' conversation below dulled along with the creaking of seats whilst the light fluttering of programs turned to a comfortable hum.

"Yes, you," Ansel replied seemingly unaffected by Brendan's voice. Florence estimated the man had the upper hand on her given that he enjoyed the confidence born from years of experience in Brendan's presence. "What do you think of our current seating arrangements?"

Brendan was silent, his jaw clenched and he said, "I find it agreeable." Florence wanted for him to continue but the man went silent. There was a stiffness in his body that she did not entirely understand, a clipped tone to his words she found...confusing. He looked back out over the balcony when the orchestra began to sound as the violinists began to warm their bows and fingers. The change in sounds caught Florence's attention and she looked away from Brendan.

Her hands twisted in the material of her skirts. Her dress pooled out around her, the warmth of the fur still around her shoulders offering her solace against the distance between Brendan and herself. There was a gulf Florence could feel growing between them, the plush seats they sat on were only inches apart, and yet...and yet...that small space of half a hand felt as insurmountable as the Atlantic. She dared to look Brendan's way then, the Scotsman was looking forward, shoulders tense, body held as taut as one of the violin strings being plucked at by the musicians below.

Florence licked her lips and opened her mouth to speak. What she would say? She did not know but she knew she must do something, say anything, to break the walls she could see forming around Brendan. The change from the smiling man she had encountered at the start of their evening was gone. In his place was a tight-lipped man she could see but scarcely hope to reach. Their situation much reminded her of when the pond outside of town froze over, the gently rolling waves of water freezing into solid floors of ice smooth enough it could be mistaken for a ballroom floor. The townsfolk enjoyed skating when this happened which gave a purpose to the cold and ice. Skating was good fun, after all.

But now with Brendan present in body only, Florence wondered where his mind had gone. Now the ice was only a barrier with no pleasure to be found. She swallowed hard at that. She had yearned for an enjoyable time with the men but the pursuit of pleasure meant nothing if Brendan was uncomfortable with it all. Perhaps the man was now having second thoughts over sharing his lover with another?

She had asked for space where love was already

present. Ansel had assured her that he and Brendan had felt lightning in their hearts at first seeing her. What if it had not been as equal as Ansel had let on? It would not be outside the realm of possibility for Ansel to want her while Brendan was less inclined.

Again she made to speak but this time Ansel's hand on her elbow quieted her.

"May I?" he asked when she looked his way. He gestured to the wrap she wore and though she was reluctant to part with the garment she gave him a slight nod, slipping the fur from her shoulders and into his waiting hands.

He rose from his seat and nodded at the opera box door to the right of them when she gave him a confused look. "I will just be a moment putting this away."

"Where are you going?" There was a desperate pitch to her voice Florence painfully recognized as panic. Where was he going? Why was he leaving her alone with Brendan encased in ice as he was? She would never manage to carry on a conversation with him without Ansel's warm presence beside her.

"There was a safe place for it in the hallway."

"It's fine here," she croaked out past a dry mouth. "Just on the seat here."

"The back of a seat is no place for a lady's outerwear and this is a spectacularly fine piece."

"I assure you it is more than all right. Why, you'll miss the start of the play," she said, scrambling for reasons why Ansel must, in fact, stay precisely where he was. Her gaze darted to Brendan who appeared to be glaring now at the stage in front of them, the chill around him growing by the second.

It was not if, but when she would need Ansel. He couldn't possibly leave her now.

"I insist in fact that you do not go out of your way to--"

Ansel waved her off already halfway to the door. "I couldn't possibly allow it. I'll just be a moment. I'll be back before the play begins, you'll see."

"Ansel, wait!" Florence made to stop him but the man was out the door before she could so much as get around her seat. She stopped where she was, hands tense at her sides and worked to stymie the heavy sigh that wanted to slip from her lips. He was gone and she was now...alone.

A rustle at her side paused her thoughts. She was not alone.

"Brendan." She turned and smiled at him. He was looking at her with a furrowed brow. She cleared her throat and shifted on her feet. The atmosphere in Ansel's absence was decidedly less welcoming and open.

What had happened in Brendan's mind and heart that had caused such a shift? Florence's frown met Brendan's still furrowed brow and the pair stared at one another in silence. They might have continued on like that, highly resembling the atrocious statues she had noticed popping up in town as of late. Some sort of art craze obsessed with new "mediums of expression and form" as Rose had lectured her on when she'd commented on one particularly curious piece that looked like a cross between a wailing woman and a peacock.

Florence didn't care for peacocks. She also didn't

much care for doing her bit as a statue form. She cleared her throat and forced the frown to leave her face. The effort of it was difficult but she managed it all the same.

"How are you?" she asked, voice soft. Below the strings were still warming their fingers, the hum of laughter and chatter ongoing but here in the relative isolation of their seats, her voice was the only sound. She waited desperately hoping Brendan added his own to join hers.

"I'm well enough."

She waited for him to keep speaking but he continued to look at her with that same furrowed brow.

"And?" She pressed, hoping it would encourage him to talk once more, but Brendan only pressed his lips together and sank back to his seat. When he looked away from her Florence grit her teeth. Suddenly, she was less concerned with the awkwardness left in the wake of Ansel's exit.

She wanted Brendan to speak to her. To look at her. For the ice around him to fracture and melt until there was nothing left between them, but how would she manage it with him looking away from her as he was?

"Are you well?" She dared to ask. Brendan's shoulders stiffened as he somehow drew into himself further at the sound of her voice. The change in posture visible to her even from the distance she was standing at.

She might have charged towards him in the hopes of eliciting an answer but the Scotsman finally spoke and Florence stayed herself for a moment more.

"Aye, I'm fine," he said again. Florence rolled her eyes, the gesture going unseen as he continued to look out over the busy theater.

"Is that so? You seem anything but."

"It's nothing," he assured her. The answer only worked to annoy her, she might even be amenable to saying it wholly infuriated her.

"Speak truthfully, or I will take my leave."

He looked over his shoulder at her then. "What?"

Florence threw back her shoulders and raised her chin slightly. "I will leave this outing immediately if you do not speak truthfully to me on this matter. What has you like this?"

"Like what?" He rose from his seat but made no move to come closer.

She inclined her head towards him. "Sitting as if you are encased in ice. As if you have no words for me, acting as if you wish to be anywhere but here."

"I want to be here. Truly."

"But do you want to be here with *me?*" Florence asked, her mind returning to her earlier thought. He did want to be here. That much was true. But did he want *her* here? That was where she lost her confidence. She had never spoken to Brendan about the lightning strike to his heart. Those had been Ansel's words, not his. She had taken Ansel's declaration at face value, and believed him on the matters of their hearts.

There had been no time to ask Brendan his thoughts on the matter. Perhaps now was as good a time as any to satisfy her curiosity. And because Florence believed in the rewards of immediate action she did just that.

"Do you want me here?"

Her question was like a gunshot in the small opera box. She half expected to hear gasps from below at the look of shock on Brendan's face. His entire body recoiled, head snapping back as if he had been slapped.

"What do ye mean?" His voice was gruff as if the words, thick and heavy on his tongue, were made of stone.

"I mean exactly as I asked. Do you want me here?" She held up a hand when Brendan made to speak. "I know you want to be *here*," her hands splayed out, gesturing at the space around them, "if you are here, then you are with Ansel. You love Ansel but the question remains: do you want *me here*."

"Why would I not, Flower?"

There it was. *Flower.* That one seemingly innocuous word at home in use for a botanical study, or hot house. That one word was fine in botanical pursuits and interests, but when used towards a woman? It was...disarming.

When used with Florence?

Absolutely distracting to the point of devastation.

She was powerless against the endearment, her skin prickling, flesh heating despite her bare arms and the generous cut of her dress. Her pulse leapt at the base of her neck. She wondered if Brendan knew she was weak to the word, if that was why he chose to use it with her now when she was asking him such things about her presence with him and his lover.

If he had not used it she might have dashed off in the same direction as Ansel, but as it was she felt herself lean forward, feet moving of their own accord in Brendan's direction.

He saw the movement, slight as it was. She could tell that he had from the way his eyes dipped to her feet before they made their way up to her face. The man took his time, gaze hot and heavy on her form until he reached her face. Only then did he meet her gaze. Florence's mouth parted slightly when Brendan's green eyes became all that she could see. There was desire and a heat so mighty it melted away the ice she had desperately wished away.

He came closer, footsteps sure and steady in their approach. There was nothing between them now. Only a foot or so separated them and Florence startled when she realized Brendan was now near enough to touch. She had been so lost in the man's eyes she had scarcely noticed his approach. For all her desire to melt the wall of ice that had separated them, now that it had all but vanished in the span of seconds Florence found herself desperately trying, and failing, to manage the shift.

She had thought herself ready for Brendan's attention but she found herself woefully unprepared for the full brunt of the man's focus now that she had it. Brendan continued forward, a hand reaching for her so suddenly that Florence was helpless to stop herself from retreating. She backed up, feet tripping and catching in her gown, as she did so.

"I-I," she began but her words failed her just as surely as her feet did. What she meant to say next was anyone's guess, but for her loss of words, her feet continued to move. She only stopped when her back bumped against the wall of the opera box. The feel of the wood at her back worked to ground her, she hadn't anticipated running into it so suddenly but now that she had its support she leaned into it.

"Flower?" Brendan had continued to move with her and was now in front of her.

She swallowed hard, forcing her hands from her skirts, and reached back to press her palms flat against the wall. "Do you want me here?" she ventured when she trusted her voice.

"Am I not showing ye?"

"No." She gave a slight shake of her head and dropped her eyes. "You were made of ice and now-I do not know what to make of you now."

"And why is that?"

Her hands pushed against the wood and she focused on the smooth feel of the wall beneath her palms. "You would scarcely look at me once we were in the opera box," she told him. "I know you wish to be here but what I do not know is how I figure into the arrangement."

One of Brendan's hands came to rest on the wall beside her shoulder. The man had fine hands. Large and well-formed, calloused but neat and clean with trimmed nails without even a speck of dirt to be seen. A feat for a miner. He had taken care with his appearance and for that she was grateful. It was far easier to dream of a man's hands slipping beneath one's skirts when said hands were well kept. Florence forced herself not to lose herself to a daydream of Brendan's touch and continued speaking.

"Ansel said that he felt as if lightning had struck him in the heart at first seeing you. That he knew right away you were a man he could love."

"Been waggin' his tongue, I see."

"And truthfully so," she said looking at him then. "He said that he felt the same when he first saw me."

"Aye, he did."

"He also said that you felt the same."

Silence met her words. Florence's palms pressed harder against the wall and if she could have pushed the wall away from her, she would have. She was surprised not to hear wood splintering beneath her hands at Brendan's lack of agreement.

She swallowed hard and continued to watch him. He was looking away from her, his jaw clenched, body once more rigid as he stood before her. She wanted to press him for an answer, for a confirmation of her suspicions-- that she was not welcome. That he was entertaining second thoughts on her joining Ansel and himself in their love, but the lights overhead dimmed just then and the words died on her tongue at the sudden darkness that fell around them as gently as any first snow.

Brendan vanished from sight in the now blackened theater. A spotlight flicked on in the audience signaling the start of the production but Florence paid it no mind. Her senses were focused on Brendan, and she willed herself to speak her fears into existence. If she did then they would cease to be her own quiet burden. If she did then the worst of it would be over.

And she might have mustered the bravery to do it if Brendan hadn't been the first to speak. He moved, clothing rustling close to her ear as his hand still rested beside her.

She could not see him now, only a hint of his form visible as he shifted in front of Florence. "Flower," he said, his voice husky and low. He sounded different here in the dark with her, and her blood began to pound in her veins.

She had not felt this way since her time with Robert. Since the time she had been called 'reckless' with her attentions. She wanted him to touch her, wanted to feel him beneath her hands rather than the hard wood at her back. She wanted...she wanted...

"Flower, I want ye," Brendan said. He was closer to her ear now, a puff of warm breath ghosting across her jaw as he spoke. Florence shivered, her hands twitched and her nails scraped against the wood as she curled her hands into fists.

"But you would not even speak to me. You hardly looked at me," she returned, her words were not a whisper and not yet a yell, though she wanted to yell, given the pull of emotion now coursing through her. She wanted to act, to reach for him, but she did none of that. Instead she continued on in a furious whisper, so as not to disrupt the production now in full swing on stage. "What would you have me think when you pulled away from me in such a manner?"

"I did not pull away from ye."

"Not physically but you were not here in your heart and that is why I ask you: do you not want me here with you and Ansel? Do you--"

He laughed then, interrupting her, and Florence might have been angry if not for his next words.

"Not want ye here?" He asked. "Flower, I burn for ye. Yer all I think of these days. Half driving a man mad with thoughts of ye."

"What?"

He raised his other hand and placed it against the wall beside her. Her flesh came alive at the gentle thump of his hand meeting the wood. The vibration of it affecting her as surely as if he had set his hand on her body and not the wall.

"I'm not as good with words like Ansel. I cannae give ye pretty words as he, but I want ye, Flower. When I look at ye, I lose my words. I want to tell ye my heart but it's no good. Dinna fret yerself."

"What?" Florence tried to understand the words but now that Brendan was speaking, his words were coming faster and faster and she cursed her woefully inadequate understanding of the man's accent. "I don't understand."

"Dinna worry if I want ye here on account of my dumb tongue."

His dumb tongue.

I cannae give ye pretty words as he, but I want ye, Flower.

So he lacked the words to speak even if his heart wanted her with them. She nodded, even if he could not see her, the gesture brought her closer to him and she realized he was only inches away from her, the side of her cheek brushing against his jaw from the slight bob of her head.

"I'm sorry, I didn't mean to press you. I should not have made my own reason for your silence."

"Shhh, none of that then," he soothed her. "There's no need to apologize, flower. Not to me."

"But I believed the worst of you."

"Aye, but ye dinna ken my heart. Will ye let me show ye, flower?"

She felt the breath escape her then. His heart. How would she survive this demonstration? What would that entail? Her body felt abuzz with nerves. There was nothing to Florence other than the skin her dress did not cover and what it might feel like for Brendan's hands to touch, no, to show her precisely what he meant.

It would be the death of her, but even still she agreed to it. She would not deny herself the pleasure of knowing exactly what Brendan meant.

"Show me," she whispered, turning her head to the side, her lips grazing against the stiff material of Brendan's sleeve.

"Show me," she urged him. He touched her then, a hand cupping her cheek gently, his calloused fingers grazed the shell of her ear as he cradled her jaw in his hand.

"No pretty words, but feel my heart here." He was close to her now, the touch of his lips pressing against her throat. He must have dipped his head to kiss her. Florence's breath became ragged when she felt him place a hand onto her shoulder. Brendan's large hand was warm and light on her skin and she shivered beneath his touch.

"I want ye," he murmured, as the hand continued to trail down her arm. Florence closed her eyes despite the darkness that was all around them. He could not see her, nor did the gesture cause any difference of sight to her, but it was instinctive to shut her eyes at the intimacy she felt in Brendan's touch.

The way he was with her now. His hands gentle on her, almost reverent in their exploration of her flesh. This was closeness.

He moved, body brushing hers as he did so. His thighs pressed against hers until Florence could scarcely stand without reaching for him. She reached then, hands coming to rest on his shoulders, fingers twisting in the material of his jacket.

"Flower, I want ye," he said again. A kiss butterfly-light dropped onto her cheek, then the space below her eye, lips caressing her temple before he kissed her forehead. He stilled there, his body pressed flush to hers one hand cupping her jaw while the other found one of hers, their fingers tangling together.

She forced herself to open her eyes. She would not hide from him, not even in the dark. He was offering her so much more than words. Brendan was offering her his body in a promise of tomorrow, of days that had not happened, but would. Days that would find them just as they were now. Her hands clung to him tighter still and she hooked an arm around the man's neck letting him hold her up.

Softness and openness, it was all undoing her like a woolen garment caught on sharp brambles and under-brush. Brendan was a forest, dark and unexplored, but for all his sharp edges and her uncertainty he was a place Florence readily gave herself to without a map or light to show her the way.

She could scarcely breathe. Her chest rose and fell in quick succession, but still she leaned into him, allowing him to steal more of her breath, more of her.

All of this and the man hadn't even claimed her mouth yet. She trembled at the thought. What would it be like when he finally did kiss her?

She turned her face up to his, or as near close as she could guess in the dark. She raised a hand to his face humming in satisfaction when she found it. "Brendan, kiss me."

"No."

Her brow furrowed at his answer. "Why not?"

"I'll not kiss ye until ye see. Do ye see that I want ye, flower?"

"Yes, I do. I see," she told him quickly. "Now kiss me." She was impatient, they could both tell, but Florence had no shame in her to own up to it. If he asked her she would agree. She was desperate for his kiss.

"No, I'll have light when I do that."

"Brendan, you can't possibly make me suffer!" She forgot to keep her voice low and clapped a hand over her mouth at hearing the production below stop. There was a gentle murmuring of voices as the theater goers wondered at who precisely had cried out, but a moment later the actors began their lines once more and she breathed a sigh of relief.

He chuckled and pressed his thumb to her mouth when she began to protest once more, all be it quieter this time.

"Another time, flower. So long as ye ken that I want ye as ardently as Ansel." He kissed her cheek, the gesture chaste despite the fire it ignited in her belly. "I should like to look at ye when I do taste yer lips fer the first time."

She stifled a moan then, fully intending to protest his embargo on kisses when the opera box door opened to their left. Light shone in from the hall illuminating what Florence knew to be entirely damning on her part as a lady. She blinked against the light and frowned at the blinding it gave her. She could see nothing, but the low chuckle and familiar voice told her it was Ansel.

"Glad to see you've taken matters in hand, Brendan," he said, coming into the opera box and closing the door behind him. He hummed in disappointment as darkness once more flooded the space. Florence blinked against the spots of light that danced before her eyes now in the dark.

"Aye, thought it was time."

"He's not a man of words but one of action, you see." Ansel told her conversationally as he came to lean against the wall beside her. Florence startled when she felt his fingers touch her hair, he twirled one strand in his fingers as he spoke. "You make a lovely couple."

"But," Brendan said, "we will make a better picture as a trio. Dinnae ye think flower?"

Once more Florence felt her legs go weak. Both men were focused on her, bodies on either side of her, fingers touching her lazily. It was enough to make a lady faint and half mad but Florence was made of sterner stuff.

This was what she wanted. It was always what she had wanted, and try as she might, she had never been much of a lady.

"A perfect picture with three," she agreed, reaching out, fingers searching for both men. She smiled when her hand landed on Ansel's shoulders and she pulled him in closer to herself and Brendan. "Absolutely perfect."

CHAPTER 8

"*Y*e'll not go off on yer own."

"But it's only down the lane. I'll be fine, really."

"The one out of town, you mean?"

Florence fought against the glare she wanted to send Ansel's way and settled for a thin press of her lips and narrowing of her eyes. Ansel chuckled at the expression and tucked his hands into his pockets.

"I see that look on your face," he told her, rocking back on his heels.

"Aye, as do I," Brendan added, coming to join Ansel. Florence crossed her arms and tipped her chin back to look at them both.

"I insist that I take my leave from you both here." She gestured to the entrance of the theater and pulled her fur wrap closer. "It will be no trouble at all and I will be home in minutes. It makes no sense for the pair of you to go out of your way to see me home."

Ansel sighed. "First you do not let us escort you to the theater and now…"

"And now ye'll not let us see ye home." Brendan shot her a disapproving look that pushed Florence's sharp eyes to a glare.

"No, I will not."

"Not up to ye. If ye want us, then ye'll have us see ye home."

Her mouth dropped open. "What do you mean it's not up to me?"

"He means what he says. It's best for all of us if you take my coat and settle in between the pair of us, hmm?" Ansel held his coat out to her. Florence shied away from the garment, not because she did not wish to wear it or have both men see her home, but because she did not know how to handle her family. There would be no stopping the Wickes-Barnes clan if she were to turn up with a pair of men on her arms.

Her mother would know. That was not the conversation she was reluctant to have. Nor was she troubled much over the inevitability of her sisters' meddling and the drama that would ensue from them seeing Ansel and Brendan. Rose would have an absolute field day over it, of that she was sure.

But even still, she was not put off from being seen home by the men on account of her sisters. No, that honor was given to her fathers. The men who raised her would surely have a thing or two to say, and ask, about the entire arrangement.

There was no way around it. The second they caught sight of them there would be questions. Questions

Florence hadn't the faintest idea of how to answer. Though…though she knew herself well enough that she was sure she would think of something to placate her fathers' interest in the men at her side.

What Florence did not know was how Ansel and Brendan would respond to being questioned by her fathers, and with the hour growing late she didn't much desire to find out. It had been such a lovely evening. It seemed a shame to end the night with such a risk.

She shook her head. No, tonight would stay perfect as it was. Her stolen moments with Brendan in the opera box, the easy conversation with Brendan and Ansel, the comforting feel of them beside her and how entertaining the production of A Midsummer's Night Dream was once they had settled in to enjoy the play. She was very glad they had the opera box to enjoy the play, the sequestered space was useful for more than stolen moments and near trysts, after all. Enjoying the theater proved to be one of them.

"I do not think I shall 'settle in,'" she returned with a toss of her head. "I'll be off then. It was a lovely evening and I thank you for it." She moved towards the bank of doors leading to the boardwalk outside but Brendan stepped in front of her with a sound akin to a gruff growl.

"Did you growl just then?" She raised her eyebrows at him but the man looked undeterred.

"Aye, I did. And I'll do it again if ye try to leave without us." There was steel in his voice, green eyes no longer the color of lush verdant forests but of cold calcite. There was no warmth for her here, only sternness and she bridled at it.

"I will be leaving, growl or no growl."

"We insist on walking you home," Ansel murmured, coming to her side.

"But really and truly, I swear that---"

"If anything were to happen to ye, we would never forgive ourselves. It's not safe fer a woman alone at this hour, flower. Listen to us."

She hesitated at his words. She could hear the concern in Brendan's voice, see it plain as day on the man's face. She bit her lip and turned towards Ansel to see the same worried expression mirrored. She sighed, shoulders dropping slightly at the sight of both men. They were right, she knew it but it didn't mean that she liked it all that much.

Even if she hadn't a clue what to tell her family, she knew the men would not allow her to walk home alone, not at this hour which presently was growing ever later.

"Oh, all right," she sighed, holding out her hands to the men. "Give me your arms then if we are to go."

"Put on my coat first." He held the garment to her once more and this time she stepped close and into it. Once it was settled over her shoulders the men offered her their arms, through which she threaded her arms before they continued towards the doors and out into the night. She was happy they were close to her, bodies lightly grazing hers, her arms warmed where they held her close.

It would snow soon enough. There was no denying the telling chill that was in the air. They had only walked a few steps when Ansel spoke.

"Why did you not want us to escort you home?"

"Aye, was wondering on that myself."

"No reason," Florence lied, nodding to a townsperson as they passed them by. Perhaps if she was lucky she would happen into a decent enough acquaintance on their way home and she could beg off with them to continue her journey homeward without Ansel and Brendan. Though when she moved a tad quicker than either men the gentle tug of their hands on her arm to pull her back between them reminded her of one simple fact: they would not be easy to lose.

These men were on a mission and that mission was seeing her home.

"No lies between us," Ansel said. "It will not help us in the long run."

Florence sighed and shook her head. She knew he was right, of course he was right. There could be no lies where love was freely given and shared. It would only sour such a sweet thing and she bit her lip as they continued on the avenue that would take them out of town. The street was still quiet and the hope of finding new company home dwindled to nothing.

There would be no one save the men with her, no one to walk her home.

"You want the truth do you?" she asked and both men hummed in agreement.

"Absolutely we do."

"Want nothing more.

She pursed her lips and raised her eyes heavenward. There would be no easy way to say what needed to be said. The delicate words and subtlety her confession would require was nothing short of what the finest orators could provide.

Florence was not an orator. So she just got on with it.

"I have no idea what to tell my parents."

Ansel sucked in a breath. "Your parents?"

"Specifically my fathers."

"Och aye."

She nodded her head falling forward. "Och aye, indeed." She lifted her head then and looked between them pleadingly. "So you can see why I am concerned about you walking me home."

Brendan rubbed a hand across his jaw and nodded, eyes trained on the dark lane ahead of them. They were now leaving town and taking the left lane that would take them to her home. It was only minutes away, there was no time for dithering when it came to a solution to a conversation with her fathers, but even so the Scotsman looked unconcerned.

"I can see that it could be...difficult," he finally said. She snorted at the word choice.

"That is putting it lightly. My fathers are notoriously opinionated and sharp shooters, the pair of them. I am loath to think what they might do if they thought you had dishonorable intentions towards me."

"Well then we can put their fears to rest," Ansel interjected with an absent pat of his hand on her arm. "We have only the most high of intentions for you."

"Meaning?" Florence asked.

Brendan's large hand came to graze across her knuckles gently. Florence's fingers automatically tightened on his arm where she touched him. "We intend to court ye," he told her, meeting her eyes when she looked his way.

"You do?"

"Of course we do. There's no other who has affected us as you do, Florence. You are singular to us. The only woman to make our hearts glad. We see what can be with you," Ansel said.

Florence felt her cheeks flush and was glad for the dark of night. At least she could keep that bit to herself, which gave her something to stand on when Ansel's words were doing the sure work of sweeping her off her feet.

Brendan had been right. Ansel could give her pretty words. She quite liked pretty words.

She smiled, though the men would never see it in the darkness. The smile was for her. Freely given and without fear of being seen. It was at times tiring to wear the mantle of the woman people expected Florence to be but she had done it for years.

The alternative was...less than appealing.

She would never allow herself to be brought low, not like she had all those years ago. Her family had forgotten it, the townsfolk who had heard about the incident from Robert's family had swept it away as if it had never happened, but Florence knew better. There were newcomers to town, ones with long memories despite their short tenure and she refused to give them even an inch to make her feel less.

Dramatic. Flighty. *Reckless.*

Those were all things Florence knew were said of her but none of it had mattered if she only acted the part. But now Ansel and Brendan were declaring a courtship, one that was rooted in true deep emotion. Oh, and then there was the way both men treated her. These two beautiful open-hearted men speaking to her and looking at her as if they truly saw her made her feel anything but reckless.

Florence tightened her hold on the men, pulling them closer to her. The move allowed her the benefit of having Ansel and Brendan close for warmth against the night's winter chill, but what she hadn't anticipated was that it afforded the men the same advantage. Ansel's hand spread out over her arm, his hand a comforting weight that worked to soothe her buzzing nerves.

She cleared her throat. "Thank you for saying that."

"Of course."

"Ye only need to tell us yer mind, flower. And we will see to it."

"Is that so?" she asked. Her house was now in sight. The glowing lights of the well-loved family home she had grown up in. The lane leading to the Wickes-Barnes home was lined with other houses but it had not always been so. When she was just a girl Florence could remember only one other homestead beyond their own on the lane out of town. Now it was cozy and well-lit, a blessing and a curse given that Florence approached now with two suitors.

"When we arrive at my home, perhaps allow me to do the talking?"

Ansel chuckled. "We will follow your lead but we will explain ourselves when the time comes."

"Aye," Brendan agreed, but he said no more. His silence, Florence knew from their time in the opera box, meant his mind was turning. She wondered what he would say when her fathers' asked his intentions. Whatever it was, it would have meaning.

"Thank you," she told them. "It will be painless, I assure you."

"That so?" Brendan asked and she could hear the mirth in his voice. "Were ye not worrying on the matter before?"

"That was then, this is now," Florence explained with a toss of her head.

"Of course."

"Now then, when we arrive I expect we will have a moment or two to collect ourselves. After that--"

"Flower--"

"I can't say if they will even be in this evening but if they are--"

Ansel cleared his throat. "Florence, it seems we do not have a moment."

She stopped in the middle of her instructions and frowned looking up at him. She could see his features plainly now in the light of the lane.

"What?" she blinked at him and her neck refused to turn her head towards her home. If it did then she might see what she hoped she would not see. At least not before she had the time to formulate a plan.

Oh, why had she wasted so much of their walk silent and brooding? She was not like Delilah who gained inspiration from brooding. She needed action and planning, and now she had time for only one.

"Your fathers are on the porch," Ansel told her.

Action it was then.

She turned her head and saw the familiar silhouette of her fathers. Both men were standing shoulder-to-shoulder, arms crossed, or at least her Daddy was. Forrest meanwhile was observing them with hands on his hips.

"Blast," she murmured, hands clutching at the men now as she took a resolute step forward. "Best get on with it then." She moved purposefully, steps speeding up as she walked up the path to her front door. She was now all but dragging a sputtering Brendan and Ansel with her.

"Change of pace then," Brendan told Ansel over the top of her head as they were pulled along.

The other man shrugged. "An interesting development to say the least."

"What now?"

"I suppose we let her do the talking as instructed," Ansel replied, cracking a smile at his partner, who was looking panicked at the prospect of speaking to two fathers. "Relax, I am confident she has it in hand."

Brendan gave a quick nod of his head. "Understood."

"I suspect you and I will have such a talk in the future if we agree on a family," Ansel continued, nearly tripping up the stairs as they came to a stop on the front porch. "May as well experience it as suitors, hmm?"

But his words fell on deaf ears. Brendan's attention was elsewhere, or rather on someone else, two someones at that.

William Barnes and Forrest Wickes.

The pair of men cut imposing figures on a normal occasion, but at night and with their daughter involved? The fathers were downright fearsome.

"Florence," Will said with a nod and a small smile. "Did you enjoy your night out?"

"I did, Daddy, thank you."

"Who are your friends sweetheart?" Forrest asked, eyes flicking between the men on either side of his daughter.

She cleared her throat and cast one last look at the men she was with before slipping her arms from theirs. "These are, ah, not my friends…"

Will looked interested at that and rubbed a hand along his jaw considering the men in front of him. "Oh?" he asked.

She stepped forward with a tentative smile on her lips. "They, ah, may I present Anselmo Ortega and Brendan Black." She gestured behind her knowing the men, her men, would be stepping close to take her fathers' hands in greeting.

"They are my suitors."

CHAPTER 9

"One or both?" Forrest questioned, eyeing Ansel and Brendan over Florence's shoulder. She could tell he had not decided on what to make of the situation quite yet and she rushed to assure her father.

"Both," she said.

There was a slight drop to her fathers' shoulders. Some of the tension seemed to leak out of them and when Forrest smiled it was genuine. "Both. That's...something to hear, sweetheart."

Will reached out and took Florence's hand, bringing her even with himself and Forrest. "When did this happen?" he asked.

"Only just," she said, blushing at the intimate question. "I met them at the singles soiree Mrs. Rosemary held, and then, again at the theater tonight."

"Wondered where you had gone off to. You had us worried, Flo," Will told her and she ducked her head.

"I'm sorry, Daddy. I didn't know what I would think of it and didn't want to get anyone's hopes up."

"Seems to me only the men calling on you should be worried about their hopes. Not you, Flo. You're the prize," he said.

"Daddy…" Florence felt her eyes prick with unshed tears at her father's words.

Forrest hummed in agreement. "He's right, sweetheart. Any men lucky enough to catch your eye should be honored to have you and to spend time with you. Are these men worth it?"

The answer came from her lips instantly. "Yes, yes, I know they are." She looked at Ansel and Brendan where they stood watching the scene play out. She could tell they were nervous but her heart warmed when she saw the men standing close and holding hands. The gesture looked so comfortable that she hardly suspected they knew they were doing it consciously, more out of instinct than anything.

It was what lovers did when support was required.

It filled Florence with joy to see it. And made her next words easier to say.

"They are worth it. They are worthy of me. I would not have chosen them otherwise."

For a moment no one said a word or moved. The tension felt like a coiled spring on the brink of snapping. What would happen when it snapped she did not know. Florence's feet moved carrying her forward and towards Ansel and Brendan. Once she was in front of them she reached out her hands to them.

Lovers reached for the other when support was required. She was not their lover, not yet, but she more than desired her share of support from Ansel and Brendan. She wished to have their hands in hers, to be a part of what they shared. Her hands shook as she held them out, but they had scarcely been raised for a moment before Brendan and Ansel moved to take hold of her. Their fingers intertwined and at that first touch, Florence felt her breath escape in a quick sigh.

She smiled seeing the earnestness in their faces. "They're worth it," she said again, looking over her shoulder at her fathers.

"Then we trust your decision," Will replied, looking pleased.

"You do?" Florence asked, unable to keep the shock out of her voice. She was now between Brendan and Ansel. The men were holding on to her just as surely as they were to the other.

"We do. We raised you, we know your heart, Flo," Forrest said, giving her a smile. "If you're sure about these two fellas then we trust your decision."

Her heart leapt into her throat. "Do you mean that?" Her earlier fears were still hovering over her like thunderclouds barely held at bay but her fathers' words were doing the work of pushing them back. Perhaps her fears had all been for naught?

"Sure we do, Flo," Will said, taking a step forward and giving her a soft smile. "We trust you, always." His eyes raised to Ansel and Brendan. "Though can't say the same for them."

Forrest sighed heavily behind his husband. "Will..."

"Means we'll want to talk to them good and proper--"

"What are the pair of you doing out here at this hour? You'll catch your death standing with the door open no less." Her mother's voice sounded and a moment later Julie was bustling out onto the porch with a pinched look on her face. "I swear that--" she stopped and drew up abruptly at seeing Florence and the men at her side.

"Oh, Flo! I didn't know you were back from your engagement. And who are these two fine men?" Julie sailed past her husbands and extended her hand. "I have not had the pleasure of making either of your acquaintances thus far. I am Julie Ann Wickes-Barnes, but you may call me Julie."

Florence's lips turned up at her mother's fussing, and in no time the former debutante had both Brendan and Ansel receiving her with all the care and grace the pair could muster between them. Though her mother had no taste for society expectations, that did not mean the woman could not wield her upbringing with precision. Brendan and Ansel were left scrambling to keep up. Brendan dipping down in an overly deep bow that nearly sent him tumbling, whilst Ansel could not for the life of him stop paying compliments, the kind that had her Daddy glaring with narrowed gray eyes. She had never seen a more tongue-tied pair of souls.

Her mother was utterly delighted by the attention. Florence smiled indulgently at her when she turned towards her daughter and asked, "Are these the pair of suitors I speculated on?"

"Speculated, did you?"

"Only a little." Julie raised her hand, two fingers nearly pinched together, indicating how very little speculating she had engaged in.

Florence laughed and nodded. "Yes, mama."

"Marvelous." Julie clapped her hands and nodded conspiratorially at her daughter. "You did well. They are well spoken and very handsome."

"Julie…" Will looked aggrieved but his wife sighed, giving him a nonplussed look. "Stop jawing over them like they aren't in front of you."

"Additionally, I said they were well spoken," her mother pointed out and then looked at Ansel and Brendan. "I am very happy to meet you both on this beautiful night and I know you have shown my daughter a wonderful time. She's simply glowing. We will have to have you over for supper this week."

Florence glanced nervously at the men. Her earlier relief at her fathers' ready acceptance melting away at the thought of Ansel and Brendan sitting amongst her family at the dinner table. It would be an ambitious task. And she hadn't even had more than one outing with them to warn them of her sisters' proclivities.

She needed more time to ease her suitors into what an evening in her family's home would truly be like.

"Mama, I don't think--"

Ansel held up a hand and gave her mother a winning smile. "That would be lovely. We would be honored to join your family for a meal."

Brendan gave a slight bow. "There would be nothing more welcome than an invitation to supper. We accept."

Florence's eyes widened in shock. Surely they must be agreeing simply to not offend? She looked at the men in disbelief, and then saw that no, she was wrong in her estimation. The men looked earnest in their words.

"How perfectly lovely! I'll plan a wonderful meal. Oh, I'll even cook it myself. I am so excited, I simply must go consult my compendium at once." Julie clapped her hands and before any of them could say a word against it she had bolted back into the house with a barely heard *goodnight*.

"Oh, dear," Florence whispered.

"I'll say. You know what this means." Forrest sighed, looking heavenward.

"We'll have to eat the cooking and look happy about it," Will said.

All three of the Wickes-Barnes family members nodded somberly, though Ansel and Brendan looked confused at the morose mood that had settled over the group. It was then that Florence knew the night must come to an end. Anything more and she was risking her sisters making an appearance. Or worse yet, her mother taking to creating a tasting tray for their enjoyment.

"I think it's time for our goodbyes," she said, giving her fathers a meaningful look. Both sighed and nodded in agreement.

"Be on time," Forrest told the men while kissing her forehead.

"And eat every scrap of food that crosses your plate or so help me," Will added, kissing Florence's cheek and pointing a finger at Ansel and Brendan.

"Aye."

"Of course, certainly."

Her fathers left then, leaving them alone, and the

breath Florence had been holding since she had first sighted her parents escaped her body. She gave Brendan and Ansel a shaky smile.

"We did it," she said, giving a little punch of her fist in the air.

"Aye, so we did, flower."

"It wasn't as bad as you made it seem. Honest."

She hummed but was not a bit convinced. "Thank you for making it as smooth as possible."

"You have nothing to thank us for," Ansel said. "You seemed to have it quite in hand without our assistance."

"I was more worried we would have to make a run fer it when yer pas caught sight of us but then ye started speaking." Brendan blew out a relieved breath. He paused and then looked up at her, a smirk on his lips. "But ye took charge, flower."

She blushed at the intimate pet name. He had called her it plenty of times before, even in the dark of the opera box while his body was against hers but it had never quite sounded like this. Now it was rich and familiar, as if the man had called her thusly every day of her life.

Intimate.

She swallowed hard and smiled at him. "I try to be handy."

"I quite like a woman who takes charge," he said, coming forward. He stopped short of her and extended a hand to her, wordlessly she placed her hand in his. Brendan bent low and placed a kiss to her knuckles. Florence could scarcely breathe as she watched, but she managed a wheeze which proved entirely fortunate as

Ansel came up beside Brendan. He raised a hand to touch her cheek lightly.

"Goodnight, Florence," he said and rubbed a thumb gently against her skin.

"Goodnight," she whispered back.

Brendan righted and nodded at her. "Till tomorrow, flower."

"Till then," she whispered, breath still short. She raised a hand to her chest, the beating of her heart felt like a bass drum beneath her palm. The men had set her body entirely aflame and all of it had been done effortlessly. A simple touch to her cheek. An endearment uttered in familiarity.

It was enough to set her swooning.

Florence watched the men walk down the path to the lane. They stopped there and turned back to look at her, hands clasped between them, perfectly illuminated by the glowing light of the street.

It was, in Florence's estimation, one of the finest sights she had ever clapped eyes on. She could look at them forever as they were. Brendan and Ansel raised their free hands in farewell and she waved back enthusiastically, heart feeling as though it might burst from excitement. She only hoped that her addition to the men would make the sight all the more perfect.

"How was your night?"

Florence blinked in surprise. She had just closed the door behind her and was scarcely aware that her feet were

130

touching the ground. It was hard to be aware of much, buoyed as she was on the cloud of happiness and joy her time with Ansel and Brendan had given her. They were lightness and warmth, so much so that she only now realized her fingertips and nose had grown cold from the winter night.

She frowned and flexed her fingers. "What?" she asked distractedly rubbing at her pink tinged nose.

"Your night. How was it? Tell me everything." Rose was there clapping her hands excitedly. She darted forward and grabbed Florence's hands. "Oh my, you're positively freezing! Come by the fire and let me warm you up."

"I hadn't noticed before," Florence confessed, letting her sister drag her into the parlour. A fire was crackling happily away with her sisters sitting in the rocking chairs her parents usually occupied.

Seylah looked up from the book she was reading at their sudden entrance and raised an eyebrow. She set her book aside.

"Where were you?"

Florence gave her sister an easy shrug, coming forward with Rose towards the fireplace. "Taking in the latest production in town."

"Ah, I heard wonderful things about that. A Midsummer's Night Dream this month, I think?" Delilah rose from her seat and made room for Florence at the hearth. "Come here, you look positively chilled. Out in this weather with nothing save grandmother's fur to warm you." Delilah tsk'd but Florence said nothing, a blush rising to her cheeks because she had done quite well in the coldness. She hadn't simply had grandmother's fur, she'd had both Brendan and Ansel to keep her warm.

"It's quite all right. I promise," she protested but her sisters would hear none of it. Seylah draped the blanket she had been using around Florence's shoulders.

"Oh, Flo. I know you are taken with fashion but there comes a time and place when you must prioritize your health and welfare." She rubbed Florence's hands between her own and clucked her tongue. "Just like mama dressing as you please no matter the weather."

Florence rolled her eyes. "The elements will not tell me how to dress."

Seylah looked up at her with a frown. "It is Montana, Flo." She said with careful emphasis as if the words would magically take root, but her younger sister grinned and leaned forward laying her head on Seylah's shoulder.

"Yes, yes, Montana this and frontier that," Florence said laughing when she heard her sister growl at her. She watched the fire and sighed happily as Seylah resumed her rubbing. "This is nice."

"Drink this," Rose said, thrusting a warm cup of tea into Florence's hands. Seylah sighed loudly and pinned Rose with a stare.

"I hadn't managed to warm those quite yet. Her fingers are likely to atrophy at this rate."

"You are always so dramatic," Florence told her, sipping primly from her tea cup.

All of her sisters laughed at that and varied answers of:
"That's quite rich."
"If that isn't the pot calling the kettle black."
"Says the most dramatic woman in the county."

Florence pursed her lips and pretended not to hear them. "I had a lovely time, in answer to your earlier question, Rose."

Rose laughed and leaned into her sister's line of vision. "I heard Papa and Daddy making a fuss out on the porch. Mama ran out as soon as she heard them grumping."

"They were not grumping."

"Are you quite sure on that account?" Seylah asked and Florence relented.

"I suppose there may have been a slight amount of grumping," she admitted a moment later. She hadn't so much as thought of them as being ill tempered with her and her suitors, but more... "They were concerned," she said.

"Why were they concerned?" Seylah asked. "You've been on many an outing with eligible suitors."

Delilah shifted in the rocker beside her and Florence cautioned a look at her sister. The two shared a knowing look on the matter. Of her sisters only Delilah knew the nature of their fathers' concern. She had met both Ansel and Brendan, after all.

"Secrets do not make friends!" Rose yelled, wagging a finger between her sisters. "I saw that look."

"As did I. Now out with it," Seylah ordered.

Florence gave her oldest sister a sidelong look. "You don't order me about just because you are a woman of the law."

"Oh, stop that," Seylah waved her hands at her. "Now tell us why you two just shared a secretive look. Rose is right. Secrets do not make friends."

"No, but they do make sisters," Delilah chimed in earning withering looks from Seylah and Rose.

"You're insufferable," Rose said, crossing her arms. When Delilah looked as if she might shake her Florence held up a hand stilling her sister's movement.

"Oh, all right, I'll tell you unruly mob everything." Her words commanded her sisters' attention.

"Every sordid detail?" Rose asked. "You promise?"

"I hardly consider my night to contain sordid de--" Florence began in protest but the faintest memory of her time with Brendan in the opera box stole her words.

Perhaps there was a bit of sordid details to impart.

"I know that look. This will be utterly delicious!" Rose cried excitedly.

Florence sipped from her tea cup and rolled her eyes at Rose. Her sister was right but that did not mean she had to agree to it.

At least not right away anyhow. *Where was the drama in that?*

"My time tonight was anything but sordid, of that I can mostly and half-heartedly assure you."

Seylah's eyes widened. "Who did you go to the production with?"

"Ah, well," Florence ran her finger along the rim of her tea cup and then continued on, "I was invited to the production by two men that I met at Mrs. Rosemary's soiree."

"Suitors?" Seylah asked.

Florence nodded. "Yes."

For a moment there was silence and Florence felt a brief panic sweep her body. What if her sisters did not understand her intentions with Ansel and Brendan? Her parents accepted her decision, but what if her sisters did not? She did not think she would survive it.

She cleared her throat and dropped her eyes, unwilling to look at either of her sisters. Delilah's heart she knew, and for that she was grateful but the silence proved too formidable an opponent for Florence and she much preferred to look anywhere but at Seylah and Rose.

Another stretch of silence filled the space around them and just when Florence thought she could bear it no longer Rose sprang into action.

"I knew it!" she cried, leaping to her feet. "I knew you were scheming to do this."

"Ansel and Brendan are not a scheme!" Florence shouted from her seat. She might have jumped to her feet if she had not been bundled in a jacket and holding a mostly full cup of tea. She was not known for her grace, not since she had been all of eleven and caused quite the scene at Peter Hill's wedding. She maintained her innocence as who in their right mind set a wedding cake as delectable as her Aunt Violet had created on such a high table, with that many hungry children, and on a hill no less. No, she had been innocent then, but the ghost of her less than steady limbs kept her from getting to her feet. A move as ambitious as that would surely put her on her backside, or worse, careening into the fire.

As it was she glared at Rose from where she sat, hands clenched tight on the tea cup. "They are not a scheme," she bit out once more.

Her sister's eyes widened, all merriment vanishing in a heartbeat. "Oh, Flo, I didn't mean to anger you. I admit I got carried away." She twisted her hands in her skirts and shook her head. "I am sorry. Truly. Do you forgive me?"

Florence swallowed past her rising anger and gave a jerky nod. How was her sister to know her heart if she had not spoken freely of the men who had swept her off her feet? "I do. I forgive you."

Rose sank to her knees beside her and hugged her tightly. Arms around her waist and face pressed to her side. "I was only having a bit of fun. You know how I speak before I think."

Florence sighed, her anger abating at the show of remorse. "I know, I know." She patted Rose's hair gently and smiled down at her. "It's all right. I just--well, they inspire me so and I did not think before I reacted either. I should apologize for yelling. I'm sorry."

Rose shrugged. "I understand but I forgive you for looking positively murderous just then."

Florence snorted. "I had no such expression."

"I've had convicts with less of a look to commit violence," Seylah interjected with a laugh. "You looked murderous."

"Well, I simply cannot control my face. If it takes to murderous expressions then the public will simply have to cope."

"Murderous looks aside. I think it's best you tell them the news of your suitors. It's growing late and we all need a good night's rest." As always Delilah was the most mindful of the time and while Florence might have normally scoffed at such mother henning she found it useful this once.

Just this once.

"Quite right." She nodded at Delilah and then regarded her sisters with as much of a composed expression as she could manage. She cleared her throat and smiled serenely, and only when Rose looked as if she might shout she said, "I have two suitors."

"Yes, we gathered that. We need more details!" Rose exclaimed.

"She's right. What is their profession? Are they new to the area? Please for all that is holy do not inform me they are two of the ranchers by the pass."

Florence laughed. "No, never that. I only enjoy Romeo and Juliet as entertainment, not my life. I am not so brave as to send Daddy into a rage. He hates them."

"Abhors them," Seylah agreed, looking slightly more relaxed. She rolled her shoulders and nodded at Florence. "Then by all means share all the deliciously sordid details of your two suitors."

"There are no truly sordid details. Only half sordid," Florence ventured, making her sisters titter with laughter.

"Then give them to us!"

"I will, I will! Gather round now for a tale of love at first sight."

Delilah looked as if she might faint at that admission but Rose looked delighted while Seylah laughed and joined Rose on the floor to listen. Florence grinned and nudged Delilah upright before she looked to her other sisters to share her story of how she encountered Brendan and Ansel. She loved them together like this, so like when they were girls gossiping over their day that for a moment Florence's fears of what life would be like without them all together under one roof abated.

She did not think of Seylah's upcoming marriage in the Summer, nor did she think of Rose's impending departure for New York City. There was only now with her sisters, the promise of Christmas spent snug with her family, and the delight of sharing new details of her love life with those she loved the most in all the world.

CHAPTER 10

*F*lorence closed the door to The Modern Dress and cast a furtive look around the busy street. It was just after two in the afternoon, and she had just finished her shift working with Mrs. Rosemary on a rather ambitious project. A line of clothing patterns customers could purchase and then take home to complete at their leisure.

It was new and innovative for a frontier town that Florence felt was too starved for quality fashion. Mrs. Rosemary's shop could only do so much to remedy the state of style in Gold Sky. This idea was just the thing the town needed. It was affordable and perfectly in tune with the town's can-do attitude. Florence knew it would be a hit. There was no way it could not. There wasn't a soul alive that would turn their noses up at the functional and well-designed collection of day dresses, work clothes fit for the toughest of work, and outfits made to satisfy the category of Sunday Best.

And the most exciting part of the new venture was

139

Florence's role teaching classes to townsfolk in need of instruction in the art of garment and dress making. She had always seen herself as one able to communicate ideas and lessons well. She had helped teach new tailors and taught the women in town simple tricks meant to extend the life of their new purchases. There had been a time when Florence had even entertained the idea of joining her mother as a teacher but she had always been pulled towards fashion. There mere idea of arithmetic and instructing perfect penmanship or helping students recite historical facts had done nothing but bored her.

It was a damnable thing to be able to teach effectively in a setting that was not a classroom.

"You have such a lovely way when you teach. You're a natural, Flo," her mother had gushed after observing her in the classroom. Florence had gone to the school house that day simply to help her mother but somehow Julie Wickes-Barnes had managed to turn over the day's lessons to her daughter, claiming she was there to "observe." What that truly meant and why her mother had pushed for it Florence hadn't known, but she had enjoyed her time with the children and in the classroom even if the subject was not where her heart lay.

Her heart lay with fashion. That was her passion, as was using her attention to detail and skilled hands to bring joy and confidence to the people of Gold Sky. Any that wore her clothing felt their best and that true beauty, a beauty that Florence believed resided in every person, was a reward she prized above all things.

Florence's teaching ability was a wildly natural thing that chafed at the idea of teachers' college. Her mother had been understanding, if remorseful, over Florence's decision to forgo formal schooling. But now? Now she would be able to combine her talent with her interest to continue to do good for the town she loved.

Florence smiled at the thought though she winced and rubbed at her temples a second later. There was no denying she was tired from the day's busy planning and pattern creating. She had been a ball of excitement, an easy thing to do when in the company of Mrs. Rosemary. The other woman simply thrived when there were new plans afoot.

She rolled her shoulders and started forward slowly. Her limbs ached and her head pounded. Had she had anything to drink that day? She had enjoyed a quick breakfast at home before she'd dashed out to the dress shop but save that she hadn't so much as paused to eat or drink. Florence had just rounded the corner, the only thing of importance on her mind was getting to Mrs. Lily's cafe as quick as her feet could manage and ordering the most decadent item off the daily menu. So focused was she that she didn't notice the man in front of her until she barreled right into him.

"Ooof!" she grunted and winced, bringing her hands up to brace herself against the broad chest she had run headfirst into. "I'm so sorry," she apologized. "I didn't see you there." She made to move away but an arm caught her around her waist and steadied her.

"No trouble at all."

A warmth spread through her at the voice and she smiled, looking up at the owner of said muscular chest.

"Brendan. How are you? I didn't think I would run into you like this but I am quite happy to see you."

"I am well. Looking for you flower."

"You were?" She beamed at him, stepping away when a passerby raised an eyebrow at their intimate position.

He nodded at her and offered her his arm. "I was. Ansel wanted to invite you to tea."

"That sounds lovely. I'm absolutely famished from the day I just had." She rubbed at her temples and this time her smile was strained. The fatigue of the day making itself known once more despite the boon Brendan's appearance provided. Brendan frowned, noticing her slight wince.

"Are ye all right?" he asked, brow creased in concern.

"Yes, I'm just a bit tired," she said, voice soft. There was no denying her energy was waning even at this perfectly early afternoon hour. She turned her head, squinting into the bright sunlight. It was a beautiful day out. The crispness of winter made everything feel sharper to her senses. There was a vividness and energy to the street and people hurrying about the main avenue. It was to be expected this close to a heavy snow on the frontier.

Winters were harsh here. November and the coming months would demand much from the citizens of Gold Sky but with everyone doing their part it would pass peacefully enough. The last snowfall had been well over a week ago, a surprising luxury in their area. The town had only just settled back into the routine of life before having an impending storm threatening to throw the delicate balance of frontier life off track once more.

"It looks as if it will snow soon," Florence offered with

a frown. "I quite liked the lack of snow. It made for a more exciting winter thus far."

"Aye, I suppose it will snow either tonight or tomorrow." Brendan touched her elbow gently and bent his head low to speak to her. "What has ye looking so worn, flower. Are ye well? Should I take ye home instead?"

She shook her head and turned towards him quickly. "No, no. I'm just--well there was quite a bit of activity at the shop today."

"Would ye like to tell me about it?"

Florence had been focused on the road ahead of her but now she stumbled from the sheer concern voiced in Brendan's question. It was easy to forget the wider world around her when her personal world consisted of nothing but A Modern Dress's four walls and the ideas and people contained within it. She had been busy drinking in the activity of the robust street with hungry albeit tired eyes. Brendan's words stopped her feet from performing even the most rudimentary task of walking and managing to stay upright. She gripped at his arm and blinked in surprise at the worry creased into Brendan's brow.

"You can talk to me about anything you like," he added, and Florence felt her heart swell.

"You truly wish to know what's on my mind?"

"Nothing would give me greater joy and if it eases the tiredness from yer shoulders I will gladly listen."

Florence smiled at him. It touched her that he would offer to listen to her worries, but more than that, the man was genuinely interested in what she had to say. It was a glimpse at the intimacy and care her parents enjoyed, what she had grown up wishing desperately for when it came time to make her own life. To have Brendan offer that to her now was no small gift and she clung to it eagerly now with both hands.

"Thank you," she told him, pulling his arm close to her. She settled her head against his shoulder. "That makes me very happy to hear."

"Ye should have someone to share yer heart with," he paused and then added, "ye will have us to share yer heart with when ye care to."

Us. Florence smiled and the activity around her softened slightly. She no longer cared if it snowed or about the sharp cold biting at her nose. He had said 'Us.'

"Ansel and I keep no secrets from the other. It makes the days easier to bear, especially when life becomes...trying."

She looked up at him. "Trying?" There was more in the man's words than he was saying. She could tell it as surely as she had heard his earlier spoken concern.

He nodded, green eyes trained ahead of them. They were now on the outskirts of town, the streets were less traveled here and there was now a lane leading out of town, towards the small lake facing the mountains. It was a serene place she had often escaped to.

"Life's not always easy when you move to a new place. Ansel came to Scotland from Mexico, and then we both made the move to New York City before coming on to Montana. It has been interesting and worthwhile, but every step of it has presented challenges for us. Havin' the other has made it easier to bear."

"Loads are easier to carry when there are more hands to make the work feel light."

"That's the measure of it, flower. And now ye have us."

She grinned. "Why limit yourself to two pairs of hands when there can be three at work, hmm?"

He laughed. "Well said."

"I'm to teach a class and there is a new business venture at A Modern Dress," she told him. "We are aiming to create a more accessible and affordable fashion option for the people of Gold Sky. Though it has experienced a boom as of late, Gold Sky still is and will always be a frontier town. The people here have a particular way of doing things and purchasing new dresses and suits for events is not often one of them."

Brendan hummed, leading her down a lane that was, as she estimated, in the direction of the lake. In the near distance she could see a home, it was a small two-story affair painted in a light blue and ivory trim. There was a porch that wrapped around the front of the home and she wondered if they had plans for a swing there. She would love a swing on the fair summer nights when the three of them would be alone here in the relative quiet the fringes of Gold Sky offered. The town was a wellspring of life but out here? Here it was calm and quiet, much like she remembered her family home in her childhood.

She adored that Gold Sky was expanding and growing with each and every day but there was something to be said for the quiet and peace of a secluded home. Florence may love drama, but she understood the need for rest and that was precisely what Brendan and Ansel's home offered.

Even from where she stood she could tell it was well built with a neat yard complete with a row of what she assumed to be rose bushes. They were hibernating now in the frigid winter but she knew they would be lovely bursts of color come spring. She spied a well and a barn along with two work buildings around the side of the home. It seemed the men's absence from town was well spent in time invested into their homestead.

It was picturesque in its simplicity. She could tell they had poured countless hours into the space.

"Is that your home?" Florence asked even though she knew the answer. There was no way it was not from the way Brendan was watching her. He was watching her as if cataloguing her expressions for later study. What she thought mattered to him. She could not wait to see inside the home the men had built, sure it would be as lovely as the feelings Brendan had inspired in her on their walk.

"Aye, it is. D'ye like it?" he asked, sounding suddenly shy. If Florence hadn't been holding onto his arm she might have melted to the ground. Who knew her knees would join her feet in rebellion?

In her defense it was quite unreasonable to expect them not to go weak at the odd mix of vulnerability, and yet still so imposing, that Brendan offered her as he watched her expression nervously. The man wanted her to like the homestead. She could see it plainly on his face. She smiled, reaching up to touch a finger to his cheek.

"I adore it," she told him. Brendan's shoulder relaxed slightly and he smiled. A thick gust of wind kicked up sending his red hair into his eyes, and out here in the quiet with the wind their only companion Florence did not stop herself from reaching for the man in front of her.

Her fingers lightly brushed against the strands before

she pushed her hand forward to card her fingers through his hair. She heard his breath catch at the gesture. She continued to move her hand until her palm brushed against his scalp burrowing into his thick hair. The wind proved relentless, freeing Brendan's hair from the low knot he wore it in.

"You have lovely hair," she told him, raising her other hand and capturing the stands blowing over his shoulders. "I've never seen it free before."

"I wear it pulled back. It's bothersome when I'm going about my day but Ansel would never forgive me if I cut it," he told her with a slight note of exasperation in his voice that had her laughing.

"Add me to the list alongside Ansel then. I too will have very strong words for you should you cut it."

Brendan's lips pulled into a frown.

"I will picket."

"Oh not you too."

Florence twisted a lock of his hair around her finger and sighed. "I believe you know what is expected from you, sir. Simply see to it that your hair never departs from you and all is well."

"Aye, I hear ye. Now then, come along before ye begin to issue additional demands."

"I think you'll find that I am quite apt to make demands even when in motion."

"Of that I have no doubt, flower but given that ye had a very busy day we will aim to keep the demands low, and the motion as well."

She pouted at his words, following behind him as he led the way to the home.

"What does that mean?"

"It means tea," he reminded her. "And that will put ye out of motion while ye enjoy what Ansel has prepared. The man is quite handy in the kitchen."

"And how are you in the kitchen?"

"I have my skills and he has his. The kitchen is not a strong suit but I do have a few dishes I can prepare well. What Ansel has made for ye today will be sure to please and not one that I have the head to prepare." He paused and looked back at her. They were now standing on the porch and he had the nervous look once more that she was coming to find endearing.

"Are ye ready?"

"For?"

"Ah, well, I've never brought a woman home before."

"Oh that," she waved a hand. "Do not worry, I am quite a lovely house guest and will use my very best manners. I swear it." She crossed her heart and winked at him. Brendan chuckled.

"I meant for Ansel to fuss over ye, not to mind yer manners, flower."

He reached for her hand and pulled her forward, interlacing their fingers while opening the door with his other.

"Ye can behave as if ye were raised in a barn for all we care but Ansel has a mothering way about him. Once he catches wind that ye were tired he will be upon ye full force."

"Oh, well I quite like being fussed over."

It was known the town over and within a few choice New York City circles that Florence Magdalena Wickes-

Barnes utterly adored being fussed over. She had made a healthy practice of accepting any and all pampering from a young age and she was more than happy to oblige Ansel's predilection for coddling.

"Perfect. There will be no shortage of it today. Just this way then is the parlor, I expect he's set up everything in there."

He nodded towards the door to the left of them. They were standing in a simple but tasteful entryway, one with hardwood floors and cream white walls and a bevy of greenery in the form of parlor ferns framed the space nicely. Stairs were at the end of the hallway, a doorway she supposed led to the kitchen was ajar beside the staircase. Brendan was leading her through an archway, the contents of which belied the simple furnishings and decoration of the front hallway.

Patterned parquet flooring and lush carpeting covered the floors here, emerald green velvet curtains, an ornate mantle with a stoked fire warmed the room and set before the fire was a table for three. A tower of tea sandwiches, a vase full of fresh cut blooms--roses to be exact--though where Ansel had managed to get them in the dead of winter puzzled Florence, next to the roses was a carafe of coffee. Fine linens and a tea service for three complete with bone china was set atop a lovely patterned silk table cloth. Around the table sat a trio of high-backed mahogany chairs, of which Florence would admit looked downright inviting after her busy day planning the new venture with Mrs. Rosemary.

"This is so wonderful," she gushed, taking a step forward. "You did this for me?"

"We did," Brendan told her with a smile.

"Indeed, even if I was the one to set it out," Ansel replied, entering the room behind them. He was carrying a tray of cakes that smelled heavenly.

Florence's eyes widened at the sight. "What are those?" she asked.

"Bannocks," Brendan answered, moving to pull her seat out for her.

"You would probably know them as scones," Ansel added helpfully. He set down the tray and then tapped a finger against the tea pot at the center of the table. "Would you serve, Flo? I have one more dish to finish in the kitchen."

Brendan clicked his tongue at Ansel. "Always over-cooking, ye are."

"I know what you're prone to do when you go hungry, so yes, I do overcook," he returned giving the man a wry smile. He stopped and gave Florence a considering look. "Are you all right? You seem a bit piqued."

"She's had a busy day. One that she will tell us all about once yer done fussin' in the kitchen."

Ansel gave a quick nod to Brendan before looking back at her. "Have a seat," he told Florence and moved to take her hand. "You do look lovely, so I hope you do not think I meant to say otherwise with my comment. I was only concerned."

"No, no," she murmured with a shake of her head. "I am more worn down than I realized from the earlier part of my day. Thank you for asking."

"Always," he told her before he bent low and kissed the

back of her hand. He glanced up at her, "You are as lovely as the sunrise," he said, giving her a wink.

"Charmer," she laughed, but there was no denying the blush that colored her cheeks. Ansel chuckled and then was off and out of the room. She was left smiling after him as his footfalls faded down the hallway. She turned to look at Brendan who was beside her chair and offered him her thanks as she took her seat. Florence sat quietly and watched as Brendan busied himself with filling their cups, hers first with a liberal dash of sugar and cream. She smiled and took the cup from him with a murmur of thanks.

"This looks delicious."

"Aye, it does," Brendan answered, taking a seat beside her. Florence jumped at a popping sound from the fire, but in truth it was not the only thing to catch her by surprise. Brendan affected her as surely as the sudden change in atmosphere, as subtle as it was. His words on their own were harmless, perfectly affable and expected but there was a touch of something more there. A lowness to Brendan's voice that she had only heard once before, in the space of the opera box.

She blinked at him over the cup of tea she had only begun to sip from. He smiled at her and served a cake onto her plate.

"What is it, flower?" he asked, watching her as she swallowed hard and set her cup down.

"You," she told him, licking her lips. "You are doing magic on me. I know it."

"Magic?" he raised an eyebrow and moved to place a tiny cucumber sandwich onto her plate as well. His large hand handled the small sandwich with grace she hadn't thought his fingers capable of. But to see him delicately set the sandwich triangle onto the plate in front of her made Florence wonder what else the man was capable of touching just so.

"Yes, magic," she said, still watching his well-formed fingers. He was now just touching the delicate side of her plate, his thumb stroking the painted pattern of the china. God she knew that thumb would touch her just as lightly, sliding along the curve of her hip as surely as it did the rounded edge of the plate.

"There's no other explanation for it," she told him with a shake of her head. She reached for him then, fingers furtively touching his. "You've sent my mind into a fury with just the stroke of this thumb here." She traced the length of the digit with her pinky.

"That so, flower? And what does that mean when it comes to thinking about my hands?" Brendan curled his fingers around her pinky and hand until Florence's hand was nearly cradled in his grasp.

She swallowed hard at the sudden change of position. "It's unconscionable," she explained.

"Aye, I can understand that," he said, laying his other hand on top of hers until Florence's fingers touched nothing but Brendan's skin. The fire crackled merrily along reminding her of the many nights she had spent with her family in their own parlor. This scene was so at odds with that homely and familiar memory that she nearly laughed. Then, she had been arguing with her sisters over some fact or bit of gossip, maybe she had read a book while her sister played the piano and her parents chatted in the background, but now?

Now she felt as hot as the flames of the fire, now she felt as if she might combust from just the simple curl of Brendan's hand around hers, the sheer fact that they were simply touching hand to hand as they were was enough to make her chest rise and fall in rapid succession.

This one intimate touch was enough to undo her and she closed her eyes briefly. A bloom of heat warmed her cheeks and moved down her body until she felt a familiar ache of want between her thighs. She squirmed slightly in her chair and opened her eyes to see that he was watching her with interest. The man had noticed her slight movement and he was hungry for more.

"You look distracted, flower."

She shook her head quickly. "No, only...thinking."

"Focused then are you?" he asked, rubbing his hand along the width of her palm and making her voice shake when she answered.

"Ah, yes, I like to think."

"What are ye thinking?"

Oh dear. She couldn't tell him that. She cautioned a look at his face and paused. There was a hunger there that rivaled the one she felt growing in her body. Perhaps she *could* tell him that.

"Just...thinking," she finally decided and Brendan gave her a slight incline of his head.

"Do ye want to know what I was thinking just then? Because I was thinking, perhaps not as focused as you were, but me mind was at work, flower."

She swallowed hard at his words. This felt like a delicious game they were both playing and she had always liked games. All of the earlier fatigue seemed to melt away at the touch of Brendan's hands on hers. If he kept touching her she might mistake herself for well rested by the end of it.

"What were you thinking?" she asked.

He was silent for a moment, eyes moving to look at the table in front of them before he met her gaze once more.

"It had crossed my mind what it would be like to touch you."

"You're touching me now."

"Aye, but not as I wish."

Her heart leapt into her throat. The pulse there quickening and once more she squirmed in her seat but this time it was to move closer to him. Their knees bumped beneath the table and she blinked in surprise at the sudden jolt.

"Oh, I'm sorry, I didn't---"

"Don't apologize for getting closer to me, flower. I wish to be much closer than we are presently."

"You do?" Her words came out far breathier than she intended and she blushed at the suddenly wanton tone that had invaded her speech. Brendan's next words banished any such embarrassment with ease.

"Aye, I do. It is a struggle to not want to pull ye into my lap and kiss ye," he told her with the same intense earnestness he had expressed when learning she was tired from her day, the same energy and intention present as when he offered to listen to her worries.

This man intended to win her heart.

She knew it.

"Is that all you would do?" Florence asked, reaching out with her free hand to curl a finger in his hair. She moved up to cup his cheek and Brendan smiled, leaning into her touch with a pleased sigh.

"Aye and much more that I cannot possibly describe over a plate of bannocks."

"Oh and why is that?"

He grinned at her. "It would scandalize them, you see. There's nothing less tasty than a scandalized bannock. Makes the cake terrible-bland."

She laughed and tweaked his hair before withdrawing her hand. "As I've never had a bannock I fear I'll have to take your word as authority on the subject of bannock sensibilities."

"A wise decision. They are a truly delicate lot," he said. "And asides from that it would not do for Ansel to return to me ravishing ye, flower."

"You would do that?" There was nothing more that Florence's body wanted than to be ravished by Brendan Black. To have him against her as he had been only a few nights before. It would be heaven and here without fear of anyone happening upon them? It was a fantasy that Florence found herself nearly demanding come to life as the Scotsman shifted and gently took his hands from hers. She loathed losing the skin to skin contact but she forced herself to keep silent on the matter.

At least, for now.

"Aye, but only," he held up a finger, "when ye asked me to. Not before. That is terribly ungentlemanly and Ansel has gone through great lengths to ensure that I am a somewhat passable gentleman."

155

"I find that hard to believe."

Brendan's green eyes darkened. "You have no idea how much restraint I have shown around ye, flower. It has been trying me patience."

Her pulse was beating frantically within her body. The skin of her hands still held the ghost of Brendan's touch. There had been a heat between them in the opera box that was undeniably true. To know he had been holding himself back? Her mouth went dry, the gentle crackle of the fire at odds with the roar of the wind she could hear muffled from where she sat.

Walking home would be unpleasant, though she suspected the men would not allow her to go it alone. Brendan would continue to play the role of gentleman then once more. But she would know different someday, by the man's own admission. He would wish for more than the light touches, the perfunctory way they would be allowed to walk with one another in public.

Even in plain sight there would be the heat of his fingers at her elbow, the warmth of his palms through the fabric of her coat, and then there was the way his fingers stroked and *trailed...*

Touches such as those could be done covertly enough with coats as adequate cover. Florence could see it now, feel it as surely as the high backed chair beneath her. Her fingers curled around the arm of the chair. Ansel would be there with them as well, the man's dark head bent low to speak to her as they insisted on a buckboard being taken to her home. The sturdiness of the wheels would make quick work of what sounded like a growing snowstorm. They would hand her up, a man pressed close and then furtive intimate touches would be easier to conduct as they pleased.

It would be incredibly thrilling and forbidden. It would have tantalized Florence any other day, or, it might have if not for her realization only a few nights before.

She did not want secrets or covert cover. She wanted boldness but on her terms, no, on *their terms, all three together*. She wanted Ansel and Brendan as they were--- and that encompassed all behavior both gentlemanly and not. The approaching sound of Ansel's footsteps broke her focus. She looked away from Brendan to see Ansel entering the room, a tray of assorted meats and hard cheeses in his hands.

His dark eyes moved over them. "It looks as if a serious conversation was happening?" He moved closer and set the tray down.

"A bit," Brendan replied. He nodded at Florence and moved to pull out the chair beside him for Ansel. "I suspect flower was at the start of a profound bit. Sit and listen."

Ansel sank down into his seat, his attention on Florence. "Then I am quite happy I finished when I did. What were you about to share Flo?"

She smiled at him, happy that he had arrived. It felt right to tell the pair of them together, even if her brain was still working out the curious details of what exactly she would say.

"May I share a secret with you both?" Florence leaned back in her chair, hands burying themselves in her skirts as she spoke.

"Please do." Brendan raised a hand to his face, one

finger pressed to his temple, knuckles touching his cheek with elbow braced to the arm crossed over his chest. The overall effect was quite scholarly and despite Brendan's previous words telling her how ungentlemanly he could behave, Florence was hard pressed to believe him. Sitting as he was presently Brendan looked every bit the part. It was terribly unfair that he could assume such a pose and look, but what was even more upsetting was how Ansel was likewise able to appear the same. Both men watched her intently. The attention bolstered her efforts at ordering her thoughts. She could do this---she must, if they were to move forward together.

"I have come into a bit of hard-earned knowledge if you will. And it would be remiss of me not to share it with you, and Ansel."

"Of course. And what is it?"

"That it matters not if you are a gentleman, and by the same token it matters just as little if I am a lady."

Brendan's eyebrows lifted in surprise. "Is that so?" He was smiling at her, just a slight turn of his lips as he leaned against the arm of his chair.

She nodded and sat up straight in her seat. "You don't know this, but for a very long time I thought it was important to be ladylike."

"Why? Ansel and I quite like ye as ye are, flower."

A bitter half smiled passed her lips and her eyes flitted to the side. "I was not raised to be worried about things like ladylike behavior. My family has their own way of doing things, as I know you've heard."

He nodded. Florence cleared her throat and continued on. "But when I was a young woman, younger than I am

158

now," she added when Brendan pursed his lips, "I found myself in a compromising position. It was not compromising because of my family's rules or sense of propriety but for the fact that things had changed in Gold Sky."

Brendan remained silent but the unasked question hung between them. *Changed how?*

Florence's fingers moved restlessly. She rubbed at the armrest beside her, foot tapping and leg beginning to jiggle as she continued speaking.

"There were so many newcomers to the area. New citizens and people are always welcome on the frontier. With the way it's isolated, and there's always more than enough work to go around for too few hands but there is a downside to more hands. And it's that those hands carried with them all the preconceived ideas of what life could, and should be, with them. This included the appropriate behavior of young ladies. Especially when said young ladies were inclined to give into the pleasures of the flesh."

The men shared a look at that. Florence ducked her head when they turned their respective gazes onto her. It was one thing to share her thoughts and experiences and quite another to do so when the objects of her affection were staring at her with open and shared lust.

There was no other word for it. She knew hunger when she saw it and Ansel and Brendan were hungry. They desired her. That knowledge should have made her happy but it only worked to amplify the sudden bout of nervousness that was washing over her.

"And it was those newcomers that made me forget myself when not even my own family held judgement in their hearts for me." It hurt to say the words aloud, to have them in the open when she had denied them in her heart for so long. For years Florence had dodged the whispers and looks from those freshly moved to Gold Sky. "Rather than admit that I was hurt or self-conscious I learned to hide it and to use it as armor. Everything I was made to feel *reckless* about," her voice caught on that one word and the men did not miss it, their eyes darkening as Florence swallowed thickly and continued on. "Anything that was perhaps unfit for a young lady, I learned to embrace and thrive under but then...but then came time to admit the truth in my heart." She raised a hand to her chest and smiled thinly at them. "I knew that I wanted what my parents shared. Their unconventional love was what had raised me and I wanted nothing less, but that meant two men to love me, and in turn love each other as surely as they did me and I them. It was then that I began to worry about what a lady was, or what would be perceived as proper. I did not want for what we had to be thought of as illegitimate, or unseemly. I wanted for those in Gold Sky to see us with the same understanding as they did my family, as the community shared with one another but that has clouded my judgement in what I could be with either of you, and the thought pains me."

"Flower..."

She met Brendan's eyes and then Ansel's. "And that was my hard-earned lesson. It matters not what others think of us, or if we are a lady and gentlemen, but that we are true to our own wants and desires. What matters in this life is that we do not keep our truth hidden, and on that account I do not care much if you are gentlemen or not."

Brendan's lips pulled up at the corner. "Are ye telling me that ye wish for me to abandon pretenses of civility and decorum?"

Ansel leaned back in his chair. "I'll allow it," he said, with a nod at Brendan. "That is if she wishes it so."

"Is this your general reaction to my lesson?" Florence asked, unsure of what to make of the men's reaction.

Ansel rubbed a hand along his jaw. "We are pained that you were worried over such things like civil behavior, or that you ever saw yourself as reckless." He lingered on the word and Florence flushed, but the man kept speaking. "We see you as a woman who knows her mind and heart. And one that is ours."

"Aye." Brendan inclined his head, the word coming out in a gruff sound that made Florence's toes curl.

Ours.

She took in a shaky breath, hands coming up to press against the tops of her thighs as she worked to keep herself from launching herself at them.

"Yours," she said.

They nodded in unison. "Ours."

"I will also allow for the ungentlemanly behavior. A ravishing I believe you called it? I wish for that."

"Are you sure?"

She gave a curt nod. "Truly. In fact, I find myself infinitely more intrigued by what constitutes as rakish behavior and why it has previously been forbidden."

"We did not wish to overwhelm you," Ansel answered. He pushed back from the table and rose from his seat.

"We understand this is an unconventional arrangement. That our wants and needs are something that is not often expressed nor found in society at large."

"Nor is it accepted," Brendan added, rising from his seat as well. "At least not in most places that we have been. It made the appeal of Gold Sky our chosen destination when considering sites for our mining venture. This is where we knew we would be able to make a life."

"Where we would be able to find a wife that would have us. Gold Sky has always been in our minds, a place to make a family. A place where we would be respected in our profession and welcome in our community." Ansel rounded the table and came to stand beside her. He put a hand on the back of her chair and Florence's breath caught in her throat, so intent had she been on his words that she hadn't quite noticed that both men had approached her on either side. Brendan moved forward, his hand joining Ansel's where it rested on the curved back. She could feel the heat emanating from both men though they moved no closer towards her.

"Is this rakish behavior?" Florence raised her hands from her skirts and reached for them, a hand on each man's side.

Ansel chuckled and gave a shake of his head. "No, not yet," he said.

"But soon." Brendan dropped a hand to where Florence's rested against his side and threaded their fingers together. "I reckon the tea will keep, mmm?" he asked Ansel.

The other man sighed and then nodded. "Yes, I

wondered if something like this might occur. Everything will keep."

"Keep? Why would you worry about the tea keeping when--" Florence's words caught in her throat when Ansel bent low and met her eyes.

"For the sole purpose of executing rakish behavior."

Brendan's hand on the back of her neck nearly pulled a moan from her. She blinked in surprise at the slight touch as Ansel reached forward, a finger under her chin gently tipping her head back to look up at them.

"Oh." The one utterance was all she could manage. That barest of syllables that she labored to speak into being, of which she was left nearly gasping. Her chest rose and fell rapidly, the strain of her dress made itself painfully felt. She had thought the structured dress of silk with all its buttons and boning had been the perfect thing for her day, but now she was left lamenting the tight fit. Damn her own handiwork that now squeezed the breath from her lungs, or rather helped the men achieve the effect all the more easier.

Her eyes darted between their handsome faces. Both alike yet so contrary that Florence could not imagine one without the other. They were perfect halves of the same puzzle and Florence never wished to end her quest to solve it.

Ansel reached for her, one hand cupping her face, a thumb rubbing lazily across her cheekbone. "You are so lovely, Florence."

"Thank you." She swallowed hard. Her tongue felt heavy and thick in her mouth, she was thirsty suddenly.

Anticipation filled her as she awaited the men's next move, next touch.

"Will ye allow us to see ye?"

"See me?"

Brendan's grip tightened on her neck while Ansel continued to stroke her cheek. "Aye. See ye." He raised his other hand to run his finger along the neckline of her dress, his touch was light, the calloused feel of his finger making her shiver when it dipped beneath the fabric of her dress. He pulled lightly on the soft material and smiled at her.

"Without this."

All at once Florence's skin went hot. Her body felt as if it were floating and the men hadn't even touched her, only hinted at what was to come, asked permission for it in fact. She felt as if she were in heaven.

"Yes, I want that but only...only if I am able to see the pair of you." Her fingers dipped beneath the coats they wore to the waistband of their trousers and she pulled. "Without these."

"That is fair," Ansel said with a nod. "I agree to it. How about you?" He looked to Brendan. The Scotsman made a show of unbuttoning his waistcoat as he said, "I think it more than fair due to the fact that I get to look upon the pair of ye."

He pulled off his coat and tossed it over the back of the chair he had once been sitting in. Ansel chuckled and looked at her. "I think he agrees to it. We both do."

"Aye, Flower."

And then both men were reaching for her, pulling her up from her seat and ushering her forward. She knew that she should be far more acutely aware of what was going on, where exactly she was going, but it was difficult to notice, or care for that matter when she had both men on either side of her. Florence felt as though her feet were scarcely touching the floor as they moved. The warm solid feel of them intoxicating. The thin material of their dress shirts did little to stop her from feeling the muscled arms beneath her hand. Her fingers tightened on their offered forearms, her thumb rubbing absentmindedly along the material beneath her hand.

Once more their presence on either side of her worked to steady her. It was easy to find the center of her world when they put her at the center of theirs. She did not think there was an instance when the men's penchant for putting her between them would not settle her nerves. She should be nervous, overwhelmed even, but she was neither of those things. Instead, she was happy and at ease.

"Watch yer step, flower." Brendan's familiar burr in her ear made her jump in surprise. She had been lost in her cocoon of contentment but Brendan's voice broke through her reverie. Her eyes had been on the men, not the path before her and she hardly registered she was being led up the stairs until she was standing on the second floor.

Florence looked up at him and licked her lips. His face was shadowed in the sparse lighting of the second floor, it was darker up here with little light coming in through the window at the end of the hallway. She saw through the window that it was dusk, snow was also blowing past from what she could see. She bit her lip at

165

the sight of snow. Getting home would be difficult at best.

"Florence?" Ansel moved, his hand settling at the small of her back and all thoughts of Florence's journey home flew from her mind.

"Are you all right?"

Florence's eyes left the window and she saw him giving her a concerned look. "Yes, I'm fine. It-I just was caught by surprise." She gestured towards the window at the end of the hall, the fading twilight of the evening casting her hand in relief. "It's snowing," she explained.

He half turned to look at the window and hummed. "So it is," he said, his hand pressing flat to her back so that his palm was pressed firmly to her. "Do you...still wish for this?"

"Yes, of course," Florence blurted out and then she colored. She should be a bit more coy, or at least she thought so? No, she gave a shake of her head. Coy was not in her nature, not when it came to these men. She probably wouldn't ever master such a thing, not even if she was with them for the rest of her days.

"This way, flower." Brendan caught her hand in his and he led her through a door to the left of them. It was pitch dark inside, only a sliver of pale moonlight to be seen in the quiet space, slipping between icy clouds.

She stopped short when she bumped into Brendan, her forehead bouncing off of his back. He had stopped at what she estimated to be the center of the room and she rubbed her forehead with a frown.

"Quite sorry," Ansel murmured from behind her and

then a second later the room was flooded with warm lamp light.

The room was furnished with only a large bed, one far too large for two bodies. It would undoubtedly be perfect for three. The bed was heaped high with pillows and quilts and Florence knew it would be a delight to sink into to be sure. Several thick sumptuous carpets of crimson and emerald covered the wood flooring. If she were to go barefoot, she would not have to worry about cold feet. A pair of matching night tables flanked the bed, one held the lit lamp and Florence smiled when she saw a small collection of books on the table. The other table held a nearly identical set up and she could very nearly imagine Ansel and Brendan side-by-side at night reading at the end of a long day. Even with both men in bed there would still be ample room for her between them. Perhaps with a book of her own, or a sketchbook where she could work on her latest designs. She smiled at the thought, the shock of running into Brendan quietly faded from her mind as she envisioned what her nights here might entail.

"Meant to make for the fireplace," Brendan apologized, turning to give her a chagrined smile. He raised a hand and touched her forehead gently. "Ye all right?" he asked, giving her a worried look when he saw the faraway look in her eyes.

She blinked, forcing herself to stay rooted in the present and nodded. "Yes, I'm made of sterner stuff. You'll see," she said tapping his chest with a finger.

Ansel took her hand. "How fortunate for us then, hmm?" She flushed when the man raised her hand to his mouth. He dropped a kiss to her knuckles and she felt her breath catch in her throat at the wink he gave her.

"I thought Brendan said you kept him from rakish behavior?"

"I do."

"Then what is this?"

He lifted a shoulder in a shrug. "Simply because I can control it better does not mean that I too am not to be watched. Taking liberties with a lovely young woman such as yourself. In fact...some would say that I am the far more rakish of us."

"Yes, I am that someone. Ye are." Brendan called from where he was now squatting in front of the fireplace. He was working on stoking a fire to life but Florence saw that he had not missed even a second of her interaction with Ansel. She wondered how much escaped either man's notice when it came to the other.

"The kindling is to the left," Ansel called out to Brendan though his eyes never strayed from Florence's face.

"So it is," Brendan replied.

An answer to her question. It appeared very little went unnoticed between the pair of them.

"May I help you get more comfortable?" Ansel asked. His eyes were moving over her face now, searching. He was asking permission before this went any further. She could see it plain as day and Florence's heart warmed.

She nodded and reached for his other hand. "Yes, please. I want nothing more in the world."

He took both her hands then and with Brendan working the fire to life led her towards the canopied bed to the left of them. "And what a happy coincidence we have then. If you will." He gestured for her to sit.

Florence sat on the bed watching as Ansel lowered himself to his knees in front of her. "And why would that be?" she asked, her breath coming out in a gasping rush. When a man took to his knees it was often with good reason and Florence did not wish to miss even a second of Ansel's reason.

He looked up, brown eyes darkening with need as their eyes met. There was a pull between them, a tension she could feel building in her chest with ever increasing pressure.

"Because, we, my dear Florence, are quite of the mind to give you precisely what you want most in the world. Isn't that right, Brendan?"

The other man rose from the now lit fire with a nod. "It is our heart's most desperate desire," he said. He gave Florence a look that could only be termed as bordering on lascivious, and Florence found that she liked it immensely. If he continued looking at her in such a way she would not be responsible for her actions and she told him as much.

"You are inviting me to act, sir," she said, meeting Brendan's eyes before she looked back to Ansel. "The both of you are."

Ansel's hands were warm on her ankles. The man's hands were beneath her skirts, fingers deftly working on easing her boots from her feet as he continued to kneel in front of her. One of her shoes slipped free with a thud and he reached higher, the slight brush of his fingers along Florence's calf making her shiver.

He paused at the slight tremor and she knew he had not missed it.

"Then by all means, my lady," his fingers were warm as he pressed them against her skin, his hand moving to grip her leg as he met her eyes. "Act."

CHAPTER 11

*A*nsel's words hung heavy in the air like the incense Mrs. Rosemary was fond of burning when they were alone at the dress shop. It was cloying and inviting all at once, like jasmine and myrrh, filling Florence's lungs with every breath until she was very nearly drunk from it. She blinked slowly, watching Ansel as if she were an observer, standing outside of herself.

He moved slowly, deliberately, his hands gentle and methodical in his treatment of her dress and underthings. Up went her skirt, the hem gathering in his hands as he pushed it higher, and higher, and still higher, until the fabric of her skirts settled above her knees.

Florence watched still as he settled himself closer to her, his body now between her legs. She had parted them, allowing him to come closer, his shoulders nudging her knees and inner thighs, and only when he was leaning in, arms braced on either side of her thighs did he pause and look up at her.

"Is this all right? May I touch you?" Ansel's question

broke the heady trance his touch had induced, and all at once Florence was no longer an observer capable of cataloging the soft and delicate way Ansel touched her, or how methodical he was in pulling her stockings free from her legs. She was present and affected, her heart leapt into her throat as if on command and she felt her entire being turn molten. Behind him Brendan stood from where he had been crouched tending the fire.

Her eyes drifted to the lively flames and Florence could not tell herself apart from what made the flames dance and writhe. She was every bit as wild and unleashed, her skin aching to be touched in a way that left no room for modesty or grace. She was a woman, all fire and need, and the men in front of her were the only ones capable of satiating her.

Florence nodded. It was difficult to trust one's voice when there was not one but two men to consider.

"Yes, touch me," she choked out. She put her hands on the bed at her sides and leaned back, bracing herself on the heels of her palms. "Yes, this is, ah, very good."

"Just good, flower?" Brendan's voice was low and soft. The timber rich and velvety, and sliding over Florence like molasses. She thought of the bannocks downstairs and their light dusting of sugar. If Brendan's voice were made physical it would be that sugar dusting, barely there but tantalizing in its sweetness, alluring and just sweet enough to leave Florence licking her fingers free of the sticky sweetness and reaching for another.

She swallowed thickly and nodded at him, though her eyes never left Ansel's. "Better than good."

"How much better?" He wanted to know.

She smiled and looked at him then. "Perhaps it's best to show you? My words are failing me." Her voice was steady but it sounded thin, even to her. She was attempting to keep her head level and cool, to show that she was not worried about matching both men in the more intimate setting of the bedroom. Florence was not, in fact, intimidated by the act of taking two lovers, but she was nervous.

It was hard not to be when her heart ached for each of them as it did. She cared for them, hoped to love them each more with every passing day and now the prospect of being bedded by the couple had her spinning. She would have kept speaking, drawing out her play as the unruffled and collected woman had Ansel not touched her.

His hands alighting on her thighs, the gentle stroke of his fingertips against her exposed flesh made her shiver. He chuckled and leaned forward to drop a kiss at the top of one bent knee. Florence found she had no more words to speak and instead watched him silently as the man continued to kiss up her leg.

"I understand the problem with language. Words can be so troublesome at times, hmm?" He kissed her again, head bent over her leg, this time it was a brush of lips chased by the touch of his tongue.

"Yes." The one word was nearly strangled from her lips and Florence stifled a moan, eyes drifting closed when he began to pepper her skin with light kisses.

"Yes," she murmured again, her voice less sure now, but there was honesty there. An openness that had not existed before was plainly heard and the men exchanged a knowing smile. The woman in front of them was blooming moment to moment and it was a beautiful sight.

"I much prefer actions to words. I find it more effective. Don't you think?" His breath was fanning across her and her skin prickled with anticipation. The heat that had begun to bloom in her body swept over her, her anticipation transforming to hunger and need. She nearly gasped when she realized she was canting her hips towards Ansel's exploring lips. Florence wanted him to keep kissing her, but she sought out the pressure in a far more intimate place.

She nodded, eyes still closed, and licked her lips. "Y-yes, I agree." She was shaking now, they could hear it in her voice, feel it in her body, of that she was sure. Though she was not a stranger to the pleasures of the flesh, of what joy and release could be achieved between a man and a woman when their bodies became a playground to explore and relish rather than hide, Florence was desperately out of her depth. No one had incited such pleasure and longing in her, not like this. It was all new again and she sucked in another gasping breath, fingers twisted in the quilt beneath her before she continued on, voice quivering as she did so.

"Will you show me?" she asked, all of the confidence she had attempted to project when speaking to Brendan gone now. She was simply a woman in need of touch, desperate to be consumed by her passion to delight in the men she would soon take as her lovers.

Ansel moved in close, crowding her until Florence's back hit the bed. "Gladly," he whispered.

"Nothing would give us greater pleasure, flower."

Brendan joined them and Florence smiled when she felt the bed dip beneath his weight. "Yer beautiful," he told her, a calloused hand coming to brush against her collarbone.

"She is, isn't she?" Ansel's fingers joined his in their perusal of her skin and Florence moaned at the sensation. Brendan hummed in answer, hand turning to trail the backs of his fingertips along Florence's skin.

"You are just as beautiful," Ansel said and she knew he was speaking to Brendan by the low and throaty chuckle he received in response from his lover. She opened her eyes to see the men had closed the distance between them. Their eyes were locked in a heated look that had Florence squirming beneath them. Brendan raised his free hand and cupped the back of Ansel's head, his fingers carding through the other man's dark locks.

"Always a sweet talker," he murmured, pulling Ansel towards him and capturing his mouth in a hungry kiss. The fire in Florence was now a raging blaze. There was no denying her desire was only multiplied watching the men kiss. They were beautiful in the way they fit together, hands reaching and mouths perfectly slanted to the other's kiss. When they parted she reached for them, a hand cradling the side of each man's face.

Ansel looked down at her and smiled. "We are happy you are here with us. There is no other woman for me."

"For us," Brendan corrected before he leaned down and kissed her as he had Ansel. He tipped his head back to look at her. "Flower, ye are perfect for us, and we will make ye feel as such."

"How do you mean to do that?" she asked.

"Like this," Ansel replied. He slipped from Brendan's grasp, the other man's disapproving sound at the movement dissolved when Ansel settled himself back between her thighs. His earlier deliberate motions were gone and Florence was left gasping at the speed of which he had her skirts pushed up and her drawers done away with, leaving her bare to both men.

"And like this," Brendan added, catching Florence by surprise. He reached for her, fingers hooking into the front of her dress. She had dressed with care that day, as she did every day if she were honest. She dressed for none but herself and there was never a day that Florence didn't believe deserved the very best her closet and abilities could offer.

That morning she had selected a pale-yellow gown with a dainty neckline trimmed with lace. She had found the effect to be lovely if a bit prim. But now? The sweetness she had seen when looking herself over that morning had transformed into perfectly debauched. The metamorphosis of Florence's neckline was significantly aided by the presence of Brendan's fingers. He cupped her breast, palm rubbing against her through the material of her dress before he moved to slip two fingers past the lace trim and beneath her neckline. He tugged on the material and Florence gasped when his free hand joined his already questing fingers to tug down her dress, taking her camisole with it to free her breasts, open to Brendan's mouth and hands. He laved her breast with his tongue before capturing her nipple in his mouth, the flesh hardening as he suckled at her. The feel of his mouth on her was singularly erotic and pure bliss, as was the feel of his hands cupping and massaging her breasts.

"Oh, darling," Ansel murmured. He gave her a look that could only be adoration before he was kissing her once more, but now his mouth was at her core. He was no longer teasing her with feather light kisses along the tops of her thighs but was lavishing that sensitive bundle of nerves with attention. Gentle caresses of lips, tongue and teeth left her gasping as her hips shot up to meet his mouth.

"Oh, yes," she moaned, her head falling back against the bed as Ansel continued to ply her body with sinful drags of his tongue. The man's touch was practiced, focused, and above all else--thorough. There wasn't an inch of her that Ansel left unloved. The scent of her arousal bloomed around them, filling the room in its heady fragrance. He shifted then and lifted his head to look down at her glistening flesh, she was growing wetter by the moment as her pleasure mounted. The men were playing her body like an instrument tuned to music that only they knew how to perform.

A ragged breath escaped her lips, the bodice of her dress constricted her breath, so much so that she nearly saw stars and she reached up urging Brendan's hands to take her dress lower.

"Please," she told him, opening her eyes to give him a plaintive look.

"Do you want this off?" he asked, fingers still plucking at her nipples and making her gasp.

"Yes!"

"How should you ask then, flower? Ask me nicely."

She opened her mouth to retort that she should answer in any way she pleased, but one of Ansel's hands tightened on her hips, his other hand moved to her channel, a finger joining his efforts. All thoughts of protest vanished at the feel of his tongue and fingers moving rhythmically in and out of her.

"Ohhh." She was writhing now, hips thrusting to meet him. "Ansel!"

"Ask me nicely, flower." Brendan tweaked her flesh and when she said nothing other than utter a ragged keen he dipped his head to capture her nipple in his mouth.

"Focus, *flower.*" This was an order, not a request. Florence could hear it in the demanding tone of his voice. She opened her eyes and looked at him then to see him staring up at her over the swell of her breast. The sight of his hands on her, fingers pressed closed to her, mouth devouring her as if she were the last morsel of food and he a dying man.

"Please," she gasped, "please take me out of my dress."

He lifted his head then, letting her flesh loose with a light pop. The sound was obscene and yet she yearned to hear more of it. "Your dress?" he purred, licking his lips.

She nodded and opened her mouth though her attempts to speak were stolen by Ansel's touch. He had increased his efforts, tongue circling her most sensitive place, ever increasing in pressure until he moved to capture her hardened bud in his mouth. He sucked and stroked at it and Florence found she could scarcely breathe let alone form words.

She was a lost woman.

The only grounding forces were the men at either end

of her, each holding her down in their own way. There was nothing but the pleasure they brought her, the pleasure they found in her body and provided for her. And so she leaned into that exquisiteness until it was all she knew.

Dimly she was aware of Brendan freeing her from her gown, the coolness of the room held at bay with the heat of their bodies. Brendan's skin was there as he had pulled his shirt and coat off as well. Ansel must have as well for there was no other way to explain the smooth feel of his muscled shoulders beneath her legs as he hooked them over his shoulders, her calves and thighs pressed firmly to his body.

On and on, higher and higher the men drove her until finally the web of pleasure and want they had woven over her went tight, and then finally snapped. A rough cry escaped her mouth, her body went tight before it relaxed and Florence laughed as she rode the crashing wave of her orgasm. From head to toe there was no part of her that did not feel bliss and she had her men to thank for it. Brendan and Ansel kissed and touched her gently, their hands and lips reverent and gentle in their work of bringing her back down to earth. Their work was complete when Florence came back to herself and opened her eyes to see both men watching her expectantly.

"Are you all right?" Ansel asked, sitting up from his place between her legs. His eyes were soft on her and she smiled. Brendan was looking at her in a similar manner and though he did not ask what Ansel did she knew he was similarly concerned. He rubbed her shoulder gently and she patted him absently.

"I am better than all right. I am," she drew in a breath and raised herself up onto her elbows so that she could look at them better in the dim firelight. "I am wonderfully and wholly satisfied in all ways, but I do have one request."

"Which is?" Brendan drawled and she smirked at him poking his chest lightly and then a moment later repeated the gesture on Ansel.

"That we, before daybreak, perform what just transpired no less than three times, but that you allow me," she pushed herself up to sitting and reached for them, a smile on her lips as she ran a hand over their respective chests, "the liberty of exploring the pair of you as thoroughly as you have just done me."

Ansel arched an eyebrow. "Are you quite sure that is what you wish?" His eyes raked over her form, nude from the waist up, skirts shoved high above her thighs and Florence lifted her chin feeling far bolder than she had since the start of their time together.

"Yes, do you find my terms amenable?" She knew they would but even so there was something thrilling asking the question, and a finger of excitement ran down her spine as they looked at one another putting on a show of deliberating her request.

"Do we agree?" Brendan asked.

After a moment, Ansel gave a slight nod. "In spades. What say you?"

Brendan inclined his head burnished ginger hair catching the firelight and gleaming like copper. "I find that I am quite in the mood to be ravished." He looked to her. "We agree, flower."

It was music to Florence's ears and she smiled widely raising herself up onto her knees in front of the men. They had taken her by surprise before, the newness of their touch sending her senses into confusion and lust but now she felt more sure of herself, clarity was restored and Florence was looking to give them a taste of their own medicine. Day break would come too soon, no matter how many hours passed. Of that she was convinced.

She pushed lightly at their shoulders and nodded at them. "On your backs then, hmm?" Their eyebrows shot up. Brendan let out a low whistle just as Ansel huffed out a laugh of disbelief.

"Bossy," he murmured. Ansel winked at her once he was settled and Florence's blood began to pump almost painfully in her veins at what was to come.

"I quite enjoy it," Brendan replied, looking up at her.

"Good," she said tossing her hair over her shoulder, "because I intend to." She was urged on by the eager look in both men's eyes as they lay spread out before her on the bed. Tonight was the first of many, and she would do her utmost to make it memorable, just as she knew Ansel and Brendan would and had.

She would not rush, she would take her time, and enjoy every minute of it.

After all, one good turn deserved another.

CHAPTER 12

"Watch your step." Ansel's hand was light on Florence's back as she stepped down from the buckboard.

It was in the early morning hours. The snowstorm that had begun to fall earlier that day had not let up, and while Florence had loved the excuse to stay warm, safe and between her men, she had thought it prudent to return home before sunrise. No doubt her sisters had covered for her whereabouts when it came to their parents. Her mother, she knew, would understand, but her fathers?

That was an entirely different matter. They would not be as amenable to Florence's time with Ansel and Brendan, at least...not right away. And not before they had been presented with the opportunity to take both men to task over dinner. After that she was sure they would be far more accepting of her overnight stays once they had truly become familiar with the men. She winced thinking of it. What she thought of as becoming familiar most likely entailed her fathers putting the fear of god into Ansel and Brendan.

She turned to look at them, they were both fussing over the borrowed jacket she had worn, a duster of Brendan's that was far too long with sleeves that engulfed her arms and hands wholly. The garment was unfit for everyday use, but proved perfect for the wintry journey to her home. She wrapped her arms around herself and breathed in deeply, the familiar scent of juniper and honey that was uniquely Brendan filled her senses and she sighed happily.

She would hate to part with the duster, no matter how impractical it was for her to wear in her day-to-day. Perhaps she could make a case for it even if there were other items more useful in terms of outerwear.

"Let's get you inside." Ansel pulled the collar of the coat up around her ears and smiled at her. He smoothed her hair back from her face before pressing a light kiss to her cheek. "It's freezing and I'll feel better the sooner you're indoors. We both will," he said looking back at Brendan who was nodding in agreement.

"Aye, it's too cold for ye to linger outdoors, flower. Off you go." He made to usher her forward but Florence rolled her eyes and moved away, yanking the coat close as she did so.

"You are both worse than Delilah. I shall be perfectly fine if I linger for a few minutes with the pair of you. It is not unreasonable that I want more time with you." She pouted when both men shot her stern looks. She placed her hands on her hips and raised an eyebrow at them. "I think you both forget I was born on the frontier. I am quite acquainted with the Montana winter and I'll not set foot indoors until I am good and ready."

"Flo…" Ansel sighed and caught her about the waist. She yelped, a rather undignified sound, when she felt herself being swung up into the man's arms.

"What are you doing?" she gasped when he started forward.

"Taking you indoors," he said, simply.

"Aye, that he is. If ye try to escape, I will bring ye back, so mind yerself."

She scowled over Ansel's shoulder at him. "You're both insufferable," she told them. Brendan raised a shoulder in a shrug as he ambled along behind the couple.

"So we have been told, but I think ye enjoy it a bit."

Ansel scoffed. "A bit? She loves it. Don't you, Flo?"

Florence's lips pressed into a thin line and she blew out a heavy sigh. There was no denying the truth in either man's words. She did, in fact, enjoy their particular brand of company. They were gentle, sweet, but also the perfect blend of strength and humor that put Florence at ease. She frowned at Ansel, who showed no signs of slowing down even with the foot of snow the man had to push through to take her to her front door. His profile was aquiline and sensual, plump lips and high cheekbones she longed to trace her fingertips along--had traced her fingertips over only hours before.

She flushed at the remembrance of it and clenched her fist, pressing it to her chest. Flashes of her night filled her minds eye making it nearly impossible to breathe, let alone maintain her glare.

Her hands in Brendan's hair as it fell over his shoulders when he looked down at her where she lay on the bed. Ansel had kissed her gently, tongue tracing her bottom lip before he'd moved to slant his mouth to Brendan's, a sound akin to a growl escaping his throat and rendering Florence unable to do anything but stare longingly at the couple. She had reached for them then, hands linking with theirs as they pulled her close to exchange passionate kisses that stole her breath.

Florence shivered relishing the memories that would no doubt pursue her well into her day. It would be difficult maintaining her focus but well worth it for the night of pleasure she had enjoyed.

"You're cold aren't you?" Ansel was frowning down at her mistaking her shiver. He couldn't know it wasn't a product of the cold and was instead the heat brought on when she remembered the feel of Brendan's hands on her hips, or what it was to have Ansel pressed to her back, his chest against her bare skin while Brendan claimed her lips in a heated kiss. She had touched them freely then, her hands exploring the planes of their bodies eagerly.

It had been exhilarating and glorious but Florence did not tell him that. Instead she only ducked her head and sucked in a deep breath. There was no sense in reigniting the passion that had left her wrung out and sated. Not here, not now that she was on her doorstep.

Instead she gave him a bright smile all together abandoning her efforts at sternness. There wasn't a woman alive that would have been able to manage a frown in the direction of either man, not when they had treated her as lovely as they had.

"I'm fine. Honest," she told him, though Ansel did not

look convinced. He merely gave a quick nod but she did not miss the careful eye he kept on her. If she so much as shivered or coughed the man would be up in arms, that much she was sure of.

"Set her down here. I'll get the door." Brendan pointed at the porch and turned to her. "Have ye yer key, flower?"

"It will be open. No key needed," she told them, adding at their shared incredulous look, "my sisters would ensure that I was able to return home undetected you see." She reached for the door and turned the knob, showing them that it was indeed unlocked.

"Very handy," Ansel commented. He looked about them and then asked, "Your fathers will no doubt ask after your whereabouts?"

She smiled when she saw the line of tenseness in his body. "You are safe. I'm sure Seylah made up a story or two. Rose would have come up with something, if not. The only thing I would worry about if I were either of you is dinner on Sunday."

Brendan nodded and ran a hand through his hair. "We will do our best." He sounded unsure, a look of worry crossing his handsome features.

Florence gave his arm a reassuring squeeze. "They will love you. I am sure of it."

"Even so, we will worry because we want to make only the best impression, which I do not think would be possible if they caught sight of ye now."

"And what is the matter with my appearance?" Florence raised a hand to pat at her hair when she caught Brendan looking at it with a smirk.

"Ye look well pleasured, flower."

She flushed and cleared her throat at his words. "Perhaps because I am, but I am entirely presentable. I assure you."

Ansel chuckled and moved closer to tuck an errant lock of hair behind her ear. "You most certainly do not, though you have never looked more beautiful." When she opened her mouth to protest he nodded at the open door behind her. "Get inside before you catch a cold, Flo, or before your fathers catch sight of you and throw us in jail."

"I do not look that obvious!" she hissed at them but Brendan merely raised an eyebrow at her while Ansel tutted.

"Debauched. You look positively fallen, though I am proud to say that I had a hand in it."

"Ye had more than a single hand in it, if I remember correctly," Brendan told him. Florence clapped a hand over her mouth to stifle the laugh that threatened to burst free and wagged a finger at them.

"You are both incorrigible."

"You are fond of it."

"I think she loves it. Adores it."

She rolled her eyes at them. "Perhaps I do, but there's no need to get cocky or complacent."

"We will do our best to remain humble so long as ye take yer leave where it is nice and warm." Brendan ushered her forward and into the house, but not before he stole a kiss from her. Florence giggled softly at the quick press of lips before Ansel took his place and she well and truly laughed then at the boyishness of the stolen kisses. Though they had shared passion and lust, given their bodies to one another that very night, there was no mistaking the genuineness of their affection for her and she beamed at both men.

"Good morning," she told them with a grin.

They bowed in tandem.

"Good morning, flower," Brendan bid her.

"Until we meet again, darling." Ansel sent a kiss her way.

They stood waiting until she had closed and locked the door, and only then once the lock slid home did she hear their departing footsteps. She sighed, and despite the cold was warm and happy. There were certain things winter could not freeze and one of those was the glow of young love, the effect of which was plain to see on her. A fact her sister Rose was quick to tell her the moment she entered her bedroom.

"Well don't you look well loved. You're glowing!"

Florence clapped a hand over her mouth to muffle the shriek of fright her sister's sudden appearance had nearly caused. "What are you doing here?"

Rose wrinkled her nose at her. "Waiting up for you. What else do you think?" Her sister was sitting on her bed looking as if she had been there for quite some time, if the pile of books and tray of tea on the bedside table was any indication.

"And I see you made yourself at home while you waited," Florence observed. She sat on the chair beside her door and began to work on the laces of her boots while Rose clicked her teeth at her.

"Of course I did, what else is a girl to do when she knows her sister is out enjoying herself? I wanted to be the first to hear every delicious detail of your lovers' tryst."

"It wasn't a tryst, it was tea." Florence wasn't lying, there had been tea after all, and a lovely one at that... even if it was well past its intended service time.

"Tea? Is that what they are referring to it as now, hmm?"

"Rose...." Florence frowned at her sister, but it only took a wiggle of her sister's eyebrow for her to laugh. "I swear, I cannot take you seriously when you look at me so."

Rose drew herself up on her knees and shoved the pile of books aside. "And what way is that? Expectantly and full of eager anticipation? I am on veritable tenterhooks for details of your night, dear sister. You cannot leave me in this state and expect me to respond in an entirely calm manner."

"No, I suppose I cannot." Florence set her boots aside and approached the bed. She was still wrapped in Brendan's duster and she fingered the cuff of the coat with a faint smile. "It was lovely, Rose. Every second of it was perfect. I wish it never had to end." A sigh escaped her and she raised the sleeve of the duster to her nose, inhaling the juniper that would, in her mind, only ever be associated with Brendan.

"Are you smelling his clothes?" Rose asked, cocking her head to the side and giving her sister a curious look.

Florence cleared her throat but she kept her hands where they were, the cuff pressed to her nose. "Perhaps," she said, giving another delicate sniff before she lowered her hands.

"You were," Rose exclaimed. "You well and truly did!"

"Keep your voice down," Florence shushed her sister with a flap of her hands. "You'll have the entire house awake before dawn with news of me smelling clothing like a lecher."

Her sister stifled a giggle and crawled over to her. "I thought it was sweet."

"Oh?"

"Yes, it's sweet that you're so taken with them you smell their clothes. You look in love, you know."

"I should hope so because I certainly feel as if I am in love, or at the very least falling very quickly."

"How quickly?"

"Absurdly so. As if I might blink, and in the next moment be there. I almost cannot even breathe without feeling my heart grow closer to theirs. Each and every breath pulls them tighter and tighter," her hands went to her sides and she inhaled deeply with a shake of her head, "I feel them becoming a part of me, stitching themselves into me where I can scarcely remember what it felt like without them." She was speaking in a rush now, words tripping and running into one another, and she knew that she sounded breathless, but Florence didn't care. She huffed out a laugh and looked at her sister.

"I sound completely mad, don't I?"

"No, not mad. Just…" Rose smiled and stopped. She reached for Florence's hand and squeezed it. "You sound genuinely taken with them, and for that I am happy."

"Every woman should be taken with their suitors. I had always hoped for what our parents had but I just," she swallowed thickly and looked away towards the door.

Beyond it she knew her family slept, her parents just at the end of the hallway, the three of them together, safe, happy, and content in the home they had created for not only themselves but their family. The Wickes-Barnes household had always been filled to the brim with warmth and love. Florence felt a stirring, the barest hope that she had nourished in her heart, that she too would find a love like theirs had bloomed into. A full and sure sense of knowing that she had been given a precious gift.

After the magic of her night with Brendan and Ansel there was very little doubt in her mind that she had been offered the opportunity to enjoy a life much like her parents.

"I just had not expected it to feel like this."

"And what does this feel like?"

Florence looked away from the door and back to Rose. Her sister was looking at her expectantly, she knew that whatever she said next would be met with support and love. And that made it all the more easy to speak her heart plainly and truthfully.

"It feels like coming home. It feels as if they had always been meant for me, even when I did not know them. And that everything and everyone until I met them was for a reason, because without any of it I would not be who I am now. And who I am now is exactly the person we all need." She sucked in a shaky breath, giving her sister a watery smile. "I know it sounds too soon and fast, that I just met them but--"

Rose moved forward and caught her hands. "It doesn't sound too soon, Flo. It simply sounds like love, and I think it is incredibly romantic."

"You do?"

"Of course, I do. Any that heard you would take it as such. I am so happy for you."

Florence felt tears well in her eyes and for a moment she said nothing. Her sister's words sinking into her slowly and surely.

I am so happy for you.

"Oh, Rose. Thank you." She threw her arms around her sister, tackling her in an embrace that sent them onto the bed and careening into the tower of books Rose had piled there. Florence winced as a book hit her forehead, but Rose simply laughed and shoved the books further aside to better return her sister's hug. Florence laughed along with her, the earlier caution to keep quiet lest they wake the house already gone from her memory. She was far too joyful to limit her merriment, and in no time at all the sisters were laughing in earnest.

"You're very welcome. Now then, are you thinking of a spring wedding, or are you aiming for the winter? I should like both but it would be quite nice to be present for the event before I leave for New York."

Florence rolled her eyes and flopped onto her back. "Oh, wedding talk already? Can a woman simply not enjoy the start of love and the ensuing passion of a night filled with--"

"What is going on in here and why are we not involved?" The door to her bedroom swung open with a resounding bang. Florence looked to her doorway to see both Delilah and Seylah standing with their arms crossed and frowns on their faces. It was evident they had come straight from bed as both were in sleeping gowns and plaited braids. Seylah raised an eyebrow at them before she pushed into the room.

"You woke me from a delightful dream," she said, making a motion for her sisters to part on the bed, "now make room for me on that bed and tell me what has you both cackling."

"We were not cackling," Florence informed her sister, but she still scooted to the side so that Seylah could wedge between them.

"Lies," Seylah muttered and gave her a poke. "This has to do with you being in the clothes I last saw you in, and your suitors, doesn't it?"

"You know it does." Delilah shut the door and shoved in beside Rose without preamble. "Now tell us."

Florence cleared her throat. "Well, I-"

"And it had better be sordid for the amount of noise you were both making," Delilah added.

"It was actually more romantic than sordid," Rose informed her.

Seylah smiled. "How lovely."

"I expected more." Delilah sighed, turning her eyes heavenward. "More in the way of salacious and titillating romantic overtures. Lustful, even." She sighed again, lips pursed.

"When did you change your tune on romance?" Seylah asked, giving her sister a confused look.

Out of all the Wickes-Barnes sisters Delilah was not the one most known for romance and daydreams of a happily-ever-after. She was at times stern, and known to be focused on her work as one of the town's librarians, a precious commodity on the frontier. The rugged places outside of cities were not known for their literature or wealth of culture. Gold Sky was an anomaly in that respect. Julie Wickes-Barnes had done her very best to instill a healthy love of reading and the belief that anyone with the drive and interest should be afforded equal access to an education. Delilah had taken that lesson to heart in a far more tangible way than the rest of her sisters and dedicated her time with single-minded focus towards her position as a librarian.

As such, it left little time for her to be idle, and even less for her to entertain thoughts of romance. It was not surprising that her sisters were confounded by Delilah's sudden demand for titillation.

Florence opened and closed her mouth in confusion before she cleared her throat. "You've always been the most reserved of us and now you are asking for the salacious?"

Delilah shrugged, eyes still focused above her. "With age a woman's needs often change and that includes amorous appointments."

Her sisters were silent before they burst into laughter.

"Appointments?" Florence asked when their fit of laughter had subsided enough that she was able to speak.

"Yes, appointments. What else would they be?" Delilah wanted to know, which only made her sisters laugh once more. "What's so funny?" She asked with a scowl looking quite put out.

"That you managed to make romance sound like a doctor's appointment, is what," Rose informed her. "We are going to have to do something about how you view courtship, and well....everything it entails between two willing--"

"And sometimes more than two," Florence pointed out helpfully.

"Any number of participants," Rose finished with a nod of thanks towards Florence. "It's not so business-like as the word appointments brings to mind."

Delilah sat up and crossed her arms. "I think it's a matter of semantics, but very well," she said inclining her head. "What happened on your...*rendezvous*," she tried finally.

"That's a much better word. Well done," Rose commended, clapping in appreciation.

"Thank you." Delilah nodded at her and then pointed a finger at Florence. "Now you. Tell us everything."

Florence blinked in surprise at her sister. "Well I--"

A knock at the door stopped her, and all four sisters looked towards the sound. "I think we woke mother," Florence whispered.

"And if she is awake then that means our fathers are too," Rose hissed with a wince.

"Oh dear," Seylah sighed, biting her lip. "This does not bode well."

"But, perhaps it's only mother and--"

"Girls? Are you all in there?" Will's voice made them go silent and Florence groaned.

"Quick, get under the quilts." Rose gave her a shove and moved off of the bed. "Get under there now," she hissed, but her insistence was for nothing as Florence needed no prompting to follow orders. She was already beneath the bed clothes with the quilts pulled up to her chin, desperately doing her best to look as if she had spent the entirety of the night just as she was.

In her own bed. In her own house. Alone.

Most decidedly not with two men she fancied herself falling in love with.

"Act natural," Rose whispered, rushing towards the door. The youngest Wickes-Barnes sister drew herself up and blew out a long breath when their father knocked at the door again.

"Girls, what--"

Rose yanked the door open, startling her father into silence. "Good morning, father!" She trilled throwing her arms wide to show that her sisters were all, indeed, behind her in bed.

"What's with all the noise this early? It's well before sunrise."

"Why we were all just here and we thought it would be--"

"Stop questioning her and move aside." Julie bustled up and poked her husband until the man moved. She cast a knowing look at her daughters as she stepped into the room. "I see we have much to talk about."

Will frowned and held up a finger. "But--"

"But nothing, I'll be along shortly for breakfast. Do not wait for me if Forrest is ready before I'm down." Julie ushered her husband back and Will backed up into the hallway at his wife's insistence.

His lips pressed into a thin line when Julie blocked his view into the bedroom. "Oh, all right."

"Love you, darling!" Julie chirped cheerfully, and before Will could think better of it, shut the door. She turned to her daughters and when Florence opened her mouth to speak, held up a finger for her to remain silent. She tilted her head to the side listening until she heard the sound of Will's departing footsteps. Only when they faded from hearing did Julie nod and drop her hand, coming forward with a raised eyebrow.

"I know you did not spend the night as you are, and judging from the shrieks that woke me this morning, you have much to tell me, Flo. Am I correct?" she asked.

"Well, yes, mama," Florence answered. There was no worry over telling her mother what she had spent the night experiencing with Brendan and Ansel. Julie Wickes-Barnes had raised her daughters to understand that love and lust were not the same, but that indulging in the latter without the former was fair play so long as they took care of their own health as well as their partner's, or partners'.

Julie sat at the foot of the bed and patted the spot beside her, motioning for Florence to join her.

"Now then, tell me everything, and I mean absolutely everything."

"Finally." Delilah sighed, scooting closer to them.

"My sentiments exactly," Rose agreed.

"On to the good stuff," Seylah added with a wave of her hand.

Florence rolled her eyes at her sisters but she turned to her mother all the same and smiled at the expectant look on her face.

"It was wonderful," she told her mother. "Everything I had ever wanted and expected from suitors." Her mother wrapped an arm around her shoulders and Florence rested her head on her shoulder, a nostalgic feeling taking root in her heart. More than once she had sat like this in her mother's arms with her sisters gathered around. Then, she had been a girl with the most pressing matters on her heart being hair ribbons, summers in New York, or the fact that Mrs. Rosemary had offered her an apprenticeship.

But now? Now she was a woman and the same comfort and love that she had been given was still freely offered and available for her to take solace in. She had thought her time with the men had made for the perfect day and night but she had been wrong.

This did.

CHAPTER 13

"*D*id you know uncle Julian will be here in a few short weeks?"

Florence raised her head to look at her sister Rose, who was bouncing on her toes excitedly.

"No, I didn't know that."

"And just in time for Christmas too! I am so excited to see Aunt Violet and cousin Claude. He said in his last letter that he had a gift for me, and I hope he brings it with them. Oh, I just love the holidays, don't you?"

"Yes, I love them." Florence smiled, watching her sister twirl about the shop. She loved seeing her sister so excited. It was something she would miss. Watching Rose when she was excited was always a happy event, the other woman's energy was infectious. It was impossible not to feel exhilarated when Rose was in one of her happy moods.

"I bet it's a new dress, or perhaps it was that mirror set that we saw when I was in town last. Oh, I hope it is, I hope it is."

"I'm sure it will be." Florence lowered her head and looked back down at the drawing in front of her. She had spent the better part of the morning arranging the patterns to be copied and printed for sale in the shop. Now she was designing a dress that had been percolating in her imagination all morning. Something fitted with enough flair to make any stop and look in appreciation, but how...perhaps, pleats at the back of the skirt?

She tapped her chin with her pencil as Rose continued to chatter excitedly about what she would do once their family had arrived for Christmas. She only looked up when the bell to the shop rang, signaling the arrival of customers.

Florence pushed back in her chair to look around the corner of the work table where she did much of her drawing and planning. It was tucked away, offering a secluded vantage point that proved useful when keeping an eye on customers while allowing for work to be done. She smiled when she saw a small group of women. There were four in total, and with the right motivation, a group like that could do wonders for their sales that week.

Florence put her pencil down and stood. Her design would have to wait until after she had helped the group of eager looking women. If she managed well with the women she could count it towards the Christmas bonus Mrs. Rosemary always included for her employees.

She had only made to step away from the table when the women came near enough to cut through Rose's continued excited chatter.

"Did you hear about the woman who has two suitors?"

"Oh, yes, I did. And you'll never guess what I heard

about the two men." The woman tittered before continuing on. Florence stopped short, a hand going to grip the table as a sinking feeling began to settle into her stomach.

"Immigrants. The pair of them. One from Mexico."

Another woman gasped while the first continued speaking. "And a Scotsman! Can you believe it? Of all the things," she said, lowering her voice as if immigrant status numbered among the unthinkable things a person could be or do. Florence felt her face flush with rage as she listened to the women talk. She really could have used the bonus to buy gifts for Ansel and Brendan, but there was no helping it now.

"They're opening a mine, I believe. A pair like that would be able to do nothing more, you know." More laughter and Florence moved to grab the pencil she had just been sketching with. The wood bit painfully into her palm as she squeezed it tightly.

"I know this place is...different, but I never imagined two men who would be willing to marry one woman. I mean, if that is their intention at all."

One of the women hummed in agreement. "Well, you have heard about the proclivities of the head school teacher and the sheriffs, haven't you?"

"Aren't those just tales?"

"No, no, they have a triad marriage. I heard it in the mercantile and everyone here just accepts it!"

"How beastly. I reckon it is only tolerated on account of the woman's family. She was a debutante before she came here. That much I read."

"A debutante!"

"Yes, from one of the wealthiest families on the eastern seaboard. She's a Baptiste."

There was a collective gasp from the women. "There's no other excuse. She went mad, I'm sure of it. Absolutely mad to leave New York for two men with depraved tastes."

The pencil in Florence's grip snapped with an audible crack. She would be promptly showing the women to the door. There was no way around it.

"Her daughters are also mad. One is even a deputy. It's no wonder the other has it in her head to take two men to bed. This town may be a place of opportunity, but I find it lacking in civility and propriety." One of the women gave a delicate sniff and the very sound of it filled Florence with a white-hot rage. She wanted to strike the woman, throw her out in the snow until she succumbed to exposure, ban her friends from the shop and every event Mrs. Rosemary hosted, which in Gold Sky was all events of import.

The women would be pariahs. Outcasts before Florence was done with them. She would make sure of it.

Rose twirled to a stop beside her. "What is it?" she asked, giving her sister a curious look. "What happened? You look absolutely furious and you broke your pencil!"

"Nothing. I just remembered that I haven't taken the trash out."

"Trash? What are you--"

Florence dropped the pencil on the table and strode towards the women. They were bent over a table examining silk scarves that had only been put out that day. They were a lovely collection of color and lace, each one more inviting than the last. These foul-mouthed women would never have one.

One of the women noticed her approach and straightened, giving her a quick nod. "Oh, hello, we are in requirement of--"

Florence lifted a hand to point to the door. "Please see yourselves out of A Modern Dress."

The woman's brows knit together in confusion. "See ourselves out? But we have only arrived. What is the meaning of this?"

"I think you'll find our shop lacking in items to your taste."

"But we have already found items to our taste." The woman pointed to the table of scarves. "These are to our taste. Now we have only arrived from Boston and we--"

"Will not be customers of A Modern Dress. Not now, not ever. Because we are simply made up of immigrants, are depraved and lack all sense of civility." Florence's voice was cold, her eyes narrowed with anger as she spoke. The white heat in her eyes at odds with the wintry chill of her voice. "We also do not care to serve those who would gossip of our parents, and seeing as you have done just that, and well," she raised a hand to her chest and smiled, "we are what we are, I cannot possibly think of anything we have to offer you. Now. Get. Out." The last of her tirade was practically spit out at the women's feet.

Behind her, Rose gasped.

"Flo..." she began, voice soft but her sister was not listening. Instead she was watching as the women spluttered with wide eyes, as it dawned on them who was speaking to them. There was a half-hearted protest but it failed before it had even begun, withering under the heat of Florence's glare.

"Out," Florence said once more, giving a flick of her finger that left no room for protest. Awkwardly, the women shuffled forward, all of whom had the decency to not meet her eyes. The moment the door slammed shut behind them Florence dropped her arm with a growl.

"Those women were the most awful humans I have ever had the displeasure of setting eyes upon," she told Rose, who was still watching the scene with wide eyes. She hadn't moved an inch since the start of her sister's rage, and even now she stood still, watching as Florence set herself into a whirlwind of motion. There was no true direction to it, with Florence making for the door to watch the departure of the women. She paced the length of the storefront until they vanished from sight and then, without pause, Florence was at the table of scarves they had perused. Her hands busy setting the scarves to rights before she was off and moving again.

"What happened?" Rose asked.

"Those women, those awful--" Florence's hands balled into fists and she growled. "Those people took it upon themselves to look down upon not only *my men*," the word was stressed and Rose smiled at it. "And myself, but they took to disparaging our family, our parents. Calling mother mad! Papa and Daddy depraved! They are lucky that I only tossed them out of the shop, and well, that I never learned to properly fight from Seylah." Her hands curled into fists and she raised them to her chest, closing her eyes as she took in a giant calming breath. It was still not enough to dispel her anger.

Florence squeezed her eyes shut even tighter and took in another deep breath. Perhaps in a breath or two she would be able to think without lamenting the fact she was incapable of providing a sound thrashing to a group of women.

"I need to speak to Seylah," she muttered, eyes still closed. "At least learn to hit a target squarely."

Rose made a strangled sound. "You've always been more of a lover than a fighter, Flo."

She opened her eyes and looked at her sister who was watching her with a worried look. "Yes, yes, I know. But that doesn't mean I don't wish for the ability to...to-" She threw out her hands. "I don't exactly know what! But I do know that I want to be able to do it when the occasion arises."

Rose nodded at the door. "And that was one such occasion?"

"Indeed. You should have heard what they said."

"I was a bit preoccupied. I missed it." Rose frowned, but her sister waved a hand at her.

"It's good that you did. Both of our moods should not be spoiled by their ignorance."

"You should not let them control your emotions. We both know you are not as productive when angry and I've not seen you like this in a long while." Rose smiled and crossed the room to her sister, putting a hand on her arm. "You should take a walk, hmm? I'll watch the shop for you."

Florence shook her head. "I have so much work to do for the upcoming workshop. I couldn't possibly."

"You can and you should. You'll be in a far more agreeable mood if you take a walk. Just a few minutes of air will help." Rose gave her a nudge towards the door. "Go on, I'll watch everything here, and Mrs. Rosemary will be back before long. You'll feel so much better and those designs will come to you without all the brooding."

"I am not brooding. I am seething," Florence corrected, but she walked towards the door all the same. She grabbed her coat from the hook and continued forward. "Thank you, I'll be back before long."

"Enjoy the walk." Rose waved at her cheerily. "And do not find those women until you've been properly instructed in quality thrashings!"

"Oh, all right," Florence laughed, the dark cloud of her anger abating slightly at her sister's words. It was difficult to stay seething when Rose was smiling at her and sending her on a walk. She was correct. There would be no creating or productivity so long as Florence was angry and daydreaming of administering a well-placed punch or...three.

Florence turned her face skyward, soaking in the bright sunshine. The snowfall from the previous days imparted a picturesque quality to Gold Sky. All around her the streets were bustling with energy and activity. The many fond memories Florence had enjoyed in her life surrounded her, wrapping her in a sense of belonging and love. Everywhere she looked, the faces that smiled and greeted her on her walk, the welcoming sight of familiar streets and walkways was almost enough to abate her anger entirely.

For that she suspected she would need something else entirely.

Something in the way of two men, and thankfully she had just the two men in mind for the job.

"HELLO?" Florence rapped on the doorway as she peeked into the office. *Ortega & Black's* was painted in gold filigree on the window of the office she had just entered. She closed the door behind her and cautioned another look around. There was no one in sight and she wondered if they had taken an early lunch. The office was neat and orderly, two desks sat side by side. Across the room was a long work table stacked with various papers and maps. Above it hung what she recognized as a cartographic map of the area. She came closer to the rendering and smiled when she recognized her Aunt's tell-tale initials in the bottom corner of the map.

V.B. inked in small script. Of course they were using her Aunt Violet's handiwork. Anyone serious in their pursuit of working the land successfully would do so. She had been the first to provide detailed maps in the area, and none had come close to matching her in the years that had passed since her Aunt and Uncle's work. They had them to thank for the Gold Sky Depot which had helped usher in new business and citizens eager to make a claim on the frontier.

In the distance she heard the familiar train whistle of an incoming shipment.

It was not often that she came to this area of town and she turned to look out the window. The streets here were narrower, less cozy and familiar but there was an intensity here that she could appreciate. Brendan and Ansel had chosen a logical place for their office. Here they were among similar businesses, and closest to the depot. The sounds of transport and business were far more noticeable here, but that was to be expected. People did not meander here, they walked with purpose and a destination, each of them motivated by the pursuit of business.

Ansel rushed into the room with an apologetic look on his face. "So sorry that we-," he stopped speaking and smiled at Florence. "Well, now this is a lovely surprise."

"Who is it?" Brendan called from a door she hadn't noticed. It was ajar and she leaned to the side, catching sight of the man adjusting his shirt collar.

She grinned and crossed her arms, pinning Ansel with a knowing look. "I see that you were preoccupied at my arrival."

He laughed, hands going to his pocket. "There are times when business must give way to pleasure, Flo."

"Pressures of the job and all that, flower." Brendan emerged from the room with a wink that set her cheeks flaming to pink. Even if she had been intimate with both men only nights before it was hard not to be affected by such a gesture, small as it was.

"I can see that," she sighed, giving them a smile that didn't quite reach her eyes. "I'm happy you are able to make time for it. There are too many people and things that rob joy these days." Florence tried for light and happy but from Brendan's furrowed brow and the raised eyebrow Ansel sent her way, she knew she had missed the mark.

"What happened?" Ansel asked gently. He came

forward until he was standing beside her, Brendan was not far behind and in a moment both men were next to her with looks of concern.

"Nothing." She gave them a tight smile. Now that Florence was here she had no desire to bring the ugliness of the women with her. It had no place, not here with her, and most certainly not with them. She wanted anything but that, so instead she nodded at the map on the wall. "She's my aunt, you know."

They were all silent. None of them willing to speak first and Florence knew from the tension in the men's shoulders they were weighing their options on whether to press the issue or not. She desperately hoped for the latter and looked away. Though she may have come this way with anger as her fuel, the furthest thing from her mind was how to thrash someone soundly. Now, she wanted to look upon the men eagerly, to drink of their handsome profiles, catalogue the way they moved and touched the other, how they touched her. Oh, yes, that would be far more enjoyable for her than discussing the earlier events.

Another long moment passed and then finally Brendan spoke, breaking the silence. Florence breathed a sigh of relief.

"Oh, is she?"

She nodded quickly. "Yes, she and my uncle met shortly before she began her work in the area. The railway, it's theirs as well."

"Industrious family."

"We are keen on a good venture."

Ansel rubbed his jaw and gave her a considering look. "As are we, and as are you, no?"

"I suppose you could say that," she agreed, but Brendan tutted and moved to tweak a lock of her hair.

"There's no supposing, flower. Yer an entrepreneur and a skilled one at that. Ye'll take the town by storm with yer designs, ye will. We're sure of it."

"And what of your mine? I suspect the pair of you will do the same when it's up and running."

Ansel took her hand in his. "Would you like to see it? The mine, I mean," he added when Florence's eyes dropped to the waistband of his trousers. "My eyes," he gestured to his face with a playful grin, "are up here, Flo."

She raised her eyes to his and winked at him, returning his gesture, and was glad to see a similar flush dusting his cheeks. So, she could affect him as easily as he did her?

How truly wonderful.

"I would love nothing more." She had been sent on the errand of a walk to dispel her anger, and so far the men had done a perfect job of lifting the dark pall of fury she'd found herself in. If a walk had yielded such results, a trip to the mine could only further brighten her day.

"But first, I have a request."

"And then ye'll come to our mine?" Brendan asked. He was behind Ansel and he leaned forward to drop his chin onto the other man's shoulder. The gesture was automatic, so familiar that it must have been done a hundred times before and Florence felt the stirring of awe at something so simple. It was beautiful in its thoughtlessness, as was Ansel leaning back into it, accepting it.

It was achingly perfect.

She sighed happily and nodded. "You must both kiss me."

"Oh we must, must we?" Ansel was smiling again, his brown eyes lighting up with mischief. By now he had recognized her game. She wondered if he would play one of his own. Her eyes drifted to the still open door of the back office and she remembered how they had both emerged just disheveled enough to prove what they had been up to with one another.

Oh, she hoped the man was up to a game. She prayed for it, in fact.

She inclined her head. "Yes, as payment. I demand it."

"Demands? Payment to see our mine?" Brendan chuckled and circled an arm around Ansel's waist. "One would think that it would be ye that should pay us for such a tour. Few have been able to claim they have had the honor, flower."

"And fewer still are able to say it of kissing me," she returned, crossing her arms. "I am offering the two of you a steal of a lifetime, a perfect price to pay for something so exquisite and rare." She raised a hand to touch her lips, both men's eyes tracking the movement closely. She liked it when they watched her like this. Intense and longing. It made her feel beautiful and powerful to know two men such as this wanted her. Wanted her and made no move to hide their hunger.

"If a kiss is all she demands for the honor of escorting her, then who are we to squabble?" Ansel asked, patting his partner's arm around his waist.

"I suppose yer right and I've never been one not to pay my due." Brendan reached for her with his free arm, the movement surprising her as he caught her shoulder and then slid his hand to her neck. His fingers tensed slightly there, the drag of his fingers against her skin eliciting a moan of pleasure from Florence that surprised her. She leaned forward in his grip, allowing him to bring her close for the kiss she had demanded. For all his abruptness the kiss was achingly sweet and tender. The first brush of his lips light and teasing before he deepened the kiss, but only slightly. It was a chaste thing that stirred her more than she would have thought, and before she realized it the kiss was at an end.

"Flower," he whispered softly, his breath puffing lightly against her lips and cheeks. She smiled, eyes still closed at the endearment. There was a rustle of clothing and a shifting of the men in front of her before Ansel moved close and claimed her lips. He did not touch her, instead Brendan's hand at her neck stayed gently pressing into her skin as Ansel kissed her. He trailed his tongue along the seam of her lips, asking for entrance. Florence eagerly opened her mouth to him.

Where Brendan had been gentle and restrained, Ansel was wild and needy. Their kisses were nothing alike yet mirrored each other in a way Florence yearned for more of each. Ansel groaned lowly, the sound driving Florence to reach for him as their tongues moved teasingly against one another, lips slanting together perfectly. She could scarcely breathe, her heart thumping madly in her chest with each and every second they touched. She curled her arms around both men, a hand at Ansel's jaw, another in Brendan's loose hair, whether from Ansel's touch or hers she couldn't say.

The thought of it was intoxicating and she gave herself over to the kiss--and the men entirely. Not a scrap of her anger was left, not with Ansel kissing her like this, all passion and need while Brendan whispered the loveliest things in her ear, hands gently brushing her hair from her face as he did so. She sighed happily when they finally parted and threw herself at both men with renewed energy crushing them to her in a tight hug that surprised them.

Rose was right.

She was a lover, not a fighter.

CHAPTER 14

"It's not much, but it's ours," Ansel said, gesturing out at the parcel of land in front of them. They were a good fifteen-minute ride from town. Their route had taken them in the direction of the lake, well past the small home she knew to be theirs. The well-worn wagon path was carefully maintained and easily traversed despite the heavy snowfall. She wondered if Ansel and Brendan had made sure it was thus. Her suspicions were confirmed when Brendan leaped from the buckboard to inspect a large dip in the road.

"It was fine just the day before," he called out to Ansel with hands on his hips.

"It's fine," Ansel replied, standing from his seat to squint in Brendan's direction. The ginger haired man was walking the length of the dip and tutting to himself.

"He will be insufferable until he's filled it," Ansel murmured with a sigh. He climbed down from the wagon and came to her side, reaching for her. "It's best to leave him to it until he's worked out how to fix it."

Florence nodded. She turned to see that Brendan was now squatting and staring thoughtfully at the dip. "You maintain this road on your own?"

"We do. At least for now. We've begun to contract workers but it was on us to have the road leveled out and travel ready. We had a bit of waiting on permits and equipment this fall, and you know what they say about idle hands…"

She nodded, but the only hands she was concerned with were the pair on her waist. Ansel's hands. His touch was warm and strong, steady and sure as he lifted her from the buckboard and set her down on the ground. Florence's cheeks heated at the way Ansel's hands felt on her waist. It was not as if his touch were erotic or intimate. To any that saw them it would simply look as if he were a gentleman aiding a lady, but Florence knew better. And what she knew was Ansel's touch, she knew far too well what he was capable of with the beautiful hands he held her with. Calloused, large, warm, and all too talented in their capacity to handle Florence's body.

She cleared her throat delicately and looked away from the sight of Ansel's fingers pressed close to her. The sharp contrast of the pale green day dress she wore and his tanned skin made her heart skip a beat. She would be lost to the tour of the mine if she did not rein her thoughts in now.

She sucked in a deep breath, inhaling the icy winter air and shivered. *Think pure thoughts. Think of only mining*, she advised herself silently. *Only of mining.*

"Are you all right?" he asked, noticing the look of concentration on Florence's face. She was looking to the side, chest rising and falling with each deep inhale she took and released. He raised a hand, pressing it to her forehead. "The carriage ride did not make you ill, did it? I told Brendan to drive less recklessly but he never listens." He turned to scowl in the direction of Brendan who had moved to his knees and appeared to be taking measurements of the hole.

"You've made her ill!" Ansel yelled at him. "Get up from there."

"No, no, I'm fine. I promise."

"What's that?" Brendan raised his head to look at them and Ansel threw a hand out at the man.

"She's taken ill due to your poor driving!"

"I haven't, I promise. I was only," she shook her head and swallowed, "I was only distracted," she told him.

Ansel pursed his lips. "By what?" he asked, dropping his hand.

"Ah, by, well, *you.*" She flapped her hands at her sides and stepped away from him. "Your hands," she clarified when he gave her a curious look.

"My hands?"

"Yes, your hands are very...well-formed."

"Who is ill?" Brendan yelled, face still lowered to the icy ground. He raised his head to look at them and saw Florence and Ansel standing close together. "Hello!" he hollered when neither of them answered him.

"No one!" Florence cupped her hands around her mouth, hoping she was heard over the gust of wind that kicked up to life around her. She blinked and turned her face away from the snow that flew into her face. Even in her haste to turn away she was not quick enough and squinted, rubbing her eyes free from errant snow.

"No one is ill!" She called out to Brendan and made to give him an assuring pose but was nearly blinded by the snow that had slipped through her fingers and she let out a muffled curse at the snow's effect on her vision. Why, she was nearly struck blind from the small bit of ice and grit! "Oh, drat, drat, *drat*," she muttered blinking furiously and rubbing at her eyes.

"Flower!" Brendan raised his head and stood when he saw Florence's form double over, hands to her face.

"Is this from my hands?" Ansel's voice sounded stricken and he rushed to her side. "Florence?"

"I'm fine." She straightened and blinked her eyes, smiling when her vision cleared of the snow. "There was a bit of snow and--"

"Flower, what happened?" Brendan rushed up to her. He reached out, catching her shoulders and turning her to him, the sudden movement pulling a less than eloquent 'oomph' from Florence's lips. She scanned his face, smiling when she saw the streak of mud across his cheek. His rust colored hair had come free from the knot he wore it in and blew out across his cheek. It was unfair for him to look as handsome as he did, but Florence thought he looked every bit like a hero from her books.

"I'm well. There's no need for worry." She reached out, catching Brendan's face between her hands, forcing him to look at her. "Look, it was just a bit of snow and Ansel's hands, you see," she explained.

"Ansel's hands?"

Ansel held up his hands and shrugged. "I claim innocence. I simply handed her down from the buckboard."

"It was just that," she gestured weakly at Ansel and then sighed, "it's no use. Show me the mine?" she tried, when she realized she would make little to no sense if she tried to explain.

She grasped both his and Ansel's hand. "Show me the mine, please."

"But aren't you--" Ansel began, but Florence shook her head.

"No, not at all, onward, gentlemen."

The men exchanged a look over her head but continued forward all the same but not before Ansel muttered, "I told you to change your ways when driving."

Brendan scoffed but said nothing. Florence shook her head, the light bickering between the men only serving to endear them to her all the more. She paused when they began down a gentle slope of dirt. It was not so deep that she would need to worry about her dress and footwear but she would need to watch her step. Snow was packed well here, and she could see the bones of lumber and stone reinforcing the small depression. At the center of it was an entrance that looked to be seven feet wide and tall. She craned her neck peering into the darkness that greeted her only a few feet beyond the mine's entrance.

"So this is it," she observed.

Brendan pointed at the beam above the mine's entry, within the dark lumber the words *Black & Ortega* was etched. "Aye, it is small but it is ours and I value it more than anything in the world."

"Except for us," Ansel cut in and Brendan chuckled, squeezing the man's shoulder.

"Of course, save ye and, well, now ye, flower."

"That makes me very happy." She smiled up at him. Knowing that she was a part of his life, his plans, of what he valued the most, of what *they* saw as precious made her heart leap with joy. For all of her talks with her mother on the matter she had never expected for there to be so much good in an arrangement such as theirs.

Ansel squeezed her hand lightly before he stepped away, walking the perimeter of the cleared area. "I do not think taking you in is a good idea, but this is a nice look at what we've been working to accomplish. There will be far more work we can complete when the spring thaw hits, but for now we will focus on hiring on experienced hands, and the more arduous nature of logistics."

"Aye, nothing but paperwork." Brendan gave her a sour look. "I hate paperwork."

"And yet it must be done all the same, dear," Ansel reminded him. Brendan's sour look ripened to downright disgust and Florence laughed when he said, "I think I ought to revisit that hole in the road. Work that out while ye handle the next batch, hmm?"

"You're not getting out of it. Not again."

"Oh, but Ansel, yer so much better at it than I."

"If I hear that excuse one more time…"

Florence clasped her hands behind her back, content to walk and look at this or that. A small building sat at the edge of the clearing and she peered in to see that it would serve as a foreman's office. Hitching posts a short distance away would provide a space for horses. Beyond that there were benches and tables beneath the framework for a small shelter. She supposed the workers would take their breaks here, and in the distance she spied a well. It was a well-thought out work space, each foot of land utilized to provide the most function. She had no doubt it would be a success.

It had to be with the energy and love she could tell Brendan and Ansel had poured into the operation. She looked at them then, grinning when she saw the men nearly toe-to-toe, both gesturing wildly as Ansel went on about the importance of initialing in the designated area while Brendan dared him to say the word 'triplicate' one more time. Their bickering brought to mind the familiar scenes of her fathers having it out over any number of things, from the mundane to the life changing. Florence loved that she was able to see them together as they currently were. It meant they trusted her to give her a glimpse of the imperfect side of them. To see that it was not all suave words and sure attitudes. This was the real them, and she cherished every second of it. It gave her a sense of peace to see them acting as her fathers did. There would be a resolution and a handshake with a kiss or two and the whole matter resolved before they moved on to tackle the next item of business.

For all the ways they were like her fathers she did not see them having an unenjoyable time at supper, and so she called out to them, "Remember that tomorrow is Sunday!"

Brendan looked at her. "Sunday?" He looked confused for a moment before realization dawned on his handsome face. "Sunday," he whispered worriedly.

"Sunday, indeed!" Ansel clapped his hands. "We will

have a marvelous time, if only someone would complete their share of the paperwork."

"Och, more of that? Can a man not worry over one problem at a time?" Brendan threw his hands up and strode off.

"Where are you going?" Ansel wanted to know and the Scotsman walked faster.

"To fix that damnable hole!"

Florence crossed her arms, watching him walk away. "Is he alright?" she asked Ansel, who only rolled his eyes.

"Yes, he's just a bit...nervous."

"But why?"

"Brendan has no family of his own, save me, and I know he wants to make a good impression on yours. It's only nerves, Flo. It'll all be right as rain by tomorrow evening, you'll see." She jerked in surprise at the news. She had not thought of Brendan's family, so focused was she on the now, and the stolen time with each of the men. How could she not have asked after his family? She glanced at Ansel to see him watching Brendan with an intent look. There was care, worry, and love in Ansel's eyes. He was Brendan's family, any that looked upon them could see it. She had not wondered after Brendan's family for that reason, but now she wished she had thought more closely on the matter.

Florence chewed on her bottom lip watching Brendan as he bent low to inspect the offending dip in the ground. "They will love him, there's no need for worry."

"I know that, and you know that, but he has no refer-ence point for such a declaration. If he is distant, that is why. But give him a bit of time and the man will work it out on his own." Ansel turned towards her with a reassuring smile. "I promise. You can trust me, Florence. Do you trust me?"

"Yes," Florence answered him without a thought because she did trust him, even if she was worried after Brendan. He knew his lover better than she and if he told her that he needed only a little time then she would accept it. "Yes, I trust you."

"Perfect." He extended his arm to her and nodded at the mine entrance. "Now come with me. We have lanterns and I quite think I would like to show you inside the mine. Even if only to frighten you into standing closer to me and becoming distracted by my...hands."

She laughed at the intonation in his voice and swatted at him as they set off towards the mine. All around them the wind blew and a light dusting of snow once again began to fall signaling that winter was well underway, and just like that all was right in the world.

"I HEARD you caused a bit of trouble this morning," Mrs. Rosemary said, causing Florence to jump. She had just tiptoed into the dress shop, her prescribed walk by Rose having gone well beyond a turn or two around the area and had spilled over to in the early part of the afternoon. Florence had hoped to slip back into the shop undetected but she should have known Mrs. Rosemary would catch her.

She always did. Always had. Florence suspected the woman had eyes in the back of her head specifically tuned to whatever mischief the Wickes-Barnes progeny were carrying out.

"If by trouble you mean I kicked out an unruly and uncouth lot of women, then yes, I did cause my fair share of trouble." Florence straightened up and met Mrs. Rosemary's eyes. There was no use in hiding what she'd done. She'd been caught fair and square after all.

Mrs. Rosemary grinned, her blue eyes dancing. "What exactly did these women do?"

"Insulted my family. Disparaged my suitors."

Mrs. Rosemary's mouth turned down, the light deepening from jovial to something that strongly resembled anger. "They did what?" she asked, voice just above a whisper.

Florence folded her arms around herself, feeling uncomfortable under the intense look in Mrs. Rosemary's eyes. She was unaccustomed to seeing her like this. There was a fire she didn't recognize in the older woman. "Ah, they said terrible things about, well... everything and everyone I care about," Florence finally opted to say.

"Those little chits." Mrs. Rosemary turned away from her with a snap of her heel. "And you banned them from ever shopping here again, yes?"

"Well I hadn't thought far enough ahead to issue a lifetime ban, but I did kick them out."

"I'll make sure they know they are no longer welcome here, no matter the circumstances. Even if they had not a stitch to wear and had their belongings swept up in a great storm. Even if they were the last paying customers in the county and I was on the verge of bankruptcy and ruin, I would not sell them a scrap of muslin!"

Florence clasped her hands in front of her and rocked back on her heels at the tone in Mrs. Rosemary's voice. There was pure venom in the place of the older woman's normal good cheer. She swallowed hard and held up a hand, trying to organize her thoughts.

"Mrs. Rosemary, I--"

"I would have them as naked as they are manner less. You must be so angry."

"Yes, but I went for a walk just now and--"

"I will settle this. Don't you worry. They will never set foot in this establishment again." Mrs. Rosemary moved to snatch up her hat and gloves, the gesture sent a flood of adrenaline through Florence. She had to act, and quickly, otherwise Mrs. Rosemary was apt to hunt the women down and see to their personal shame. Florence had been angry before, burning with rage in fact but her time with Ansel and Brendan had quite laid that to rest.

If she dwelled on it for long then she would grow angry again, and if she did that she had no prayer of finishing the designs for the upcoming workshops.

"Oh, where are you going?" Florence sidestepped in front of the other woman and held out her hands. She cleared her throat when Mrs. Rosemary's eyes widened in surprise at Florence's tone. "I mean to say, we have so much to get done before the workshops! They are in a few weeks' time and then it will be Christmas shortly after that. Why, I only have half the designs done and we really must buckle down now." She smacked her fist against her palm for emphasis.

"And the work will be waiting for us to finish it *after* I confront those horrible women."

"Oh, but must you?"

"Well…yes, yes, I must." Mrs. Rosemary lifted her chin. "I am honor bound to do so, as a trusted family friend. I'm your godmother for goodness sakes and this will not go unchecked."

"But what if we banned the women after I finished the designs?"

"Why is the timing important, Flo?"

Florence leaned back against the table with a dramatic sigh. "Because I am incapable of creating in a timely and orderly manner when I am encompassed with rage, and those women are like a match to me. I am liable to catch fire and burn out without ever accomplishing any fruitful work. I will not be able to think straight if those women are walking around town clucking that we've banned them from the shop. I nearly tried my hand at thrashing them today, before I realized that I have no idea what a thrashing entails. I couldn't design a thing until I calmed down which is not good for our deadline, and I'm already so woefully behind."

"And so you want me to ban them after you finish your work?"

"Yes. I imagine I can finish it all within the next week or so, and once I do you are free to ban whomever you like for the rest of time immemorial."

"Time immemorial?" Mrs. Rosemary stroked her chin. "I quite like the sound of that. It's dramatic in such a lovely way, don't you think?"

"I do." Florence bobbed her head, readily agreeing.

"I grant this request and then reserve the right to

proceed with all the drama the situation deserves. Is that agreeable?"

"It is, it is. I fully support your right to drama. You know that I am a fan of it, a lover of it in fact. I will help you carry out whatever plan you so choose to ban the women, if you only wait a little."

"Until after you've completed the workshop designs."

"Yes, that. Most assuredly and foremost, *that.*"

Mrs. Rosemary clapped her hands excitedly. "Then I agree. I am excited to set those harpies straight. Running their mouths like that, and in my place of business, your place of business. Why I ought to--"

"Mrs. Rosemary," Florence held up a hand to stop her from speaking, "you promised."

"Oh, I know, I know. It's just so incredibly hard to stop when I start." Mrs. Rosemary sucked in a deep breath and sighed heavily. "I will refrain at your request because I love you."

"And I you. Thank you." Florence held out her hand to Mrs. Rosemary. "Now give me your gloves and hat."

"But what?" Mrs. Rosemary frowned, holding the hat and gloves to her chest. She eyed Florence with a wary look. "Do you not trust me to stay put?"

"I do trust you, but I also know you. Now hand them over." Florence wiggled her fingers to which Mrs. Rosemary sighed loudly, and most notably, dramatically, before she slapped the hat and gloves into her waiting palm.

"I am so put-upon in this world. Cruel temporal existence."

"Unappreciated in your time. Your sacrifices will be heralded long after you've passed."

"The unfairness of it all."

"A statue will be erected in your honor. Ballads sung of your sacrifices." Florence smiled when Mrs. Rosemary perked up at that. The blond grinned at her. "You always craft the most beatific fantasies. And where would they put this statue?"

"In the town square of course. Future generations will be able to best study your likeness with such a placement."

Mrs. Rosemary clasped her hands to her chest and sighed happily. "How lovely. I adore the future."

Florence hugged her, the women embracing tightly for a moment before they parted. Mrs. Rosemary patted her check and smiled at her. "I love you, Florence. Please remember that when I am sour at not being able to tell those chits what I think of them."

"I know you do. I love you as well. With all my heart."

"That's enough sweet talk, you. Now show me the designs that you've completed. We can see what needs to be done before we have them made into patterns, hmm?" She wrapped an arm around Florence's shoulder, pulling her close as they walked towards the worktable.

"Here they are…" Florence glanced nervously at Mrs. Rosemary. The woman was a family friend and they were extremely close, but first and foremost the woman was her mentor. Everything Florence had learned of fashion, she had done so under Mrs. Rosemary's tutelage. What she thought of Florence's work mattered immensely to her, and so Florence watched her nervously. Mrs. Rosemary picked up the sketchbook, eyes moving over the pages as she began to flip through the designs.

"Ah, it could do with a bit of polishing but I hope you can see the merit in the work, rough as it is." Florence twisted her fingers nervously and cleared her throat.

"They're wonderful, Flo." Mrs. Rosemary lifted her eyes from the book to look at her with a warm smile. "Absolutely stunning. You've done so well with this."

"Truly?" Florence blinked in surprise.

"Well and truly. Better than I anticipated. This work is so very modern but perfect for the frontier. These pants here," she turned the notebook to Florence and tapped the page, "this is stunning work. Any woman would be happy to do her work in these. Well done, Flo!"

"Thank you." The infectious energy from the other woman had her smiling brightly. "Thank you, you taught me everything. I am just--I want this to go well."

"And it will! It will be a hit. The absolute sensation of the year." Mrs. Rosemary gestured wildly with the notebook and turned to look out at the shop. "I can see it now. The eager faces, the happy customers, the beautiful designs all over town. It is just the thing this town needs." She whirled towards Florence then, surprising her with the sudden movement. "You will be the talk of the town, no, the state! People will beg for your designs by the time this is all well and done. How thrilling!"

"Yes, but first we must finish the work…"

"Oh, that will happen. We will not pick fights until it's done just as you made me promise."

"Right, right."

"Now then, give me that pattern sheet there." Mrs.

Rosemary held out a hand to Florence, head already bent over the notebook. "We have work to do if your notoriety is to grow."

Florence hurried over to the table and grabbed the stack of paper, but no sooner had she turned towards Mrs. Rosemary than the other woman asked, "Is all banning and fighting outlawed or is it permissible to squabble? I can get quite a bit across with a well-aimed squabble."

"No fighting, banning or squabbling. You promised."

"Oh, all right but I want to go on the record as not liking it, not even a little bit. Thank you so much for the paper, dear."

Florence gave the woman a wry smile and handed her the stack of pattern paper. Mrs. Rosemary began to fuss over the designs in her notebook. Florence watched for a moment before turning to the worktable behind her. She rummaged for her latest half-finished idea for a small collection of lady's separates. The pieces would be versatile, sturdy, but still fashionable making them useful for all manner of occasions. The addition to the designs Florence had already penned would make for a well-rounded wardrobe any Gold Sky citizen would consider practical and well suited to frontier life.

The thought of seeing her designs come to life was more than enough to help inspire Florence. Besides, if there was work to be done there would be peace. Mrs. Rosemary would not have the free time necessary to exact revenge. There was an excited gleam in her blue eyes, and Florence was grateful for the distraction their work posed. If not she knew it would have been impossible to make her mentor agree to begging off from telling the troublesome women exactly what she thought of them. Florence's pencil began to fly across the paper before her, after all she had a duty to add to the work required to keep Mrs. Rosemary occupied and well out of a confrontation.

"Duly noted, Mrs. Rosemary."

CHAPTER 15

"*Y*ou look nervous."

Florence pressed her lips into a thin line and glanced out of the window. There was a snowstorm underway and she watched the flakes fall with ever increasing speed. The weather had worsened considerably for the better part of the past hour. Any that were out were risking their safety and wellbeing. It wasn't safe or smart to be on the road, and she knew nearly all in town would be indoors.

On an evening like this it should be all, not nearly all. And it might have been if not for one very pressing Sunday dinner. Florence knew there would be at least two souls on the road. Two foolhardy and romantic souls that she suspected would risk quite a bit to be at her doorstep within the hour.

Ansel and Brendan.

"I am," she said, raising a hand and resting it lightly against the window glass. "I know they're coming tonight." She raised her eyes to look at her sister's reflection in the glass. Rose crossed her arms and moved to come stand beside her sister.

"Perhaps they won't."

She shook her head. "They would have sent word. I know they are coming tonight. They wouldn't miss it."

Florence knew as much on account of Brendan telling her rather ardently how much tonight mattered to both Ansel and him.

"We wouldn't miss it for the world. We'll be there, flower. Come hell or high water, and the weather be damned. Rest assured."

She bit her lip and sighed. Then the words had seemed romantic and devoted. The kind to make her stomach flutter pleasantly, but now? Now they were worrisome and her stomach was no longer fluttering pleasantly but tied in knots. Knots that induced her to deem dinner as unnecessary. There was no way she could eat, not the way she felt now, sick with worry as she was.

What if they were on their way and had become stuck? What if they were lost? What if they fell ill?

The worries swirled louder and louder until Rose's hand on her arm startled Florence from her worries.

"You're brooding," Rose told her.

"I am not, I am worrying. There is a distinct difference in the effect and method."

Rose tugged gently at her arm. "They are safe. Please come sit down. Staring out the window and worrying yourself to death will do nothing but put your nerves on edge. You'll be a wreck for dinner, and that will do no one any favors when you have to keep a level head."

"But I cannot help it, Rose. How am I to sit when they

are out there, in *that*," she jabbed a finger at the window, "infernal weather?"

"They wouldn't want you to worry. I have no idea of their character and even I know that." Rose held up a hand when Florence made to protest. She crossed back to take her place on the settee "Now come and sit beside me," she said, pointing at the space beside her.

Florence bit her lip. She knew her sister was right. It wouldn't do for her to be a nervous wreck when the men arrived. She knew they were on their way and it pained her to think it might be all for nothing if she were unable to calm herself enough to make it through dinner.

If the men were putting in the effort to arrive by dinner time she could do her part and remain calm, or at least achieve a semblance of it. Her shoulders slumped and she sighed heavily, giving Rose a tight smile that didn't quite meet her eyes.

"Very well," she agreed, moving to take a seat beside Rose. Her sister gave her an approving look once she was settled and held out a book to her.

"That's better," she murmured, when Florence took the book. "You'll enjoy that, I think. It's a dramatic serial that I only picked up yesterday. I devoured it in no time at all."

"Just the thing for keeping anxious thoughts at bay, hmm?"

"Precisely."

"Thank you," Florence smiled at her sister and this time it was a bit more genuine. She leaned back against the settee and opened the book. If her sister swore it was engrossing then at the very least she would be able to lose herself for a bit in the story. The pair had been reading for all of twenty minutes, Florence's worry lessened by a truly engaging tale of a librarian-turned spy bent on revealing the true identity of an antiquities thief, when there was a rap at the door. She jumped up, the book falling by the wayside and hurried towards the door.

"It's them!" she told Rose over her shoulder. "How did I not hear them?"

"I told you, it is an engrossing tale. Good writing trumps all, even worries over beaus."

"True, very true. Thank you for the book." Florence pointed towards the door. "I'll be just a minute. I have to let them in before--" Florence's words cut off abruptly, the words dying on her tongue when she saw her fathers stride past her and make for the door.

"Oh no," she whispered. She hadn't wanted Ansel and Brendan to be greeted by her fathers immediately. The men of the Wickes-Barnes household were known for their intensity, and her fathers, she knew would be in fine form when greeting suitors.

"Papa...Daddy. Just a minute, please!" Florence called after them. "Wait for me." She hurried forward to stop them but Forrest had the door open before she'd even managed to take two steps.

"Well aren't the pair of you a sight for sore eyes," he greeted her suitors. Florence peeked around her father's shoulder to see that blessedly Ansel and Brendan were standing and looking no worse for wear, only slightly snowed upon. There was a dusting of snow on their hats and coats and they were slightly red-nosed but that seemed the extent of the weather's effect on them. She let out a sigh of relief and smiled at them.

"You're safe," she gushed, pushing past her fathers and throwing herself into the waiting arms of Ansel and Brendan. She wrapped her arms around them as best she could and raised herself up on her tiptoes. "Oh, I was so worried for you. I knew you would come," she told them, her voice muffled from being pressed to their chests, "I knew you would, but *why?*"

"Why what?" Ansel asked.

Florence drew back glaring at them. "Why did you come in this infernal weather?! You could have gotten lost, or worse, hurt. It's only dinner."

"It's not just a dinner, flower. It's dinner with yer family."

"Our first dinner with your family."

"Yes, but it was foolhardy of you to come all this way in this weather."

"All the same, we would gladly do it again and it was hardly any trouble at all." Ansel turned her gently back to the door and gestured for her to go inside. "But you will catch your death if you stand out here with us, Flo."

"He's right sweetheart. Come on in." Will reached out a hand to her. Florence lifted her head from the men's chests and gave the appendage a sour look.

"But then I have to let go of them," she said.

"Sweetheart." Forrest rubbed at the bridge of his nose and shook his head. "Come inside. You're letting the heat out and these two are freezing from the journey."

Florence pouted, but she extricated herself from the men all the same and stepped inside. Once they were all inside Will gave the men a critical look.

"Did you ride here? Need to tie up any horses?"

"No, sir, we walked. Didn't want to chance the animals on our outing," Ansel answered, and her fathers let out a collective hmmm that Florence couldn't quite interpret. She looked to Ansel and Brendan to see that they were similarly wearing confused looks at the sound.

"Hello? Are our guests here?" Her mother's voice floated its way from the kitchen and Florence cleared her throat, grateful for her mother's interruption.

"Yes, mama, they're here!" she yelled back not paying much attention to what was considered an appropriate indoor voice for a lady.

"They're here!" A shout from upstairs had Florence wincing. She had been so concerned over how her fathers would receive her suitors that she had forgotten one important element: her sisters.

"Yes, they are, hurry down!" Rose yelled from the parlor. The shout set off a chain reaction of hurried footsteps, giggling shouts, Seylah nearly tripping down the last few steps of the stairs, and Rose nearly sending Delilah crashing to the floor in her rush to get closest to Florence.

"How do you do?" Rose thrust her hand forward in greeting. "I am just so pleased to finally and formally meet you. I've heard nothing but lovely things."

"The pleasure is all ours. I am Anselmo Ortega." He bent low over Rose's hand and took it in greeting.

A slight flush rose in her sister's cheeks and she lifted a hand to her chest. "I'm Rose." She glanced at Florence and gave her a wink. "I get it," she whispered too loud to go unnoticed in the silent foyer.

Florence nearly slapped her forehead at the starry-eyed look her sister was now sending Ansel's way.

Then it was Brendan's turn to introduce himself. The Scotsman flashed a warm smile Rose's way, taking the hand Ansel passed him. "We are delighted to be here. My name is Brendan Black," he said, giving it a slight squeeze.

Rose tittered nervously, the hand at her chest moving to pat at her hair. "Charmed," she murmured demurely, earning an elbow to the ribs from Florence.

"Behave," she warned her sister but Rose only rolled her eyes and grinned at the men in front of her.

"But that's boring. You taught me that." She winked at Florence, who gasped and started forward with a clenched fist. She might not be skilled at a thrashing but she could quiet her sister all the same, if she put her mind to it. All of the sisters had grown up wrestling and even now they were no strangers to scraps with one another.

"I am serious, you little--"

"I am so pleased to have you in our home, gentlemen. I apologize for our lack of hospitality. To have you standing here with snow dripping from you and in the drafty entry. My apologies." Julie bustled forward, taking both men's hands. "My husbands will take your coats," she said, giving a quick nod to Forrest and Will, urging them to action, "Please, call me Julie. I am so happy you are courting Florence. She's quite taken with you both."

Florence blushed and grit her teeth but allowed her mother to continue on. The men now had their coats taken from them and their hats and scarves being put away by her fathers.

"Please, come with me. We will continue the introductions at the table, I think. That way I can make sure you're being well seen to and in a far more hospitable atmosphere," the last was said with a meaningful look to Will who was looking torn between wanting to throw the men out and perform his duties of hospitality. Julie extended her hands to Ansel and Brenda urging them to come with her.

"Thank you," they both said in unison, taking her hands without another word. They walked with her mother into the dining room and Florence felt her heart clench at the sight of them walking along, docile as lambs. It was an endearing thing to see and she smiled, falling into step with her sisters while her fathers brought up the rear.

"Please, make yourself at home, sit here," Julie gestured at the seats nearest to them. "Florence, take a seat between them, just here. Rose, Del, Seylah, on this side if you please, with me." Julie directed her family with the precision of a practiced general and before long all of them were sitting at the table laden with enough food to feed them all twice over.

Introductions were made with just as much precision and guidance. Florence watched on with a glow of pleasure warm in her chest. There were no uncomfortable silences or awkward moments, not with her mother's practised hand smoothly orchestrating it all.

Julie Ann Wickes-Barnes was many things to many people--a teacher, mother, frontierswoman, and questionable cook, but she above all things remained what she had first been.

A debutante.

The proof that she had not forgotten her schooling or practiced social charms was evident by how effortlessly the conversation flowed, how at ease she set everyone during the first courses and drink arrangements. She flitted to and fro, holding out refreshments with a practiced hand, only taking her seat once everyone had been seen to.

"We cannot thank you enough for your hospitality. This is very nearly a feast," Ansel said, accepting the platter of grilled meat passed to him. There was food enough, and perfectly prepared, as her mother had little to do with its preparation save deciding upon a menu. Florence and her family owed much to their cook who ensured none went hungry, or became ill from her mother's well-intentioned attempts at the culinary arts.

"Oh, we are happy to finally have you here for a meal. I've heard so many lovely things about the pair of you from Florence." Julie smiled at the men serenely, her expression giving no hint at the intimate details Florence may or may not have shared with her mother and sisters only days before. Florence was wonderfully lucky that her mother was in possession of the impeccable skill in schooling one's expression when there were salacious details at play.

By the same turn, Florence was woefully burdened with three sisters lacking in the art of secret keeping. A giggle from Rose prompted Florence's attention and she nearly dropped the saucière in her hands. To varying degrees, each of her sisters were giggling or blushing, Delilah the latter while Rose was heartily engaging in a muffled laugh behind her hands, while Seylah looked caught between the two.

"Gravy?" she blurted out, thrusting the saucière into Brendan's hands. "Rolls?" she asked, shoving the yeast rolls against Ansel's chest. Both actions worked to distract the men while she kicked out at her sisters, the satisfying sound of her foot hitting the women's knees brought a smile to her face.

"Oh, are you well? Do you need to leave the room?" she asked her now glaring sisters.

Rose rubbed at her knee. "No, I'm quite well," she kicked Florence back who stifled the gasp that nearly escaped at the blow, "aren't we, Del?"

"Yes, quite." Del added her own kick to Florence's sore knee. "But Flo looks a bit piqued, does she not?"

Florence gripped the edge of the table, leaning forward with a glare. "Oh, I'll show the both of you piqued."

"Or how about we all calm ourselves. This is a nice family dinner, after all. Is it not?" Seylah was there now, leaning between her two sisters and pointing a knife at Florence. "We wouldn't want to ruin all the effort mama went through to put this together, now would we?"

"Oh, you're such a dear, Seylah always thinking of me." Julie winked at her daughter and snapped her linen napkin down firmly across her lap. "Now gather yourselves. All of you. This is a family dinner. No mischief."

Brendan and Ansel exchanged looks that all at the table could plainly interpret as panic, while Will and Forrest merely chuckled. Forrest sighed and sipped at his lager.

"You'll have to get used to it," he said, giving the men a knowing look.

"There's no way around it. Don't fight it," Will added.

Ansel remained silent but nodded solemnly at the men at either end of the table.

"Ah, seems like sound advice." Brendan continued to plate his food.

"It is, it is. Now, before we discuss where your people are from, and where the pair of you met, I have something I'd like to ask." Forrest leaned forward in his seat and set his glass down, the thud of it reverberating so loudly in the now silent dining room that Florence swore she felt it in her toes. She bit her lip while her father considered his words. Her Papa had always taken great care with his words, there were few times that she could remember him speaking rashly, and she knew now was no different. His words would have weight, the question a heavy one and her mind raced trying to puzzle out what precisely was he going to ask and why was it taking him so long to speak?

The room collectively held their breath. Her sisters gripped their silverware a bit too tightly, her mother appeared to be praying silently as she waited on her husband, and even Will leaned forward in his chair, awaiting his husband's words.

"Do you love each other?" he asked, and then gestured between Ansel and Brendan with a flick of his finger. Florence felt her chest go tight at the simple but important question. *Did they love each other?* And then, because her father was not one to do anything in half measures, he asked, "Do you love Florence?"

241

"Papa…" Florence murmured when she trusted herself to speak. "I don't think that's a fair question, and when you've only just met them. It's too…" Florence's voice trailed off and she looked away from her father's blue eyes that were now on her. She swallowed hard when the words she wanted to speak didn't come. How could she say that it was too big of a question? Something that frightened her so much to think of that she did not, would not, and perhaps could not just trust herself to dream of?

She was falling for the men, yes.

But were they falling for her as quickly as she was them?

Yes? No? Perhaps…she didn't know. There was in her mind quite a bit of difference between feeling as if one had been struck by lightning at first sight, and an entirely different matter of introducing love where it already lived.

"It's too what?" Ansel asked. He placed a hand on her arm and rubbed at the skin beneath his fingers. "Flo?"

She shook her head. "I don't know what I mean to say, and dinner is not the place I thought this would occur."

"I think it is as good a place as any." Brendan was now touching her. He smiled at her encouragingly. "Ye have nothing to fear, flower. Not from us and certainly not here. This is your family. They love you." He paused and looked at Ansel, the other man giving him a slight nod before Brendan cleared his throat and proceeded. "And we love ye."

Florence's head snapped up, eyes wide as she looked from Brendan to Ansel and back again. "What? You what?"

"We love you," Ansel said, echoing Brendan's declaration. "From the first moment we saw you. But propriety did not allow for us to lead with that at the dance."

Brendan scoffed. "I told ye I didn't care what was proper."

Ansel sighed. "No, but you should when there is a lady involved." He looked back at Florence and smiled warmly at her. "We didn't want to frighten you, not even when it seemed as if you felt the same for us. And you do feel that way?" His final words were a question, one that was not entirely sure of the answer. She could hear it plainly in his voice, they all could, just as they could see the worry on his and Brendan's faces. There was no looking away from it. Not even if they wanted to. Not in a room as small as this and six pairs of eyes moving from Ansel to Florence to await her answer.

She finally had the good sense to put down the fork in her hand. There was no accepting declarations of love when one was clutching a utensil, even one as laden with delicious potatoes, to their chest.

Her fork out of the way, Florence took a deep breath and nodded at the men on either side of her.

"I love you," she said, her heart beating out a staccato rhythm her chest hurt to contain as she looked upon both of them. It was so achingly hard to order her thoughts when they were looking at her as they were. Faces open, eyes expectant and above all else--loving. They were not afraid to be vulnerable in front of her, in front of her family, and it gave Florence the boon she needed to keep speaking, though her voice trembled slightly.

"I love you both."

CHAPTER 16

*T*he dinner that followed was a happy affair. Florence supposed it was the only possibility after she and her men had exchanged declarations of love. There was no doubt they would marry, that the men on either side of her had only the best of intentions and reasons for wanting her with them. Everyone at the table could see it plainly, most of all her parents. Florence could see it on their faces as they looked on the three of them throughout dinner.

It cheered her considerably. She knew they would trust her decision, support her in any way necessary, but to know they were at peace and secure gave Florence all the confidence in the world. Her relationship with Ansel and Brendan was healthy and happy, it would continue to flourish as they deepened their connection. She did not even work to contain the smile on her face throughout the night. Nothing could touch her, not when she was surrounded by loved ones. There only good food, good people, *good love.*

The Wickes-Barnes household was full to the brim of it, if any looked on she would be surprised if they could not see the affection spilling from the seams of the home, overflowing from the windows and doors until it steeped every inch of the drive and lane, on and on until the town knew of their love.

She smiled thinking of the image. It was a fitting thought, Gold Sky covered in the love of her family, witness to the romance between herself and the men she had chosen for herself. The men that had, in turn, chosen her every bit for themselves. She had grown up here, from a girl to a woman, learned to live and love, learned what life could be if she trusted herself. She would build that life with these men and she was happy to do it in Gold Sky, the town and people that knew her and loved her.

It was all falling into place and by the dinner's end Florence had quite forgotten about the snowstorm raging outside, the one that had continued to blow and fall during the time her family had spent with her men.

It was only when it was time for goodbyes that they had opened the door to stare at the several feet of snow that were now on the ground. The snow would be up to the waist of anyone that went out in it. Under the light of day would be one thing but now in the pitch black of the Montana night was an entirely different matter. A very dangerous matter that brought back all of Florence's previous anxiety at the weather and Brendan and Ansel's safety.

She turned to them with a shake of her head. "You're not going anywhere," she said, holding out her arms as if needing to bar them from the door. "I will not allow it. Not in this weather."

"Oh, it'll be all right, flower. Just a bit of hard walking for us." Brendan gave her a reassuring smile, but one quick scan of the sky from Will had the older man shaking his head and shutting the door firmly.

"She's right. It's not safe out there. The pair of you will bunk here tonight."

"Ah, but--"

"No, buts, there's rooms aplenty," Forrest said, jerking a thumb behind him in the direction of the guest room on the first floor. "We built seven bedrooms but only had four daughters. There's a sizable bedroom downstairs here that will be big enough for the pair of you for the night."

"If yer sure it's no bother. We can make the journey, I assure ye," Brendan said, but her fathers waved the man off.

"It's not safe. We can't allow it," Forrest said, already setting off for the bedroom. "Will and I will get you set up."

"I'm glad that's settled," Julie remarked, before she pressed a hand to Brendan and Ansel's cheek. "If you need anything at all, let me know. There will be warm tea in the parlor later if you so choose. Goodnight, gentlemen, I'm so happy to have spent the evening in your company."

"Ma'am."

"Goodnight, Mrs. Wickes-Barnes."

Her mother smiled, still in the role of the debutante and gathered her sisters with her. "Ladies, let's be on our way. Florence would no doubt love a moment of peace with her suitors."

Florence sent a look of silent thanks to her mother as she herded her sisters on their way. Rose, of course, turned to wiggle her eyebrows knowingly at Florence but blessedly said nothing as their mother ushered her up the stairs. When they were alone, Florence breathed a sigh of relief, her shoulders relaxing the moment her sisters' skirts disappeared from sight. She looked to Brendan and Ansel to see they were watching her expectantly.

"It seems we are spending another night together," Ansel murmured. She blushed and crossed her arms before closing the space between them.

"Yes, but unlike that night..." her voice trailed off and she looked towards the room her fathers were busy setting up. Overhead she could hear her sisters and mother's footsteps as they readied for bed. Her family was all around her, the home she had grown up in a solid, comforting place, which meant there would be little privacy in the halls her family roamed. "I'll not be able to be in your company."

Ansel and Brendan nodded in tandem. "We thought not. "

She smiled up at them and rested a hand on each of their chests. "But it doesn't mean that I won't be thinking of you every hour of the night."

"And what will ye be thinking of, flower?"

Her fingers tensed slightly pulling at the fabric beneath her hand.

"Now that will have to remain a secret," she said looking up at the men, her eyes darkening slightly with want. "If I tell you..." she smiled and looked away. "It would not make for an entirely family friendly night." She moved to take her hand away but Ansel caught it and raised it to his mouth.

"Goodnight, Flo." He kissed her knuckles.

Brendan mimicked the gesture. "Till tomorrow, flower."

Once more, just as the first and all the times after and before, Florence's breath was stolen by the men she adored.

"Goodnight, gentlemen." She moved away and up the stairs, only stopping to chance a look behind her when she was atop the staircase. They were still standing there, hand in hand as they smiled up at her and Florence was positive she had never seen a more perfect sight. These men were as much a part of her present, and above all her future. It made sense to see them here in the place of her past and it was as if they had always been there, in the halls of the place she had grown into a woman. She leaned against the railing, lifting a hand in farewell.

"Goodnight," she said again, but this time with the addition of, "my loves."

The men beamed at her, the words lighting them up from the inside. Florence would have lingered, happy to look down at them for the remainder of the night if her fathers had not appeared to grab the men by their arms.

"To bed then," Will said gruffly, marching Ansel and Brendan from the hallway while Forrest pointed up at Florence.

"That means you too, young lady."

"Yes, Papa," she laughed, stepping away from the railing. She went to her room and dressed for bed, all around her the sounds of a home full of love settling in for the night lulled her to sleep. It was the best night's sleep Florence had ever enjoyed.

When Florence awoke the next morning it was not to a calm home, nor was it to a quiet one, it was, in fact, to a household that had been wide awake and for quite some time too. She could tell from the loud voices and the sound of feet hurrying that she was one of the last to rise. A cursory glance out the window showed that it was early yet, the early morning sun just barely coloring the sky a blush pink.

She frowned, sitting up in her bed. Why on earth was the house as energetic as it was if it was still early in the morning? And if the upstairs was this active, then that must mean... a resounding slam of the front door and a round of excited voices propelled her from her bed. There was no way Ansel and Brendan were not in the middle of the fracas, their bedroom was only down the hall from the front door.

She had to get downstairs and quickly. For all she knew her family had recruited the men to join in the morning's excitement. Florence dressed as quickly as she could, nearly tripping as she burst from her room and into the hallway.

"What's going on?" she called, rushing towards the stairs, her only thought was getting to the bottom and perhaps rescuing Ansel and Brendan from her family's machinations. She could hear voices from the kitchen and dining room, but paused, unsure of which way to go. Thankfully the decision was taken from her when a familiar face emerged from the kitchen.

"Uncle Julian!" she exclaimed.

Her uncle smiled at her. There was a kitchen towel thrown over one of his shoulders, his sleeves were rolled up and there was a streak of flour across his cheek. He was a handsome man, her mother's twin, and looked so much like her even now that it never ceased to surprise Florence. His hair was graying at the temples, a recent development but Julian Baptiste was still as boyish as ever and winked at his niece as he gestured for her to come closer.

"Good morning my dear! How are you?"

"Good morning." She rushed forward, hugging her uncle. "When did you get here? We didn't think you would be here until after Christmas." Instantly her mind began to skip ahead and she counted the weeks and days that she had left with Rose's presence. Would her sister be leaving sooner than expected? It would be their first Christmas apart and she had hoped to put it off for another year.

He hugged her back, dropping a kiss on the top of her head. "Violet and Claude were feeling restless so we came early as a surprise. We had hoped to make you breakfast as an added surprise but I fear we woke you instead?"

"Oh, yes, but what a wonderful surprise to wake up to."

"Your fathers were not quite of the same opinion before dawn," he chuckled, and she rolled her eyes. "They were far more amenable when we told them the biggest part of our surprise."

"What's that?"

"That we will be joining you for Christmas. We decided to come early and enjoy the holidays here in Gold Sky with the family. Your mother was overjoyed at the news."

"And so am I! Is everyone else awake?" she asked. They were now walking towards the kitchen where she could hear the cacophony of her family's voices. The volume made sense knowing her aunt and cousin were in attendance as well. She cheered thinking of the fine family holiday they would enjoy, all thoughts of Rose's absence pushed away. She could and would handle that when the time came, but for now she was happy to have her family close.

"They are, and I even met your suitors. They are fine men, if I say so myself," her uncle told her with a nod. She flushed, but smiled, pleased that her uncle thought to give her his approval, subtle as it was. Her family's opinion meant the world to her. Uncle Julian's counted as one such and she grinned at the scene in her kitchen. Her cousin Claude was at the stove with Brendan at his elbow, the Scotsman was watching intently as Claude instructed him on the proper technique for making crepes.

"Good morning!" Rose waved at her from the counter where she was preparing coffee. "It's about time you got up, sleepy head."

Florence stuck her tongue out at her. "I like to make an entrance," she drawled, coming up to where her aunt was rising from her seat. "Aunt Violet. I'm so happy to see you. I've missed you so much."

The other woman embraced her, hugging her close. "I missed you too, Flo. I'm very excited that we made the decision to surprise everyone." Aunt Violet inclined her head towards Claude and Brendan while pointing at Ansel who was standing with her fathers, drinking a cup of coffee. "They are very handsome, and so well-mannered too. Claude thinks so as well."

"Oh, he does, does he?" she asked, raising an eyebrow at her cousin who was now flipping a crepe with practiced ease.

"Yes, Claude more so on the side of good looks but he's always shared your taste." Violet winked at her.

"He has," Florence giggled. "I'm very happy you're all here. I had no idea what all the commotion was this morning and I'm glad that it was you, and not anything else given the storm."

Violet winced and looked out the window. "The storm was unfortunate. We managed to get to town before the worst of it hit but decided to wait until morning light to make our way here. I hear we missed a beautiful dinner."

"It would have been far more beautiful if you had been there," Florence told her.

"And more delicious too," Julie added, sidling up to them. "No one can match your culinary skills, I'll have to have you give me some pointers on my pies. I've reached a new level of baking, but I think just a bit more fine tuning and my apple pie will finally be perfect."

"You've been trying to perfect that recipe for nearly two decades," Florence reminded her.

"Twenty-four years to be exact," Seylah added from where she sat with her sisters.

Forrest and Will turned in tandem looking at Julie first and then at the room. "Her pies are perfect," they said at once and none missed the tremor that passed through the lawmen's voices, well save for Julie who preened in front of her husbands.

"Thank you. It's nice to be appreciated." She blew a kiss at the men and Forrest looked relieved when all talk of his wife refining her pie skills ended.

"Good morning, flower," Brendan greeted her. He held out a plate to her that was stacked high with crepes. "I hope yer hungry. I've received quite an education in the way of preparing crepes. Here is my morning's labors."

She laughed, taking the plate from him. "I assume Claude had a hand in your education."

Her cousin turned to her, pushing his curls back from his forehead with the back of his forearm. "I did. It seemed only proper to prepare the man for a successful tenure with the family. Everyone knows how important crepes are in this household, and mastering the fine art of the crepe is a must."

"It's true," Florence said. "Crepes are my mother's favorite. There's no family breakfast without them, and I see you've done your shift as cook." She glanced round at the busy kitchen, each of her family members were holding a plate and eating a stack of crepes she had no doubt Brendan and her cousin had prepared.

"I mainly supervised," Claude told her. "He's a natural. You picked wisely, Flo."

She smiled, leaning forward to kiss her cousin's cheek.

"Thank you, Claude. I'm happy you're here, and that we get to spend Christmas together. It's almost too perfect to believe."

Claude hummed, plating another crepe onto the plate he held. "I agree. I quite needed a change from the city. It was a bit too...stifling there." Her cousin's face was hidden from her, his back to her now but she could hear a note of sadness she did not recognize in his voice. Claude and she were so much alike, and there was only one thing that could put such morose feeling into either, especially when in the company of family.

"And of Damon?" Florence asked quietly.

"He's no more, or rather, I suppose he is but is more with someone else on the banks of the Seine."

"Oh, Claude, I'm so sorry." Florence set her plate down and hugged him tightly. "You deserved far better than him. He is a lout and a lecher. I hate him."

Claude chuckled and leaned close to press a kiss to her temple. "Thank you, Flo. You always know what to say. It's a lovely quality and what I love the most about you. Well, next to your spite. Please do keep speaking poorly of the man that broke my heart."

She smiled leaning her head against his shoulder. "I promise to devote a solid hour before dinner to the task of ridicule and spite."

"Perfect. All that I could hope for and more, cousin." Claude sighed happily.

"Who is Damon?" Brendan asked.

"My beau, or he was. Now I know not who he is, or whom he does whatever it is that he does whatever he does, with," Claude told him with a defiant toss of his head.

"Yes, he's a blight," Florence readily agreed despite the fact that she had dined many times with Damon, and happily so, but that had been before he'd hurt her cousin. "An absolute terror."

"I see." Brendan pursed his lips and then said, "A terror it is. Happy to have y'here with us rather than in the city with such foul beasties, Claude."

Her cousin beamed at him and dipped into a slight curtsy that had Florence rolling her eyes. "You're very welcome, Brendan. And might I say that it is truly a gift with such handsome company."

"Oh, stop it you." She swatted at his arm and he chuckled, moving away to take the plate of crepes to his mother.

"You cannot expect me to behave when you have such delicious specimens for suitors, Flo. Absolutely unconscionable of you."

Violet nudged her son. "Do try and behave, darling. We've only just arrived."

"If I must," he sighed.

"Good morning," Ansel murmured, coming up to them and kissing Florence's cheek. "How are you this morning?"

"Well, well, I was only mildly panicked at hearing what sounded like a circus down here when I awoke. I hope my family did not scare you too terribly."

"No, it's quite nice being in a family home again. It's been some time since we've had the pleasure of it." He looked to Brendan and gave him a smile. "Not since Scotland, hmm?"

"Aye, not since then." He looked to Florence and smiled before he scanned the room once, the man took time letting his eyes move slowly over each and every person before he turned back to her. "We miss the sounds. It's nice, ah, to be in such a place. Thank ye for the opportunity, flower."

"You will always have a family and a home so long as I am with you." Florence took his hand. "I promise this, to the both of you. Where I go, family exists, even if it is just the three of us." Her words should have surprised her, but they did not. She felt them in her bones, each and every word was a promise she fully intended to keep. She raised their hands to her lips pressing kisses to their fingers. "I love you, and you are now my family."

Brendan reached for her as did Ansel and the three embraced tightly. "I love you," Ansel told her and then he looked at Brendan telling his man the same. "With all my heart."

"A perfect fit for us, flower. I love ye. I do."

Florence felt as if her heart was fit to burst, and she squeezed them tighter still, only loosening her grip when she heard Brendan struggle to breath. "Sorry, sorry," she laughed, "but it is hard to mind my manners when I am this happy."

Brendan gave her a returning squeeze that set her to yelping with laughter. They were well and truly in love. It would be a magical Christmas, after all. Her family continued on with their breakfast, though not without them all sharing a knowing look at the trio's display of affection.

CHAPTER 17

$\mathcal{F}$lorence could not remember a time she had been this busy, perhaps the year she'd turned sixteen and had to fend off advances from callers after her coming out. That had made for one interesting vacation to New York City. She had never left her grandmother's side for fear of being caught by an eager bachelor in pursuit of a well-connected wife. She had scarcely managed to have a day to herself with so many callers and invitations that had been extended.

Yes, that summer and fall had been...arduous, but it had been the kind of busy that left her worn and tired. Mostly because it was at the request of people she cared little for. Yes, her family in New York mattered and meant the world to her but the men seeking her hand?

They had been inconsequential, as had the influential members of society. And that had been why the *busy* of her sixteenth summer had felt heavy and draining.

Now? This *busy* was entirely different.

This busy meant that her workshop would go off

without a hitch, it meant that she was with her family, surrounded by those she cared for the most. This kind of busy offered her nights with her men, times when they were alone and the hours were long and sweet, and times when they were not but the conversation and meaningful looks were enough to carry her forward.

This kind of busy saw her helping her sister plan for her journey to New York, meant that Claude had an ear to vent his broken heart to, and time with her family trimming the tree her fathers had dragged in only that week at her mother's request.

Oh, this was the best kind of busy. No doubt about it.

Florence loved this kind of busy. It was energizing in a way that left her eager for the next busy day. Today's business at hand was the start of her workshop series. An afternoon of teaching the fine art of dressmaking and blind stitches awaited her and Florence couldn't be more pleased. All of the frantic planning and designing was well worth it, as was all the efforts Mrs. Rosemary made to network and drum up interest in the classes.

It had all been quite too much for Florence to manage, and she was forever grateful for Mrs. Rosemary's continual support and help. She might have managed it without her men--her suitors. She smiled thinking of them. Brendan and Ansel were a worthy distraction, if any were to take her time from work and family. But if she were lucky, the men would be a part of her family in the official sense before long.

Already Brendan had been awkwardly hemming around the question she knew he wanted to ask. He'd tried to take her by the jeweler twice in as many weeks, but at the last second lost his nerve and instead directed her towards the bakery next door. She quite enjoyed the cake she had received from feigning ignorance at their intended destination. Ansel was far more refined at it, delicately asking her preferences for the future, when she might care to wed, and what the ring on her finger might look like--in the strictly hypothetical sense, or so he had insisted over lunch the previous day.

All around her the world was changing, her day-to-day constantly evolving and she was glad her men were a part of that change, would be a part of the change of tomorrow and all the days after. On the shop floor of A Modern Dress all the clothing displays and tables had been cleared and moved to create a makeshift classroom for the evening's event. There was a lightness in her step as she moved about the shop getting the space ready, which consisted of a pack of neatly tied patterns along with all the basics necessary for creating that evening's garment— a smartly tailored jacket.

The attendees would be sent home with homework to finish the jacket alongside a pair of simple but delicate pants. They would present their work at the next week's workshop and Florence could already see the clothing they would create together in her minds eye.

It was going to be a magical evening. She could feel it.

"Florence, are you ready for tonight?"

She looked up from the table where she had been arranging a set of tailor's chalk, "Yes, I'm quite ready for everyone," She looked around with a raised eyebrow, "or at least I believe so."

Mrs. Rosemary turned and surveyed the room with a

tap of her finger against her chin. "Yes, I think you're all set. I can't see a thing out of place, and you'll be so happy to know that I've heard nothing but excitement in town about tonight's workshop."

"Really?"

"Yes, yes, of course! Your skill is known and the good people of Gold Sky are hungry for a taste!"

"A taste?" Florence asked, feeling a finger of nervousness touch her spine.

"Yes, a taste!" Mrs. Rosemary waved her hand in the air excitedly, already moving about the room with the energy Florence was well accustomed to. "They want to take a big ol' bite right out of you, Flo and I couldn't be happier."

She swallowed hard and looked out at the room but this time it was with a shiver of anticipation. What did Mrs. Rosemary mean? Did she want to be bitten by the town and what exactly would that entail?

"What's wrong dear? You look nervous."

"It's just…" she gestured lamely at the room.

"Just what?" Mrs. Rosemary came to a stop in front of her with a quizzical look. "What is it, Flo? You look like you've seen a ghost."

"I'm a bit nervous."

"But why?"

"What if they take a big bite of me and find me not to their liking?" she asked, unable to keep the note of impending panic from her voice. "What if they hate the way I taste?" she asked, shaking her head.

"Well then we'll make them eat it anyways."

"That's not what one usually does when something tastes bad. People send the food back."

"Oh, pish," Mrs. Rosemary waved a hand. "That's ridiculous. If people are hungry, they will eat and the people of Gold Sky are hungry for a solution to their fashion needs and penchant for frugality. You are that solution!"

"I suppose you're right."

"I know I'm right." Mrs. Rosemary tapped a finger on Florence's arm. "You will be wonderful. You are a natural teacher and I cannot tell you how excited I am for you." Mrs. Rosemary swallowed hard and smiled at her. "I never had children, but Anthony and I have always seen you as a daughter. I am so very proud of you, Flo. You've grown so much."

Mrs. Rosemary's words touched her. Proud of her. Like a daughter. She blinked against the tears that stung at her eyes.

"Mrs. Rosemary..." She inhaled a shaky breath and opted to hug the woman rather than continue speaking. "Thank you," she whispered, wrapping her arms around Mrs. Rosemary tightly. "I love you. I love you more than anything."

"And I love you, just as everyone will that comes to this workshop. No one is going to send you back and if they do they'll have me to deal with."

She laughed and sniffled, managing to hold back her tears. Happy tears, but tears all the same would not be a good impression with the workshop set to begin in only minutes.

"I'll make sure to spread the word. Thank you."

"Of course. Now get your smile in place. I'm sure they'll all start arriving any minute and we want to look our very best for them, now don't we?" Mrs. Rosemary patted her cheek with a smile. Florence nodded and let Mrs. Rosemary usher her forward and set her into motion directing her to her place at the head of the room. No sooner had she taken her place did the door open and first attendees began to arrive.

"Welcome, welcome!" Mrs. Rosemary tittered greeting the attendees. "Please take your seats and ready yourself for a wonderfully productive evening with us at A Modern Dress!"

FLORENCE SANK down into her chair with a heavy sigh. Her feet were sore, her fingers ached, and her back felt as if she had aged forty years in the span of one night.

She had never been happier.

The night had been a success. Wildly so. She smiled, rubbing at her tired eyes as she leaned into the plush material of the settee. It was calm and quiet in the parlor, a far cry from if she had been in her own home. As it was she had been spirited away by Ansel and Brendan for a quiet night of rest after her big debut, though she much thought the men's idea of rest might vary wildly from the rote definition. But she suspected it would be far more enjoyable.

"You were a hit then?" Ansel asked. "An absolute sensation?"

"I did well enough," Florence answered, eyes closed as she relaxed in her seat.

"She was a right hit. Dinnae listen to her. Stop being so modest, flower."

She smiled and opened her eyes to look at both of the men. They were sitting across from her, each in an armchair wearing similar looks of interest.

"I am not being modest, I'm being factual. I performed adequately."

"Adequately? Is that why I saw a room full of people looking as if they had enjoyed an educational and productive evening?" Ansel asked, leaning against the arm of his chair.

"Aye, I agree. They were all happy as could be and with finished garments to boot. Ye did wonderful, flower. There's no shame in owning up to that fact."

"And Mrs. Rosemary could not stop singing yer praises. Besides, Claude even said it and ye know the man tells no lies."

It was true. Her cousin was honest to a fault.

Florence opened her mouth to refute the men, but she closed it again, because it was true. Mrs Rosemary had been over the moon at her showing, and then there was the woefully obvious fact that Florence was indeed side-stepping her success.

But why?

"Very well. You're right. You're both right. I did a wonderful job. The evening was a success."

"Wonderful, that's the spirit." Ansel clapped his hands and moved to hand her a snifter of brandy. "Take this then. You deserve it."

Brendan nodded in approval and lifted his glass in acknowledgement. "For a job well done. Let us raise our glasses to yer triumph."

"Here, here!" Ansel clinked his glass to Brendan's and when they both looked expectantly to Florence she giggled and raised her glass to theirs.

"Oh, all right," she laughed. It was hard not to be affected by the men's joviality. Their good mood buoyed her up pushing the tiredness in her limbs away. "Then what are we toasting to, hmm?" she asked, leaning forward to be able to reach the men's glasses with her own.

"We are lifting our glasses to the wit and beauty of the one we love."

"And to her ability to dazzle any and everyone in her presence. Our flower is wonderfully amazing."

"She sounds like a lovely woman." Florence flushed, lips turning up into a smile at their words of praise.

"Oh, she is," Brendan agreed, clinking his glass to hers.

"The loveliest. There are none like her." Ansel stood from his seat as they all cheered and took a long swallow of his drink. "And we are so lucky to have her with us."

Brendan inclined his head, glass going higher. "Here, here!"

"That's enough! The two of you." Florence laughed and waved a hand when the men looked fit to go on. "Normally, I enjoy being praised and doted upon," she began, a muffled laugh and an arched eyebrow from her men had her pursuing her lips and starting over, "oh, all right, I love being adored, but what woman doesn't?"

"None."

"She exists not."

"Correct, now as I was saying," she continued, shaking a finger at the men who were now openly laughing. "But I feel as if this moment should be shared."

"Shared how?" Ansel asked.

"Shared in the way that I extend kind words and flattery to the pair of you."

"Oh?"

"Mmm," Florence hummed and sipped her drink. "The pair of you have made my life magical."

Brendan made a face but Ansel looked interested. "Do go on. In what way?"

She laughed. "Magical in the sense that I feel as if a happily ever after is allowed to me. That my wants and desires are not so strange. I had hoped as a girl, and searched as a woman, for a love like this," she swallowed hard and forced herself to keep speaking even as she felt the force of her love for the men in front of her threatening to knock her flat as surely as the gales of wind outside were capable of doing, "but in all my dreaming, my desire to have what my parents enjoyed with one another, I never thought it would be like *this.*"

Her fingers tightened on the brandy glass, the tinkling of the ice inside deafening to her ears and she breathed in slowly taking great care that her breaths were measured and even. It would be easier to go on speaking if she maintained a semblance of control.

Grand declarations always were more manageable when there was a veneer of calm. At least she supposed so, for Florence had never made such a grand declaration, not like she was at the moment, not as she was about to do. And so she breathed slowly working to keep her voice from trembling or rushing as she went on speaking to the men. They looked as if the house could fall down on their heads and they would scarcely notice, so long as Florence did not stop speaking.

"I never imagined love could be this good. Feel this right, with not just one person but two. There's knowing and understanding, and before you, I knew that romantic love could be good and right and true, but now I understand it to be so. Love isn't something I daydream of, it's a fact and it's a fact because you both loved me. In turn, you let me love you and that has been one of my life's greatest gifts." And then because she had been raised to have manners even when baring her heart she added a hasty, *"Thank you."*

At that Florence stopped speaking, and congratulated herself that her voice only trembled slightly, that her hand only shook minutely when she raised her glass to her lips and took a much-needed drink. She winced at the burn of the alcohol but welcomed it all the same after her bout of words.

"This is strong," she informed them. "Very good."

"Florence."

"Flower."

She smiled tightly at them, unsure of what to say or do because in that moment it was as if every part of her was cracked open and bare to her core. Every bit of who she was, what she felt for the men she loved, all of it, her hopes and dreams, the wants and promises she had long nurtured as a girl to womanhood was on full display for them.

"Ye dinnae need to thank us."

"Not for giving us your heart. For allowing us to be with you."

Her eyes drifted closed, the warmth of liquor on her lips matching the buzzing in her veins. It was enough to make her light headed. The men stirred, the creaking of chairs and the sound of clothing rustling as they rose from their seats made her breath come quick. The creak of floorboards signaled their approach and her eyes opened when they came near. She looked up to see Ansel and Brendan on either side of her.

"Hello," she murmured, lifting her glass to her lips to take another sip.

"Hello," Ansel husked, watching the movement of her glass. His eyes dropped to her throat when she swallowed and he lifted his hand to touch her, his fingers lightly curling around the nape of her neck. He leaned close, trailing his nose along the line of her jaw, the gentle touch making her breath catch.

Brendan caught her hand and raised it to his lips. "You belong with us," he said, pressing a kiss to her knuckles.

"Always," Ansel murmured. "Always with us." He tightened his hand, the pressure increasing on her neck and sending a shiver down her spine. She tipped her head back until she was looking up into his dark eyes.

"Kiss me," she whispered. The man obliged, slanting his mouth to hers in a kiss that made her knees go weak. Heat pooled in her belly at the brush of his tongue against the seam of her mouth. Florence's lips parted eagerly under Ansel's and she moaned, leaning into his body. The strength of his frame grounded her when Brendan reached for her, one hand pressed flat to her back. He turned her towards him, breaking her kiss with Ansel before he drew her close and captured her mouth in a passionate kiss. The heat that had been slowly building in Florence ignited like a wildfire.

Hands reached for each man until her questing fingers found them. She circled an arm around each man's shoulders until she was pulling them into her body, pressing herself between them eagerly. She relished the feel of Ansel and Brendan beneath her hands, on either side of her, muscular bodies caging her in and making her nearly pant with want.

There would be no even breathing or calm displays.

Not when there was flesh to caress and kiss, bodies to explore and eager hands to do it with. Not when there was so much Florence felt and for all her words, had still not explained in full. Her affection for them bubbled up in her, the effervescent feel of it imparting a desperate need to touch them, and to be touched in turn.

She pulled away from them, taking her lips from theirs to gasp, "Take me to bed," before she surrendered herself once more to the passion she felt. All pretense of calmness gone and dispensed with. She needed them. *Wanted them.* And she would have them. All of them, together with her, just as they had always been meant for one another.

Ansel swept her up against him, carrying her easily towards the bedroom on the second floor. Brendan went ahead of them, working quickly to stoke the fire and turn down the bed while Ansel tried to make short work of undressing her, but the man was thwarted by her clothing and its damnable buttons.

Florence made a mental note to opt for simplicity and ease, no little frills to deter seeking fingers in her next design. Who knew fashion would slow her efforts as it did now? Ansel's fingers fumbled with the buttons at the back of her dress and she swore before setting to work on them herself. The small pearl buttons down her dress front proved difficult, slipping from her fingers just as she meant to grip them. It took all of her willpower not to demand he simply rip them off, but she knew it would make the next morning difficult if she meant to get home in any sort of presentable state. And so they worked on her dress in silence, the room slowly filling with firelight and warmth as Brendan's efforts succeeded. He joined them, toeing out of his boots and pulling his shirt free, baring himself to Florence's wandering fingers before he set himself to unbuttoning Ansel's shirt as well.

"How am I to concentrate on these infernal buttons when you're both touching me so?" he asked. Florence simply hummed as she continued to kiss his neck and Brendan raised one shoulder in a shrug.

"That is fer ye to figure. Not us," he told his lover. Florence laughed, undoing the top button of Ansel's shirt. Her lips found the flesh exposed by her efforts and she undid another button, and then another adding inch after inch of beautiful skin for her exploration.

Brendan's hands were at Ansel's waist, fingers nimbly undoing his belt and pants buttons with an eagerness Florence intimately understood. She wanted Ansel out of his clothes as desperately as Brendan. The only thing she desired more was for both men to be as such.

One man at a time. One man at a time.

Her train of thought was enough to aid her in getting Ansel's shirt fully unbuttoned. Her fingers running over the planes of his body eagerly, but at the first brush of her fingers against his heated skin her resolve to take both men on singularly was lost to her.

Why one when there were two? She needed them undressed and she *needed it now.*

"Quicker," she ordered between breathless kisses. "He has too many clothes on," she told Brendan.

Brendan smiled, working Ansel's belt free. "Aye, flower," he said, turning his head to kiss the side of her jaw.

"Do not distract me with kisses. Help me undress him," she replied, enjoying Brendan's peppering of kisses all the same.

Ansel raised an eyebrow at his lover. "She's right, you know. I am far too clothed to--"

Ansel's trousers hit the floor with a satisfying rustle that brought a smile to Florence's face. She placed a hand on Brendan's chest drawing him up from where he had begun to kiss her collarbone.

"You next," she said, pulling away when he reached for her.

"I agree," Ansel shucked his shirt away, and when Brendan looked fit to protest he kissed the other man slowly, pushing him back on the bed behind them. "You are entirely too clothed and I believe Flo has made her wishes known. Undress, sir."

"Yer both bossy," Brendan muttered, though his lips were turning up at the corners.

"You love it." Florence kissed him, shoving aside the

leather suspenders he wore. "Now kiss me." She set upon him then, buttons coming undone beneath her hands just as surely as Ansel worked his trousers free. Brendan cupped her face with his hands and kissed her deeply, Florence moaned at the brush of his tongue against hers. Her moans were claimed eagerly as they kissed and Florence's entire world narrowed until it consisted of only the men she desired.

"I love you," she whispered.

"We love you," Ansel whispered back, moving forward until he was pressed flush to her back. Brendan broke their kiss, his focus set on pulling her dress free.

"Now yer too dressed," he informed her. "And that cannot stand, flower." She might have shivered from the still cool air of the bedroom if not for Ansel's bulk at her back.

She leaned back against him when he urged her to, hands at her shoulders guiding her until she was settled firmly against his chest. She tipped her head back and looked up at Ansel. He was handsome, focused and most all he was theirs. He met her gaze, eyes darkening slightly before he closed the space between them and kissed her. The kiss was slow and delicate, at odds with everything Florence could feel building in her. Inside she was a rage of emotions and want, a spinning storm held at bay by the barest of threads and all the while Ansel continued to urge her to greater heights. He did it all with the gentlest of touches, an almost chaste kiss she would have thought impossible pressed between both men as she was, but even so, there it was, and Florence welcomed it.

Brendan's hands landed on her thighs, his work of

disrobing her from the waist up complete, his fingers sliding along her skin lightly before he shoved up her skirts. It seemed he was now changing direction and motivation. Florence lifted her hips slightly helping him work her undergarments off. She might have moved more save for that bare inch but Ansel's hands cupping her breasts as he continued to kiss her kept her precisely where she was.

"You're beautiful," Ansel murmured, lips grazing her ear as he spoke. He rolled her nipples in his fingers making her gasp as he did so. He moved and kissed her cheek. "You're beautiful and perfect. Utterly perfect for us," he told her, punctuating his words with light brushes of his lips he trailed from her ear to her jaw. She arched her back eager for more of his touch and when he moved to cup her breast, fingers still stroking her nipples, she sighed in bliss, her head settling against his shoulder.

"Love seeing the pair of ye above me," Brendan groaned, his eyes moving over them hungrily. "Never seen anything so beautiful." He sat up, hands bunching her skirts above her thighs as he did and kissed her firmly. His naked chest pressing Ansel's hands firmly into her breasts while they kissed.

Brendan drew back, his eyes moving to Ansel as he pushed himself up onto his knees.

"Get her skirts free."

"Mmm." Ansel shot the other man a smile, pulling Florence up onto her knees. She gasped at the sudden movement, Ansel's hands firm on her body as he manipulated her into a position suitable to undressing her completely. Her legs and body finally stripped bare

Brendan caught her against him and pushed her down on the bed, her thighs hugging him when he settled between them, hovering over her. She relished the heavy feel of Brendan's body. There was little more that she loved than to have her lovers against her. Florence's body sang at the feel of both men's hands on her as they put her where they chose, she welcomed the sureness she felt in their grip. She would rather be nowhere else than exactly where she found herself. In bed with the pair of them.

It was a heady thing to feel this wanted, needed, this desired. How had she gone on without them in her life? The thought of living without their presence, even unknowing of their existence was a life she balked at. Had she never gone to that dance or allowed Mrs. Rosemary to play matchmaker what would her life be like now?

She would have missed them, felt it deeply, even if she had not known they were real. That they existed and that the place beside them was specifically meant for her.

Ignorance was not bliss where they were concerned, not a bit.

Ansel slipped from the bed. Florence tracked his movements, watching as he was rummaging in the bedside table. He returned to the bed a moment later, a small glass jar in his hand. He unscrewed the jar and applied a liberal amount to his fingers before he placed the jar beside them. She recognized it as a jelly she'd often seen her mother use to treat cuts and burns her fathers suffered from their work on the ranch. It was a rich and thick substance Florence and her sisters favored to remove their makeup as well. Very useful that little glass jar was. But what was he using it for now?

When Ansel caught her giving him a curious look he held up his hand showing her his slicked fingers and simply said, "Necessary, very necessary, isn't it, darling?" He was now speaking to Brendan and had dropped one hand behind him. He gripped Brendan's hip with his free hand while he touched his lover slowly. Florence's mouth parted when she realized where Ansel was touching Brendan, that he was working first one finger and then another into his lover.

Brendan gasped at Ansel's touch.

"Yes, very," he agreed, his voice now more a groan than intelligible words. She struggled to push herself up on her arms. She wanted to see them together, like this as they were but Brendan's hand on her chest pushed her back onto the bed.

"Have to have you, flower," Brendan whispered, his lips trailing over her chin. He kissed her once, then another time, before he pushed himself up to look down at her. "I need you."

"Then have me," she told him. She felt the head of his cock slip between her thighs and gasped when the blunt end of it rubbed over her core. It felt heavenly, that gentle pressure increasing with each swivel of his hips. Brendan dropped his head to kiss at the column of her throat, his lips and teeth setting the skin there aflame, just as he did the rest of her. She was wet now and Brendan praised her for it.

"That's my flower. Open and so welcoming to me, ye are," he whispered, breath puffing deliciously along the sensitive skin of her neck. Florence arched her hips towards him. If she did not have him inside of her she

274

would fly apart and all at once the passion that had been simmering within her boiled over.

"Take me," she told him, reaching up to thread her fingers through his loose hair. She tugged on the long strands bringing his face level with hers so that she might look into his verdant eyes.

"Take me." She hooked a leg around his waist, dimly aware that her toes skimmed Ansel's shoulders in her movement. She pulled Brendan down into a messy kiss that left them both panting. Brendan moved forward, arm braced beside her head, the other holding the leg she had wrapped around him. He held her tightly to the curve of his body, the length of his arm pressed to her while he guided the head of his cock deeper into her.

Florence gasped when he entered her, the delicious stretch of him making her eager for more and she moved her hips in time with his shallow thrusts, taking more of him. She wanted him to fill her, to take her like this until they were both spent and sated, their limbs heavy with lovemaking. They would not move, not for hours, so exhausted they would be, but before that? Before that they would spend just as long locked together like this taking their pleasure as one. Or they might have if it were only the pair of them, but as it was, it was they not. They were blessed with a third in their love.

"Ansel," Florence whispered.

A muffled groan at Brendan's back came in reply, and the man above her gasped. "Ansel, indeed," he sighed, body trembling. He was behind Brendan, she could see him now as she tilted her head to the side catching sight of his body. Leaner than Brendan's bulk but muscled and

275

just as beautiful to her. He was on his forearms and knees focused on Brendan's arse, and Florence nearly keened at the sight of it. They were gorgeously perfect this way, sensuous and alluring in a way made all the more perfect for her affection and devotion to them.

Ansel raised up from his place on the bed and took to his knees behind Brendan. He leaned forward, a hand on the man's shoulder for a moment as he leaned close to whisper in Brendan's ear. "Are you ready for me?" His voice was rough, and Florence thought of gravel crunching beneath a wagon wheel, or flint striking steel. She felt herself grow more aroused still as Brendan nodded and husked out a shaky, "Yes, goddamnit. Take me." His voice held none of the breathiness Florence's had, but the words were the same, the sentiment exactly matching. At least she was not the only one to lose herself to that aching feeling that could only be sated by the stretch of a cock. Ansel chuckled and nipped Brendan's ear, causing him to gasp.

"Manners," he reminded him. Ansel looked up then locking eyes with Florence. She lifted a hand from Brendan's hair and their fingers interlocked. He raised them to his mouth and kissed her fingertips.

"That's perfect," he said, voice vibrating against her fingers, "Make love to her, we want her to feel you tomorrow, don't we?"

Brendan moaned in answer, head falling forward at Ansel's words.

"Don't we?" Ansel pressed, and this time he did so as he guided his cock into Brendan with his free hand. "Just as you'll feel me tomorrow, darling. I know you love that feeling, hmm? The one that only I can give you."

Brendan lifted his head and uttered a shaky, "Y-yes."

The breath was punched from her lungs when Florence realized what was about to happen, what was already happening. They were going to love her, yes, that much had been a given the moment they had set foot inside the bedroom, much like the last evening she had enjoyed with her men. But this had not happened then, she had not witnessed them loving the other as such and her heart sped up at the thought of it.

She was to be included in their lovemaking entirely.

Her blood could have been made of fire in that moment, so molten did she go beneath Brendan, and still the fire grew until it consumed her when Ansel began to thrust in earnest. The men's motions matched and synced, and Florence could feel it all. Their bodies fit together perfectly, all three of them, the feel of Brendan inside of her only amplified by Ansel's answering movements.

Florence had the dim thought that she would not last long. Not with all three of them like this. Scarcely had the idea formed in her mind then she found herself plummeting over the edge of her pleasure. It happened so suddenly that her body went rigid and she cried out, screaming her lover's names as she flew apart beneath them.

"Brendan! Ansel!"

These were the only two words she managed to form before her cry devolved into a sob. She could not think past now, there was only this moment, the one with all of them, the waves of their pleasure breaking over them in relentless waves.

Above her she felt Brendan tense before he shouted his release, he trembled as he worked to keep his weight from crushing her. Ansel gasped as he climaxed, one hand coming to heavily land on the bed beside Florence as he did so. He moved, gently pulling away from Brendan, and came to lay beside them, Brendan likewise moved so that he was on Florence's other side. Florence frowned at the loss of their bodies and hated that she was no longer connected to her lovers, and so she threw her arms wide, yanking them close until they were a pile of tangled limbs.

Ansel chuckled, Brendan's rumbling laughter joined his and Florence simply smiled.

The glow of their lovemaking cocooning them in a swath of warmth and contentment. Their laughter ended and a quiet descended like a warm and welcome blanket. All three of them were silent save for their breaths, and the odd pop from the fireplace, as they clung tightly to each other in their bed, this place that was only theirs. None of them said a word, for in that moment of perfect silence there was everything Florence had ever hoped to find: safety, acceptance, and above all else *love.*

EPILOGUE

"Will you have a Christmas wedding?" Rose was looking at Florence expectantly when she raised her head from the design in front of her.

"What was that?" Florence asked. Her mind had a tendency to wander when she worked, and her sister's question was lost to her.

"Will you marry before Christmas?"

"Well, we haven't exactly set a day." Florence raised a shoulder in answer. "Why do you ask?"

"She wants to know if we'll be able to make an event of it. Your wedding, I mean," Claude added helpfully.

"Ah, I see now."

"Well, I thought it might be a cheerful thought, to have a lovely event before I left for New York. Uncle Julian is talking that we might leave sooner than expected due to a business falling to shambles."

Claude pulled a face. "I hate business. I would much rather stay here with the rest of the family. I feel as if I can breathe here without the weight of the city on me."

"Then stay?" Florence asked. She paused and then said, "You aren't needed for the business whatever it is, are you?"

He chewed on his bottom lip for a moment and then shook his head. "No, I'm not. Father can handle it all neatly. I wasn't much involved in it to begin with. I've no head for business really."

"That's because you're like me," Rose sang cheerily. "We are dreamers."

"Ah, but you create," Claude pointed out, wiggling the pencil in his hand at her.

"You create as well," she returned and he shrugged, tucking the pencil behind his ear.

"In a way, I suppose."

"You do, writing takes discipline and grit. Delilah says as much about her own work. You should ask her to help you with your craft."

Claude smiled faintly and looked down at the notebook he carried with him. He had it often, tucked close as he was prone to begin writing when he was able to. Now it was closed, the edges of the worn journal turning up from constant use and from him rolling it up to fit in his pockets when necessary.

"I suppose I could..."

Rose clapped her hands and pointed a finger at Florence. "Then it's settled! Why, you could even take my room so that you're close to the others. What a wonderful time it will be. I'll run and tell the others now!"

"Rose, wait!" Florence tried, but her sister had already dashed out the door. When Rose put her mind to something there was no stopping her and Claude's presence in

Gold Sky had seemingly become her number one interest. She sighed and gave her cousin a put upon look. "There's no stopping her. By the time we return for lunch she will have planned the remainder of your year here."

He laughed and looked out the window where Rose's form darted around a corner. "That may not be unwelcome. Not after…" his voice trailed off and he sighed, "not after Damon," he said finally.

"He's a vile human. You're far better off without him."

"Thank you, cousin." Claude's smile was faint, a sadness in his eyes that Florence could not abide and so she rose from her seat and held out a hand to him.

"Come on then, I think we've worked long enough. Mrs. Rosemary has written off this week due to the holidays." Christmas was in three days' time and there was a flurry of activity in town in preparation of the town's festivities to celebrate the joyous day. Christmas in Gold Sky was a time of year that everyone looked forward to. It was, shockingly, not a time when presents or purchasing was at the forefront of everyone's mind. No, that honor went to the town wide celebrations they all loved so dear. There would be a town dinner, the Christmas play her mother oversaw every year, and even a lovely ball that would no doubt be just as entertaining as last year's.

That year had seen not one but two engagements. Perhaps this year it would be her that announced such happy news. Her palms prickled at the thought. But she said nothing of it to Claude and took his hand in hers once more.

"What do you say to a cup of tea at Mrs. Lily's?"

"I would say yes and thank you very much."

"Perfect. We can return later and do a bit more work if it falls in line with our plans, but I think spending the rest of the day in town would be a better treat." She bustled about the shop turning off lights and making sure to secure the back door before she locked the front door behind him. Once it was all done, they set off arm-in-arm towards Mrs. Lily's. Florence had just begun to wonder if the cafe would be serving her favorite chocolate cake that day when Claude pulled up short and nodded ahead of her.

"Florence..." He stopped then and she gave him a curious look.

"What is it?"

"Those are your men, are they not?"

"Where?" she asked, but she was still looking up at him and so she did not miss the roll of Claude's eyes. He turned her to the side so that she was looking out in front of them.

"There you, ninny. Walking towards us."

"Yes, yes, it is. And you're the ninny." She pinched his side making him yelp and leap to the side.

"If it didn't look as if a romantic gesture were about to happen, I would retaliate," he threatened and this time it was her that rolled her eyes.

"Oh, what are you talking ab--"

"Flower?" Brendan's voice stopped her from further questioning her cousin and she looked to the side to see that he and Ansel were now in front of her, but they were not standing, instead the men were kneeling in front of her.

"That's what I'm talking about," Claude laughed, but

she only managed to lift a hand in acknowledgement. All her attention was focused on the men at her feet.

"What are you doing?" she whispered, though she knew precisely what they were about to do. She wanted to hear it, as did the number of Gold Sky citizens gathering around them with excited looks on their faces.

"Publicly declaring our devotion. Asking you to forsake all others." Ansel extended his hand to her and a ring gleamed in the afternoon light. It was a rose gold band with a light-yellow diamond at the center sparkling in the sun.

"Will ye do us the honor of marrying us?" Brendan held out his hand to her and her eyes landed on a simple gold band of scrolling filigree work in his hand.

Florence's eyes moved from ring to ring and then up to the men's faces. She knew what she would say, they knew it too from the happy looks on their faces. She suspected even the townsfolk holding their breaths for her answer knew, but the words were stuck in her throat. She swallowed thickly, praying her voice would not fail her at this momentous time. She was a woman of many words, one that always spoke her mind and here she was shocked into silence by the men she loved.

Drat and double drat.

She might have resorted to scribbling her answer in the dirt at their feet if not for one thing. Though they were each holding a ring out to her, they were holding each other's hands between them and the sight found Florence's voice for her. She had never seen a more perfect sight than the men she loved baring their hearts and asking for her hand as they held onto each other for all to see.

"I do," she blurted out, reaching for them and taking their hands in hers. The rings were pressed into her palms and she squeezed them tightly as she said again, "I do. I will marry you both."

Her answer let loose an excited cheer from the crowd around them, Claude was the loudest of them all, and a moment later the men had surged forward lifting her into their arms as they peppered her face and hands with kisses.

"I love ye, flower."

"You've made us the happiest of men."

With shaking hands the rings were slipped on her fingers, one on each hand and Florence was unable to stop the tears that suddenly pricked at her eyes. The emotions were bubbling up and out of her like a well-spring and before she knew it she was crying in earnest. Ansel and Brendan exchanged pained looks when they realized their fiancé had now succumbed to sobbing openly.

"What do we do?" Brendan asked.

"I haven't the first clue," Ansel returned in a panicked tone, but then he cleared his throat and then in a calmer tone asked. "Are you well? What can we do?"

She laughed even as she wept. "I'm fine. I swear."

"Then why are you crying? We hate seeing you cry, Florence."

She wiped at her tears and lifted her eyes to see them both wearing a look that could only be described as sheer terror. "Oh, stop it you two. These," she pointed at her face, "are joyful tears."

"Joyful tears?" Brendan said, as if he were testing out the words to see how he felt about them. He shook his head and looked to Ansel. "I don't understand."

"Neither do I."

"Oh, you two…"

"I think she needs tea and cake," Claude interjected. He clapped a hand on either man's shoulder in congratulations. "To celebrate the happy occasion, you see. It will also make her stop crying."

"No it will not! These are good tears," she insisted, but Claude leaned close to her with a sigh.

"Allow me to get us free cake, hmm?"

"Oh, all right."

"Perfect." He tweaked her nose and ushered them towards Mrs. Lily's cafe. "Now then, you'll find that cake is always the way to stop tears in this family, and I heartily welcome you to it."

Brendan and Ansel exchanged wide eyed looks but they nodded at each other after a moment and looked to Claude, waiting for him to continue.

"Tell us everything," they said and Claude nodded conspiratorially.

"I knew you were smart men. Now then, marrying a Wickes-Barnes woman is not for the faint of heart as you will see…" He continued forward, gesturing as he spoke, and the trio fell into step behind him, their arms linked and eyes on each other.

"No, not for the faint of heart," Brendan agreed. He

looked to Ansel who was gazing at Florence in the soft-eyed way that lovers reserved for one another.

"And that makes it all the more worthwhile," Ansel said.

On they walked with the cheering crowd bidding them happiness and well wishes. On they went through the streets Florence had grown up in and watched change. Even now as she looked around the preparations for Christmas were slightly different from the last to accommodate for the town's expansion and growth.

All things changed and would continue to do so. She had learned as much in her years that change was the one constant to count on. And *'all things'* meant even the love she held in her heart for the men on either side of her. Of that she was undeniably certain would change. It would continue to grow and deepen, to mature and strengthen with each passing year. Their love would grow as steady and as sure as any oak until she could no longer remember her life without them.

The life they would build in Gold Sky would change as well, and even if she was uncertain what shape the town's future would take over the years, Florence knew one thing: she was happy to greet it with the men at her side because change with them could only bring good.

Florence had always been partial to good.

THANK YOU!

Thank you for coming along on Florence, Ansel and Brendan's love story. This ménage was special to me and I loved every romantic second of their time together! You might be wondering which Wickes-Barnes sister is getting her story next and the answer is none. Never fear though! What's coming is just as good. :)

Leather and Lace is a historical lesbian romance novella that takes place at the same time as Julian and Violet's story—Hearth and Home.

You may remember our leading lady, Mary Sophia James, who made her debut appearance in Julian's book at the side of her less than savory mother Sarah James. We are not all our mother's daughters, nor should we be defined by weak hearted moments and that is why I chose to continue Mary's story arc. She is a wonderful woman, if pressed into a difficult situation by circumstance and I hope that you find the joy of redemption and freedom that comes with no only finding true love but learning to love and accept oneself. *Plus, there's a bit of mail-order, arranged marriage, kind of secret baby with some forced proximity sprinkled on top.*

Writing this story was a fully joyful experience for me and I am eager to share it with y'all.

Sign up for our newsletter e-mail list at https://bit.ly/2PCKCZl and *don't be shy about reaching out through social media! I pretty much live for that stuff.*

Reviews help eager readers find new authors to love and I welcome all reviews, both positive and constructive. Drop me a shout and I'll love y'all to the moon and back!

Turn the page and fall into the beginning of Mary and Alex's love story!

EXCERPT: MARY AND ALEX'S STORY

"*W*hatever is the matter with you? Please, do keep up, we haven't the time for your wandering, Mary." Sarah's James's stern voice cut through Mary's pounding headache.

The pair were out on their daily walk about town, and Mary had been struggling to see through the blinding pain at her temples. It was difficult to keep up with her mother's brisk walk in the best of times, let alone when she was having difficulty walking in a straight line.

"I'm sorry, Mama. It's just that my head--"

"Stop dawdling, Mary Sophia." Her mother's tight grip tugged at her elbow and pulled her forward to match her step. "I heard there was a new batch of bankers and investors coming to town, on account of Julian Baptiste's efforts with the railroad depot. If we make it to the cafe then we have a good chance at catching their eye."

Mary frowned, still rubbing at her temples. "What do you mean '*we*'?"

Her mother let out a titter of laughter and turned to

give Mary what she supposed was her attempt at coquettish.

"Well, two arrows are better than one, now aren't they dear?"

"Are you saying that you are intending to find yourself a suitor?" Mary drew up to her full height despite the pain she suffered. "Are you aiming to marry again?"

"Keep your voice down! Good god, you would think I had never spent the money to send you to finishing school screeching like a fish wife!" Her mother berated her at a volume far more at home in a saloon at midnight than on the town's main avenue at midday.

Mary glanced about furtively and stifled her groan at seeing the attention they were attracting. Her mother's near shouting was doing wonders at making them stand out in Gold Sky. She didn't estimate it was quite in the way her mother wished for them to gain attention.

"Now come along and do walk with your back straight. Remember your lessons on posture and grace for heaven's sake, Mary."

"Yes, Mama," Mary replied automatically. So oft had she said the words that her response fell from her lips with little thought. And for her part, Sarah James, so used to having her wishes fulfilled by her daughter, did not think twice at the barely there response.

"Now then, pinch your cheeks, and I wish you had thought to apply a bit of rouge. You look so pale in the daylight. We simply must get you in the sun at more regular times."

At that Mary found her tongue. "I love the sun, but you say it causes freckles."

Sarah James clucked her teeth and nodded in agreement. "Right you are, right you are. The sun is no place for a woman like you."

Mary would have scoffed if her headache hadn't redoubled its efforts to lay her low. There would be no scoffing, not when she was nearly blinded by her pain and the sun overhead. Instead, Mary hurried along behind her mother, and before long the cafe her mother spoke of came into sight. She breathed a sigh of relief when her mother slowed her pace and let loose of her arm.

"There it is. Lily's Cafe, or some such. It apparently has decent food, unlike the establishment we were turned out of like common riffraff," her mother gave an indignant sniff. Mary bit back the remark about their behavior, her mother's in particular towards Julian Baptiste's new bride. The cook had been nothing but efficient, her meals tasty, and she'd always had a smile for her when her mother's back was turned.

Mary's cheeks burned with shame thinking on how she had kept her mouth shut when she should have spoken out. Of how she had followed her mother's lead in attitude and decorum towards the other woman. It was hard to remember who she was when her mother's hand was so tight on her neck. It was as if the older woman's grip tightened as surely as Mary's corset and stays did with each and every day of growth.

A hand strayed to her belly and she sighed when it growled. She was hungry, no doubt due to her morning sickness. If she were lucky her mother would allow her the time to eat...maybe if she did manage to catch a man's eye then she would be invited to lunch with him? The thought perked her up and she lifted her head to see that her mother's keen eyes were, for once, not on her.

Now her mother's emerald gaze was trained on a far bigger prize than Mary.

"Bankers," her mother breathed, hands practically rubbing together in anticipation, "and lots of them. Come close and quick, Mary. We will have to pick out the one for you."

"I don't feel well, mother," Mary said, but her daughter's protestations fell on deaf ears, Sarah James waving a hand at her.

"Posh. Stand up straight and smile, dear. Men like a woman who smiles."

Mary clenched her jaw tightly. She didn't trust herself to keep her mouth shut without the extra effort, and fortunately, her mother mistook it for smiling.

"Now, then, that one looks quite good. He's young. That means he won't understand what's *happening* until it's too late."

The happening was the baby. The baby that Mary wanted. She had begun to tire of hearing of it in the abstract, or as a thing---or even worse, a problem.

"It's a baby, mother. Not a 'happening'," Mary blurted out before she thought better of it. She clapped a hand over her mouth with a muffled gasp once she realized what she'd done. The words fell fat and heavy in the dirt between them with a nearly audible thud. Mary blinked and watched as her mother slowly turned to her, the older woman's face nearly red with frustration.

"Watch your tongue, girl."

"Yes, mother."

Sarah James sucked in a deep calming breath and ran a hand over her skirts with a shake of her head. "On better thought, I think it may be best that I go on, on my own."

"Your own?" Mary asked in confusion. Her mother allowed for so little alone time that the suggestion surprised her.

"Yes, alone. I see an older gentleman in the bunch that I think would quite enjoy an introduction. You may use this time to do as you please."

"Truly?" Mary's heart soared with joy and for a moment she forgot about her painful headache. Who knew when her mother would next leave her with a moment's peace? The moment must be seized and savored, enjoyed to the fullest in whatever small way she could find in this frontier town.

"Yes, truly. It's not as if anything worse can happen to you," Sarah James bit out, giving her daughter a cold look. The words should have stung, but Mary found they didn't so much. Not when there was the promise of an after-noon hour spent away from her mother.

Her mother stepped closer to her and lowered her voice so that none but they could hear her words. "Now stay out of trouble for the next hour, hmm? I will return then with lunch for you, courtesy of the rich gentleman I have in my sights, if all goes well."

She balked at her mother's assertion that the man in question had money, how could one even tell such a thing from a glance? She had known more men than she could count that dressed as a dandy, though were penniless and feckless in business matters. Her father had warned her against tolerating the attentions of such men, *and yet here she was all the same.*

She wrapped her arms around herself, shoving away the dark thought. She forced a smile as fake as any she sent her mother's way and nodded quickly.

"Yes, mother."

Sarah James came to touch her daughter's cheek lightly, a hand cupping it briefly though the woman's eyes were still not on Mary. She did not see her daughter, not now and not ever. She tapped Mary's cheek lightly before she was gliding away again, her voice rising as she walked away.

"Have a good time, darling."

Mary raised her hand in farewell, a genuine smile, the first to grace her lips in quite some time. "Enjoy your meal, Mama!"

Sarah James raised an eyebrow at her daughter's sudden cheeriness but the woman said nothing and in a moment's time she had swept into the crowd of bankers. Mary watched in fascination as her mother introduced herself to the man she had chosen, one hand extended to him while the other was pressed demurely to her chest. The man rushed forward to instantly take her mother's hand and that was all Mary allowed herself to watch before she turned on her heel and set off down the avenue. She was certain her mother's plan for the man would proceed as her mother willed it. There was no sense in wasting her precious free time to witness it.

Mary walked forward with a smile on her lips. She was free. Well and truly, if even only for an hour.

"What to do, what to do?" she mused, swinging her

hands happily. She turned to look down the avenue and saw the public square bursting with activity. Townsfolk were hurrying to and fro with full arms and hands. An assortment of tables and benches stood in the normally neat and tidy square. A stage was being built at the center of it, the red maple tree planted there, though small, served as the perfect backdrop. She took a step forward, eyes on the workers quickly putting together the stage, her mind on what sort of music she might hear that night, if she was able to talk her mother into an outing.

If her time with the new banker went well, Mary wagered she had as good a chance as any to convince Sarah James that a town event would be just the thing to celebrate her new introduction to 'a gentleman of means.' Surely the pair would need a place to celebrate their acquaintanceship, plus there was the added benefit that her mother could--

"Excuse me, miss." A voice interrupted Mary's scheming, and she turned with a start.

"Oh, I'm sorry, I didn't see you there."

Because you were laying plans to get your way, like your mother.

Her cheeks burned bright at the voice that was growing louder by the day. What if it were right? What if she was every bit her mother's daughter and prone to schemes and well-crafted plans? What if the girl she had been under her father's care had been nothing more than a figment of circumstance, and not who she truly was?

"No trouble. I have a habit of appearing unexpectedly." The speaker, a woman, a whole head taller than she and solidly built. The woman had a neat bob, her chin length sleek blond hair framing her face prettily. She had wide brown eyes, full lips and a dusting of freckles that lent an air of sweetness to a woman that otherwise seemed anything but. There was a look to her that spoke of strength.

The simple outfit of work trousers and a white work shirt made of thick durable material rolled up her forearms, thick leather work gloves covered her hands and a red bandana hung from the woman's neck perfectly setting off her blond hair. If Mary was to wax poetically she might even liken the woman to the Montana frontier.

Raw. Beautiful. Wild.

"I just, ah, need to get past you to the stage there, miss." The woman held up the bundle of lumber in her arms and Mary jumped to attention. Here she had been gawking like a love-struck girl, while the woman had been trying to go about her business and with a load of lumber no less!

"I apologize. I was dawdling. Awful habit of mine," Mary explained, hurrying to get out of the woman's way and she winced when the beautiful blond fixed her with a curious look. "And now I'm blathering on as well. I--can I help?" Mary offered when she could think of nothing else to say. She should be silent and leave her to her work, but she wished with her entire being to stay close to the woman.

She watched with bated breath as the woman walked past, head high and arms strong. She turned her head to look at Mary, a wide smile on her full lips. They were pink like the roses in their garden in Texas. How she used to love those fresh cut flowers before the summer wilted them.

"You are a lady. I could not ask you to dirty your hands, miss."

"I am no lady," Mary laughed, and against her better judgment, fell in to step behind the woman. She could be bothering her; Sarah James would be quick to point out that Mary certainly was, but until she was told so she could pretend that the woman enjoyed her company.

"I have a nose for ladies, and you are a lady. Frontier is an odd place to find one as fine as you."

"You're a lady, too."

The blond grinned and set down the load of lumber she was carrying beside the frame of the stage. She pulled off her gloves and gave them a shake, slapping them against her thigh.

"What is your name?" she asked, eyes lowered purposefully to her gloves.

"Mary. Mary Sophia James."

"That's a beautiful name." The woman raised her eyes to Mary's. "The kind made for beautiful ladies."

Mary blushed. Her heart beat quickened in her chest at the words, and if she was not mistaken there was a gleam of something familiar in the woman's warm brown eyes that beckoned her forward. She knew that look, the furtive, quiet, but telling look of a woman *noticing her.*

How she had dreamed of finding that look in the one she wed.

The woman tucked her gloves into the pocket of the trousers she wore. "My name is Alex. Alex Pierce."

Mary's brow furrowed. "Alex?"

"Short for Alexandria. My mother had an unhealthy love for all things Egyptian, you know, as all upper-crust women of her age and predilection were want to do."

Mary laughed and nodded, remembering her own mother's craze over the beautiful Egyptian items many of their peers had shown off in their homes. Her father had forbidden it, firmly deciding the lot of it was thieving much to her mother's dismay.

Mary had always thought her father right, but now that she was looking upon Alex she was glad that the craze had led to one thing of beauty. Alexandria suited the woman in front of her, so perfectly she could think of no other name so beautiful. She looked away quickly and smiled, willing the adoration she felt welling up in her to abate.

"Your name is lovely. I am happy to make your acquaintance."

Alex gave her another smile and inclined her head. "And I am happy to make yours Mary."

"Call me Minnie." The request fell from her lips faster than she could process it and she blinked in shock at herself, though Alex paid no mind to it and nodded.

"Minnie, then. Are you new to town? I've not seen you around I'm afraid."

"Yes, I am. I've only arrived a few weeks back."

"Are you alone?"

Mary shook her head. "No, I am here with my mother. We are looking at settling in the area."

"Curious place to think of settling. Two ladies on their own in a place like Gold Sky."

"How do you mean?" Mary asked as she tucked her

hands behind her. There was a knowing tone in Alex's voice that caught her attention and she leaned forward waiting for the woman to continue speaking.

"People come to Gold Sky to escape their past. To get away from whatever bad is holding them down in the normal world."

Mary's mouth dropped open at Alex's no-nonsense words and clear reading of her situation. But how did the woman know she was running, or rather being dragged by her mother, from her troubles?

"You sound as if you know from experience," Mary observed and Alex raised a shoulder in a shrug.

"I do. I'm no different than any seeking refuge from their past. Gold Sky is my escape, same as most here."

"Same as me?" Mary asked. She held her breath waiting for Alex to respond. The blonde tucked her hair behind her ear and ambled forward with a curt nod.

"Of course, same as you. We are all in search of a safe place to land, and Gold Sky is that for me. Must be something mighty big for you and your mama to come alone. Perhaps someone?" Alex rocked back on her heels, that same knowing tone in her voice but this time it had Mary rushing to answer.

"Not my Papa. He's long gone," she said. "Passed away nearly a year now."

Alex's eyes widened slightly. "I'm sorry for your loss. A loss like that can force a move...is that what prompted your search for a new home?"

"In a way," Mary hedged. She clasped her hands and dropped her eyes, much preferring the sight of her shoes than the earnest look in Alex's eyes. If she looked too long she might say a good deal more than she should to a stranger. That would not be a good idea. No matter how beautiful they were. "We need a new home and this place is as good as any, possibly better than most," she finished when Alex continued to look at her with brown eyes she knew saw far too much.

Alex hummed. "Fair point. The town is quite hospitable to all people, no matter their lifestyle."

Lifestyle. Now that piqued her interest.

"What do you mean by that?" Mary asked.

"I mean to say people are free to live as they choose here. Free to *love* and live as they choose. Free to be the person they wanted but were never allowed to be where they came from."

"Oh." Mary swallowed hard and looked up at her. "And what truth were you allowed to live in Gold Sky that the world denied you before?"

"My right to love who I chose," Alex replied. Mary blinked and looked towards the other woman. They were still standing beside the stage, but now Alex moved away from the structure, away from the other workers and Mary was powerless to stay where she was. Wordlessly she followed behind Alex, straining to hear the other woman when she began speaking again.

"Do you really want to know?" Alex asked, her voice was gentle and soft. Words measured.

"Yes, of course," Mary breathed as they came to a stop a fair distance away from the hustle and bustle of the town square. They were alone now, at the far end beside the church where it was quieter. It was a pretty little church, painted white with windows framing the double doors, a steepled tower held a bell that Mary knew rang sweet and true. Alex ambled towards the steps and dusted off the bottom with a sweep of her work gloves.

"Would you care to sit?" she asked, gesturing towards the step.

Mary smiled at her. "Thank you," she murmured, taking her seat. She had not been treated so kindly since society had estimated her in possession of a large fortune. It did more than its fair share to kindle a warmth in her, one that was entirely aimed at Alex, and Alex alone. When she sat, the other woman came forward and sat beside her on the step. They were still far enough apart that they were respectable to any that looked upon them, though Mary had found women often were able to skirt the lines of respectability because theirs was not a love many recognized. An attraction such as that was allowed to exist under the guise of friendship and a closeness particular to women. But any who knew where to look knew different.

Mary was one such person. She prayed Alex was as well.

When they were settled and quiet for a moment, Alex began speaking. "I came to Gold Sky out of necessity," she said. "I was not born to a family as accepting as I would have hoped. Though by the same measure I expect I am not the daughter my family hoped for."

Mary frowned and turned to look at Alex. The blonde was staring straight ahead, her eyes on the workers still setting up in the town square. There was no image finer than the sight of Alexandria Pierce's profile warmed by the glow of the early afternoon sunlight, even with her beautiful features as somber as they were.

"I am interested only in the fairer sex, and that is a wrong my family could not forgive."

Mary's back straightened with a snap. "A wrong? What do you mean to say? It is not something you can control or choose, it just is."

A smile spread over Alex's face and she turned her head to look at Mary. "Oh, I know that. Glad to know you think so too. It is not us that are ignorant, but our families."

Mary crossed her arms with a shake of her head. "It isn't fair. None of it is fair, and they expect us to simply pretend that nothing is--" her words stopped and she blinked realizing what she had been saying, what secret she had just exposed to a near stranger. "I mean to say that in theory," she said weakly.

Alex hummed. "In theory, yes, but something tells me it isn't all theory for you, Mary. Is that why you've come to Gold Sky?" Warm brown eyes met Mary's green at the question, and she twisted her hands in her skirts.

"No, not, I mean not..." her voice trailed off and she winced sucking in a deep breath at her jumbled explanation. "I mean that it isn't *just that,*" she finally finished."

Alex leaned back, elbows braced on the step behind her. "So it is that, at least partly then?"

"Well, ah, yes. It is, but Mama isn't so concerned about that. She was convinced I would marry well in spite of my desires. She's far more concerned about another matter altogether."

Alex pursed her full lips. "And what might that be?"

Mary shook her head and twisted her hands together. "I can't say."

"Whatever it is, I assure you it is not as shameful as you think. You are not a bad person, no matter what people have led you to believe."

Mary laughed bitterly and looked away. "You scarcely know me, and I, you. Just because I am taken with you does not--"

"You're taken with me?" Alex abandoned her relaxed pose and sat up to face Mary. "I suspected as much."

"Yes, if you must know, and I am not ashamed of it."

"That's right fortunate as I find myself equally taken with you, Minnie."

Her heart squeezed at the casual drop of her name. *Minnie.* She found she loved the sound of the name on Alex's lips.

"I like the way my name sounds coming from your mouth," she confessed. The admission made Alex's cheeks flush and the woman chuckled, the low and slow sound of it making Mary's toes curl in her boots.

"Never had a lady tell me something pretty like that."

"I told you before. I'm no lady."

Alex rested her hand in the space between them. She moved then, to the side, hand sliding until it was nearly brushing the edge of Mary's skirts.

"Liar," she said but her voice was light and teasing, the sound of it making Mary smile.

"For some reason I do not guard my words with you," Mary said. "Scarcely an hour and I've already told you a secret."

"And I with you. Concerning, isn't it?"

"Truly, but you already knew that, didn't you?" Mary asked. She was never this...direct, hadn't been in quite some time and she liked the feel of it. Like an older worn and loved coat, a favorite that she had lost track of and now that she'd found it she reveled in the familiar feel of it.

"I did, I did," Alex admitted with a grin and a wink. "I would be lying if I didn't admit I hoped for such a secret when I first saw you, but the second secret is a different matter altogether."

"Ah, yes...that." Mary smiled ruefully. "I should guard my words but it has been a long time since I have been able to speak so freely. I feel more myself and that is because of you. Thank you, Alex." She looked down to where Alex's hand still rested beside hers and hesitated before moving it closer.

"My pleasure, Minnie." Her hand inched closer until their pinkies touched and Mary sucked in her breath. "You can keep talking to me. I'll not breathe a word of it to another soul."

"Why would you do that for me?"

"Because once upon a time, someone did that for me, and it made me who I am." She moved her hand closer, their pinkies sliding against the other in a gentle stroke. Mary's hand tensed at the gentle brush of Alex's finger but she relaxed a moment later and scooted closer to her.

"I'm pregnant," she whispered, voice thick with emotion. "My mother brought us here after I proved inept at securing a marriage to the father." She frowned and sighed quietly. "I never did understand men very well, but that is...to be expected."

"Men are challenging. Women are not."

Mary smiled at the gentle stroking of Alex's finger against hers. It was soothing in the very best way and it kept her talking when she knew she should have kept her mouth shut.

"I don't know about that. I've known quite a few challenging women in my time but they do come with less...complications," she said, her free hand coming to rest on her stomach.

"You don't have to keep running. It doesn't matter if you have the baby." Alex paused and swallowed. "Do you wish to keep the baby?"

"Yes, with all my heart," Mary answered in earnest. "The father meant nothing to me, not in any sense of the word. I did what I did because of my mother."

"Your mother?"

Mary gave a quick nod, just a tilt of her chin but it was a nod all the same. "Yes, my mother. She has certain expectations for me and for us. She thinks Gold Sky will be a new place for us to start over but in order for that to happen--"

"You need a husband."

"Yes." Mary bit her lip. "It's a complicated thing."

"I don't know about that," Alex replied, and she moved until she was covering Mary's hand with hers. Alex's hand was warm, gentle, and most of all strong. She could practically feel the strength radiating from Alex and into her from that simple point of contact. Mary sighed in relief welcoming the grounding touch. She turned her hand up so that they were touching palm to palm.

"Why do you say that?" she asked.

"If you need to be married that's one thing, but why must it be to a man?"

Mary's eyebrows rose in surprise at the question. "Because I am only allowed to marry a man?" she asked in some confusion, but from the snort Alex gave her she wondered if there was another solution she had not considered.

"Not in Gold Sky. You know of it's accepting nature, yes?"

Mary blinked in surprise. She had heard stories of the town's progressive stance, knew first hand from seeing the way people lived here. Why there was even a woman with two husbands but what did that mean when it came to her and her situation?

"What do you mean?" she asked when she trusted her voice not to waver.

"In Gold Sky there is more than one way to be married, Minnie, and one of those ways is *without* a man."

Get Mary and Alex's full story on May 20th, 2020!
PRE-ORDER NOW!

ABOUT THE AUTHOR

Rebel Carter *loves* love. So much in fact that she decided to write the love stories she desperately wanted to read. A book by Rebel means diverse characters, sexy banter, a real big helping of steamy scenes, and, of course, a whole lotta heart.

Rebel lives in Colorado, makes a mean espresso, and is hell-bent on filling your bookcase with as many romance stories as humanly possible!

ALSO BY REBEL CARTER

Heart and Hand: Interracial Mail Order Bride Romance (Gold Sky Series Book 1)

Hearth and Home: Interracial Mail Order Groom Romance (Gold Sky Series Book 2)

Honor and Desire: Friends to Lovers Romance (Gold Sky Series Book 3)

Love and Gravity: Multicultural STEM Romance

New Girl in Town: Older Woman Younger Man Romance

Auld Lang Syne: Highlands Holiday Novella

Made in the USA
Middletown, DE
09 October 2020

21518321R00187